Tattered Men

Tattered Men

Michael Williams

SEVENTH STAR PRESS

Cover art and design: Enggar Adirasa

Cover art in this book copyright © 2019 Enggar Adirasa & Seventh Star Press, LLC.

Editor: Karen M. Leet

Published by Seventh Star Press, LLC.

ISBN Number: 978-1-948042-86-4

Seventh Star Press

www.seventhstarpress.com

info@seventhstarpress.com

Publisher's Note:

Tattered Men is a work of fiction. All names, characters, and places are the product of the author's imagination, used in fictitious manner. Any resemblances to actual persons, places, locales, events, etc. are purely coincidental.

Printed in the United States of America

First Edition

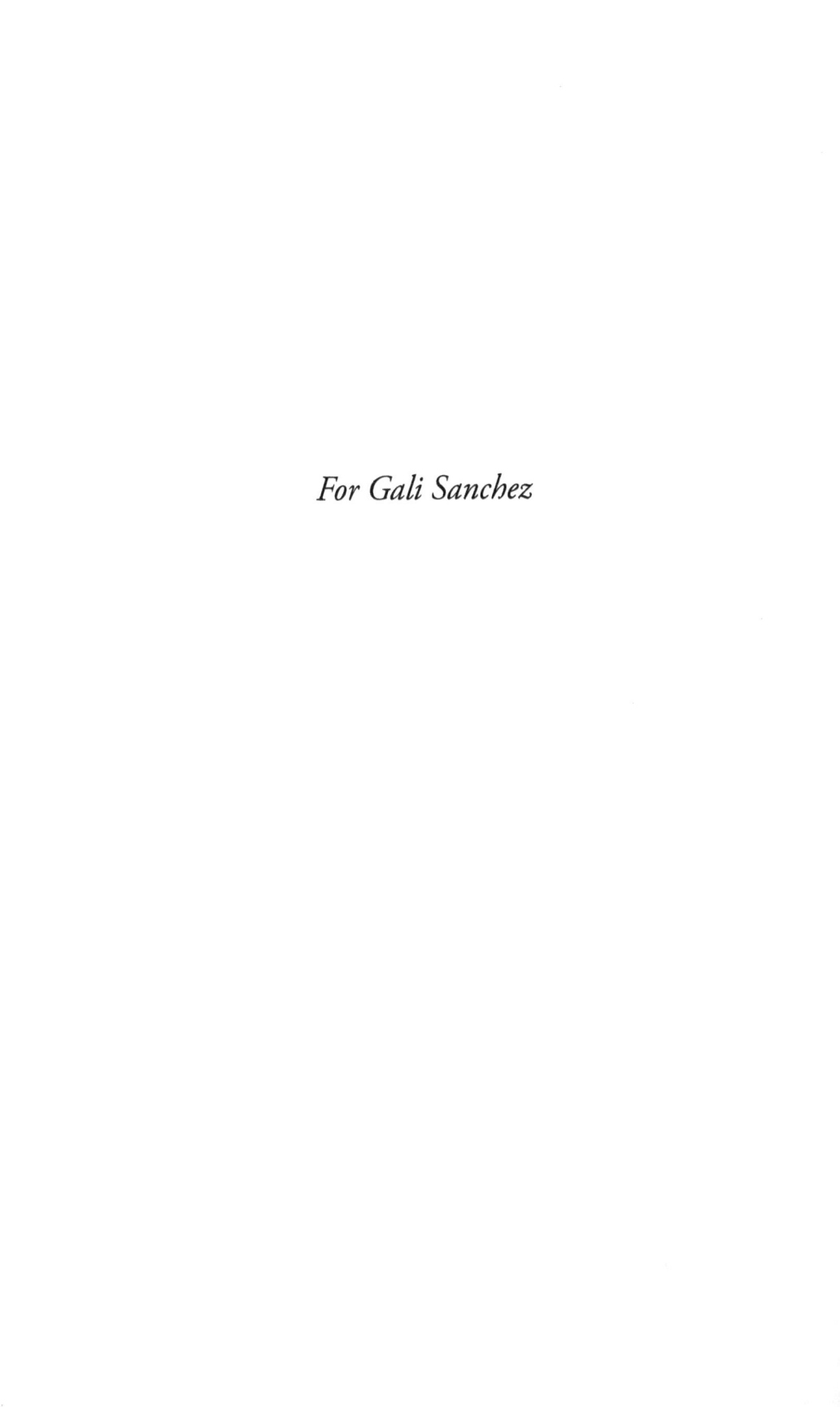

For Gali Sanchez

1

Two days after Tommy's body washed up on the bank, the police came to visit Mickey Walsh.

It was a Lieutenant McCarthy or McCartney—Mickey didn't catch the name, not quite. He was in plain clothes, black tie and short-sleeved white shirt against the sweltering July weather. Tamar went back into the bedroom to still the birds, and Mickey offered the lieutenant a glass of iced tea, which he sugared up like a native and then didn't touch. He apologized for interrupting lunch, broke the news about Tommy, then seemed to look away respectfully to give Mickey a chance to take it in.

Of course he didn't look away. He watched on a slant, gauging Mickey's reaction just in case. Mickey knew how it worked: he'd had a grandfather and an uncle on the force who'd have done the same, but they were both beat cops and probably not as smart as this one, who sat there softly drumming his pencil eraser on the clipboard until the birds calmed down to Tamar's shushing and the apartment was silent and the air conditioner kicked in.

So how did you know the decedent, Dr. Walsh? he asked, looking up at Mickey with that heat-flushed Irish face that took

1

him back immediately to the old neighborhood and put him more at ease. *After all,* Mickey told himself, *I am middle-aged, middle-class, and white, therefore not an automatic suspect, and the detective might well know I'd had police in the family up in Vermont.* It wasn't that he had things to hide, mind you: he'd known Tommy Briscoe only on speaking terms, and hadn't seen him in a month.

The lieutenant nodded and wrote something in his notes. Then asked when Mickey had last seen him, which was over at the amphitheater in Central Park, singing with the midnight choir the night of the thunderstorm.

So, about two weeks ago? the lieutenant asked. Which was probably about right.

All the while Tamar was glaring at Mickey through the bedroom door, simmering with those narrowed eyes that Southern women put on when they would really like to air a grievance but know it would be improper. At times like these, Mickey dreaded her: he hoped the lieutenant would stay for lunch now, for dinner—hell, move in if he liked—but it seemed the questioning was almost done.

You wouldn't know if Mr. Briscoe had any enemies, would you, Dr. Walsh? the detective asked, and Mickey offered the opinion that the enemies of homeless men were often sudden and dramatic. The cop shrugged, looked down to his notes, and Mickey instantly felt pompous and regretted elaborating.

Then the lieutenant asked about Falcon Holly and Magnolia Court. Then Melvin Burruss, and Mickey wasn't so sure on the third name, not until it was clear that some people called Burruss "DJ Mel B." Norm Titus and Wayne Humphrey were also subjects of interest, and of those two Mickey knew only enough to attach names to faces. He also knew enough to keep quiet, because if he were looking for suspects, that was where he would look first.

But when it came down to it, Mickey never quite believed that anyone who knew Tommy would do him in. T. Tommy Briscoe was a sweet soul who must have slipped from the bridge

2

or roamed too far from the banks while drinking, swept away by some residue of design in the water, something no doubt left over from other times, deep layers of felony that underlay the old and crumbling center of the city, made the town eat its own.

After the lieutenant left, Tamar came halfway out of the bedroom, standing gaunt in the doorway like some hypercritical heron. The parlor contracted, and Mickey remembered where the front door was. After offering the conventional condolences—*Sorry about your friend* and *Wasn't that one of the people at John Bulwer's?*—she began a slow interrogation. Why had the detective come to visit them? Did Mickey know this vagrant well enough to warrant interrogation? Was it really so that he had seen Tommy Briscoe a safe fortnight ago (she actually used 'fortnight'), and if so, why would he be considered as a helpful witness?

None of this Mickey could answer, though he suspected simply that the police's net of inquiring had been cast wide. Which was unpleasantly not enough for Tamar, who would rather win the debate than learn anything new. So she continued from there, explained how Tommy's death would be good for Mickey in the long run. The less time with the gang at the bar and the book store, she said, the more time for finishing his own book and perhaps getting tenure at long last.

Mickey felt like a drink already. The Oscar Wilde opened at noon, and it was sunset somewhere. And Salvages was next door, the haven of books and John Bulwer—Iron John, Bookstore John, the neighborhood's Dharma Bum and sage. Bulwer was the one to provide solace after bourbon, so Mickey begged off the promised lunch he had been preparing when the police came to call, heading outside into the steam and blazes, bound northward through the court and the park, past the Witches' Tree toward the primary crossroads of Fourth and Fellini, at the juncture of strangeness and resignation.

***

His walk led him past the park's outdoor amphitheater. It was one of Tommy's favorite haunts, an epicenter in a city not often nor overly kind to vagrants. The grounds sloped gently toward a stage at the park's southeast corner, the century-old landscaping design still imposing a pattern. Mickey stepped off the sidewalk and wandered through the tiered seating.

Already July had singed the grass so that it crackled underfoot and browned in the pockets of light by the tennis courts and fountain. Mickey passed under the pergola and sat down on one of the benches. The amphitheater was the site of the city's Shakespeare summer festival—free plays, well attended in spite of the heat. Tommy and his crew had been accustomed to lie low on performance nights, but they would often come over to watch the plays. The old boy had some college, and the plays he chose to attend were either magic or tragic. This year, *King Lear* would go on without him: he would miss the ultimate play of the humbled monarch, the old man dispossessed on a heath in hostile weather.

Thou art the thing itself, Mickey whispered into the intermittent birdsong and the muted sounds of the city, the words eventually overwhelmed by a rising ratchet of cicadas. *Unaccommodated man is no more but such a poor, bare, forked animal as thou art.*

Mickey had sat in this very spot—the last tier of the amphitheater, his back to the pergola—and envied Tommy Briscoe. Had seen him seated up the slope on a battered linen duster, sometimes with his cohorts glittering and sometimes alone and drab. Mickey was sure he had romanticized Tommy's life, that there was a whole dimension of hunger and nastiness in the world of a *bare, forked animal,* and that his own marriage to Tamar, cramped and floundering as it might seem, was what his students called *white people's problems* by comparison.

So instead of some primal life on the heath, Mickey would

go to the Wilde for bourbon, to Salvages for books, and home of an evening when the cages were covered and the bride slept alone amidst paintings and parakeets—when the world of his apartment was quiet and dark and thereby more endurable.

King Lear was on for tonight, but for now the stage was empty. The set design was abstract, geometrical—not the craziness of Dolores Starr's mess of mirrors and inclines that had pretty much ruined George Castille's *Hamlet* two seasons ago, if Castille hadn't ruined it himself to begin with. And on the summer after, this had been the stage where lightning almost struck Tommy for the second time, when he'd drawn those kids into a kind of concert, complete with instruments and backup singing by Falcon and Magnolia.

"Gimme Shelter," they were playing when the storm hit. A *King Lear* song if there ever was one.

A grubby white cloth was draped improbably over the balcony like a flag of surrender, and it took Mickey a walk onto the stage and close scrutiny to recognize a linen duster, a ragged thing that might or might not have been the coat Tommy wore on his non-Elvis nights, the one he would spread across the grass for his seat when *The Tempest* or *Midsummer Night's Dream* had been in the offing.

Mickey climbed the backstage steps to the balcony and looked out over the park. The pergola, the crouching bronze lions at its end, extended across his line of sight, to their left the lovely little Mission Style Information Center, beyond them the glittering spout fountain and a line of mulberry trees over by Sixth Street.

The odd design on the back of the linen duster was visible only from where he stood. Half a rectangle, a perpendicular line rising from the center of its long side:

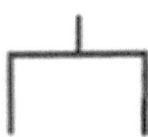

It was black and colorfast, marked in some indelible ink that you wouldn't have expected Tommy to carry. For some reason Mickey was wary of moving the coat: let the stage crew do what they liked with it later in the afternoon.

As for now, he was bound for the Wilde, and entered the bar a little after its opening at noon. He was the only customer, and the shady dankness of the place was consoling. Thanh was working in his customary crisp white shirt; he poured Mickey a bourbon, then returned to a spot at the end of the bar, where he thumbed his smartphone over what Mickey assumed were video games. Mickey asked him where Alan was and Thanh laughed, then rested his cheek against his steepled hands.

"Overslept," he said softly. "I leave him drowsing, because he need it."

The Oscar Wilde had been on the block since its owner, Alan Stack, came back from Vietnam. It started as a watering hole for the neighborhood, when this part of town was at its seediest and most decrepit: Alan said that at first it was right between a head shop and a beauty salon. Things changed, in the 80s, when for a time the bar and Dry Salvages were the only occupied buildings, then Stack found his establishment between a wig shop and a barber—what his partner, Thanh, called "a hair part on the street."

These days, the Wilde was a neighborhood pub until around 9:00 in the evening, when it transitioned smoothly into a gay bar for older men. Mickey had seen it happen once, seated at a corner table with a glass of bourbon and a copy of *Portrait of the Artist as a Young Man*, only to look up and find himself the youngest person in an all-male room.

But the bar was quiet this early, virtually empty. Mickey motioned to Thanh to turn on the television, and the afternoon news burst onto the screen, Ed Merz, the city's perennial and most reliable anchorman, going on about a riverside festival and tomorrow's scheduled 5K run through the old part of the city. Thanh groaned at the second news item, and Mickey understood why: bourgeois East End weekend runners, spandexed and well-watered, blocking traffic in this part of town on their vanity semi-marathon, while the residents sat on their porches and watched the pageant.

"So you do well, Dr. Walsh?" Thanh asked, still holding to a Viet formality even after knowing Mickey for five years.

"Well enough," Mickey said, never knowing whether to address him as "Mr. Thanh" or just "Thanh," or "Pham", given the protocols of Asian names.

Thanh had come over to join Alan in 1973, his own family either dead or scattered. He was only a teenaged boy when he rescued a wounded Alan Stack after a firefight during the Tet Offensive. There had to be a story there, and Thanh's calm and geniality sat side by side with the sharp attentiveness that made for almost the perfect bartender. Today, though, the planned run was evidently ruffling his Buddha nature. "More of a mess," he observed. "Good thing they go up 3rd. Is a block away." He wiped his hands with the bar cloth dramatically, having had his say on the whole matter.

Mickey nodded and tilted the bourbon in the glass, amber angling over the ice and that grainy, astringent smell.

Then Merz came back on center screen, the logo behind him a police chalk outline of a murder victim. The newsman announced, in that resonant voice familiar for a decade in the city, that two men had just confessed to the murder of homeless man T. Tommy Briscoe, whose body was drawn from the river early Thursday morning.

"You going to Salvages after you drink, Dr. Walsh?" Thanh asked, eyes still on the television screen. "'Cause if you do, you tell Mr. John. This he would wanna know."

ॐ

Mickey first saw him through plexiglass and myth.

Tommy was already a legend at the university. Famous for a sequined lamé jumpsuit, for a high pompadour and low sideburns. Famous for haunting the park south of Fourth and Fellini, for camping in the pergola by the stone lions, and in the backstage of the amphitheater during winter off-seasons. Famous as well for Elvis impersonations and as the front man of T. Tommy Briscoe and the Brischords, Central Park's midnight choir of the homeless and the derelict and the addicted, music of the fifties and sixties dispensed on perilous street corners until the it had become the soundtrack for the neighborhood.

Known ultimately for a small but provoking role in the history of the city. Electrified once (and years later, nearly a second time) within nearly a fifty-year span by errant lightning. Swept up and planted elsewhere by the '74 tornado. Chorus leader in a disastrous production of Euripides' *Bacchae*. Shot by a Zen Buddhist while stealing copper pipe from underneath Salvages Book Store, then miraculously restored to health at a downtown showing of silent films. Prophet, flaneur, saint and pervert, bearer of a number of names and titles, recognizable from appearance, girth, and by his habit of sleeping off hangovers in encased bus stops along the southern edge of the old city.

Mickey knew him at once that morning. Knew him by glitter and reputation. Didn't go near him, but instead congratulated himself on having recognized a local legend: it was the kind of sighting that was good for starting conversation before class, that might well earn some much-needed street cred among his terminally hip grad students, who Mickey could tell regarded him as already too old and too far down the academic pecking order to know anything useful.

But this first glimpse of Tommy he would remember—the first of only several of the man whose memory, about two years later, would occupy his life and spark his undertaking.

On that day when he saw Briscoe asleep at the bus stop, he knew only the outsides of the story. He would gather the rest through the stories of two other aging men—through Alan Stack, who owned the Oscar Wilde, but mostly through John Bulwer, whose store he visited that melancholy day when the city learned of Tommy's passing, that day when the boys confessed.

✳✳✳

Everyone in the neighborhood knew John Bulwer from Dry Salvages, the bookstore on Oak Street two doors down from the Wilde, a center of counterculture, shelves sagging with Beat poetry and fantasy novels, windows boarded against burglars and the city's constant humidity, so that you were sometimes lost in shadow when you approached the farthest stacks.

Mickey first went there about a year after he was hired by the university, astonished that a bookstore lay scarcely a mile from campus and that nobody had bothered to tell him. He signed a check for a pair of battered paperbacks--Tenzin Chogyel's *Life of the Buddha* and the old book on heroes by Otto Rank—and after looking at the titles, Bulwer looked at the signature.

"Mickey Walsh," he drawled, regarding the customer over his scuffed, half-frame sunglasses, his swirl of curly gray hair shadowed by the beam of an old tensor lamp. "Are you the Mickey Walsh the English Department won't admit exists?"

Mickey figured that he was, and Bulwer tore up the check and gifted him the books, saying that considering the circumstances of where he had ended up, Mickey would "need both *samprasada* and *cojones*."

Samprasada and cojones. Serenity and balls.

Mickey liked the image of himself as a renegade, a dirty secret. It was funny and embarrassing and flattering all at the same time. This simple observation earned Bulwer hundreds of Mickey's dollars in business, as Dry Salvages became his go-to bookstore over the next five years. Mickey often stood in the background for Salvages' events and celebrations, avoiding the small audience of lingering hipsters and Bulwer's bizarre and erudite assistant, the one people called Daddy Chrome. He eavesdropped from behind the poetry shelves or from halfway down the Spec. Fic. aisle—the one where the floor had collapsed in a 2008 earthquake and where, lacking the money for full repairs, Bulwer had posted a cardboard sign reading, *Beware: Here Lurketh Great Nyarlathotep.*

It was there, in the midst of shadow and Lovecraftian gods, that Mickey would listen in, while Bulwer held forth on Hunter Thompson, on Coltrane or Rimbaud or Joseph Campbell. It must have been like college was back in the '60s, but now it was poignant: the freewheeling ramble of a poor man's higher education not a mile from a university where classes were geared to business and marketing careers that the declining city lacked the resources to fill.

It was strange that Mickey never met Tommy Briscoe at Salvages. Only months before his death, Tommy started to drop by the store. It was there that most people heard firsthand of what he called his *exploits and deeds*, rather than catching the whiff of rumor around the university or the neighborhood By then the store—once the haven of fedoras, slouchy beanies, ill-informed talk about *Miles* and *Mingus*—had moved toward a gentler fare. Self-published urban fantasy lay stacked around and over Bulwer's desk, Henry James supplanted by *Hunger Games*, Mark Twain by *Twilight*. It was no longer Mickey's kind of place, nor Bulwer's either, and Tommy supposedly came there for the comfort and free coffee.

And for the stories. In an attempt to make the place a version of what it once was, Bulwer had established what he called story sessions at the store on Thursday nights. You could come to Salvages to tell or to listen: it could be a story you made up, a reminiscence, something out of a noteworthy book that you retold for everyone's or no one's benefit. All Bulwer's young following were supposedly there—Max Winter, of course, who might well inherit the store, and his girlfriend Ellie, the one who'd been burned in the movie theater fire. Apache Downs, the sf/fantasy blogger, and his perpetual sidekick Billy Shepard, and always Daddy Chrome, wizened and tall and probably straightening the inventory even while the stories went on. Mickey could only guess at what took place on these nights: he had yet to attend because he taught an evening class on Thursdays. But Bulwer had seemed encouraged by what went on there, and had invited him to drop in when the term ended.

✳✳✳

Bulwer was on the phone when Mickey entered. He looked up, signaled like he was hailing a cab—*just wait, it'll only be a moment*—and saying *yes, yes, it's what I suspected* to whoever was on the line.

Then Bulwer set down the phone and shook his head. "That was Daddy Chrome. Titus and Humphrey confessed."

Mickey nodded and sat down. The two newest members of the Brischords—young men in their early twenties, probably, and tweakers, from their tendency to gaunt and to bad teeth. Mickey knew there was nothing a tweaker wouldn't do, but even in that light, drowning Tommy seemed like a step beyond.

"It's hard to believe," he said at last.

"Even though," Bulwer muttered, lighting a Marlboro and

offering Mickey the pack, never remembering that everyone else had reformed. Mickey took one anyway, and Bulwer put on Keith Jarrett's *My Song*, some of that difficult jazz from back in the '80s that he was always trying to get everyone to like, some scramble of horns and piano that they all were supposed to make sense of.

Neither of them had much to say, so Mickey told Bulwer about the trip across the park and thinking he'd seen Tommy's old duster on the stage, and the symbol or sign on it, and Bulwer shrugged.

"Hobo signs," he said. "I haven't a clue how to read them, but ask Chrome when he comes in. He should know."

"Hobo signs? I thought those went out of use in the Depression."

Bulwer grinned sadly. "Tommy looked them up. He said that vagrancy had a genre, its form and duties. He even made the signs into some kind of code among the Brischords. Nostalgic, romanticized stuff. You didn't know him that well, did you?"

"And now I never will," Mickey said, drawing on the Marlboro and realizing how much he had missed them.

"No," Bulwer conceded. "But there is this." He pushed an old-school cassette tape across the counter. "Got a dozen of these. Tommy's life story, as told by. They ramble now and then—the alcohol would rise up and wrestle him down, and then the sentences would become garbled, the events suspect. But something happened during the story sessions, Mickey. It was like he narrated himself into a new man—that's the best I can describe it, and it doesn't do justice to what happened. In those last few months, he was transformed, gone full bodhisattva in his generosity and love and insight. I don't know whether the stories he told to us are what brought him into this newness, or whether the newness reshaped the stories once he got to where he was going and looked back on his memories."

Mickey stepped back from the counter, his eye on the cassette. "And you managed to keep these? After—"

"Yes. I was afraid they might be confiscated as evidence,"

Bulwer admitted. "But now that the boys confessed, I suppose the tapes are kind of public domain, that we can keep them. And I was thinking of talking to you about them anyway."

Mickey guessed what was coming. Most novelists who work at or around a university have the occasional student—usually elderly and almost never interestingly old—who approaches after class, claiming to have "a life story that would make a good book." He had learned early on to avoid such characters, but this was John Bulwer asking, no tedious old geezer. And Bulwer respected Mickey, and this life story was one of a man they both knew, potentially a tale of hazard and romance and *exploits and deeds*, and something Bulwer had said about the last months, the change in T. Tommy Briscoe, made Mickey think that it wouldn't hurt to see what Bulwer had on tape.

But Bulwer didn't make the offer. He suggested Mickey take the tape home and see what he thought, but Mickey imagined Tamar's stare as she overheard whatever unruliness passed for Tommy's life story, and it occurred to him how contagious chaos is: if he brought this work home, he figured, his house would never be the same. He imagined more of Tamar's retaliatory retail: a new silk rug, perhaps, and certainly another bird. He imagined the chilly silences between the waves of birdsong. Nonetheless, Bulwer was difficult to refuse, and the whole idea of Tommy transformed was the stuff of novels rather than mild and harmless memoir. So he pocketed the cassette and promised, against his better judgment, that he'd listen.

The tape could sit in his library carrel with unfinished things, until down the road he had to answer for it.

वेदवेद

But letting it lie there wasn't enough: Almost at once, Mickey wanted to return the tape. Though Bulwer had been subtle and polite about the possibilities, a writing project lurked in the hints and suggestions, and Mickey's patience had worn thin for such a thing. After all, he was in his early fifties, ignored in the world of his colleagues, teaching four or five classes a term so that the tenured faculty could pursue whatever life of the mind they could scavenge at the university: it exhausted him now when anyone placed even a solitary demand upon his talents.

That is, if you could even call them talents: Mickey had a drawer filled with novel outlines and the first paragraphs of short stories, but his energy failed when he sat down to write anything. His scholarly work-in-progress—a reader's guide to mythological modern novels (Hesse, Joyce, Mann, Lawrence, Faulkner, the covered ground of a worn subject) —was already the subject of mockery in his department, because the cast was all-male, most of the writers passé, and Mickey's German (Hesse, Mann) was rumored to be only high-school level (in this, his colleagues were actually generous: his German wasn't even *that* good). But the ridicule wouldn't matter if he never finished the book: after all,

Mickey was far better at imagining than at following through.

So a favor for Bulwer might well end up as one of many distractions. Mickey could see that already, and decided to duck out early. Knowing that Salvages had a website, he dashed off a quick email to Bulwer, telling him how *at this time, with summer classes underway and my scholarly research at a crucial juncture...* all of the dodging phrases of someone too educated and too lazy for his own good. All that before Bulwer even asked.

But on Monday, Mickey decided to leave the tape at his carrel.

He had almost forgotten it was in his pocket during the idleness of Saturday evening, and Sundays he usually spent in oblivious hibernation while Tamar went to services at Heart Ministries, the venue for the Rev. Aldo Wooters and his charismatic flock. Mickey would lie on the couch drinking Killian's and watching baseball, basking in the generous space the apartment offered in her absence. Over the last year, home had become even less a refuge, more a gauntlet of disapprovals. Tamar was again seething at his being passed over for tenure track, but it was not the university that angered her as much as it was Mickey himself

He slept on the sofa now, with no formal announcement that this would be his resting place. Instead, it had been more a silent, tidal ebb and flow of sleeping arrangements in the apartment. Tamar kept to the bedroom, her entourage a baker's dozen birds. Two parrots, three finches, a half-dozen parakeets the last Mickey had counted. A mynah and a macaw. Each time he completely disappointed her, she took in another. The lucky thirteenth—a parakeet—had come on the heels on the previous addition—the mynah, which she had brought in the week before, thereby launching her summer of disillusion. The apartment was so loud Mickey soon moved to an army cot in the kitchen, further than the sofa from the bedroom, as far away from the noise as he could get without sleeping outside on the curb. Whistles trailed from the bedroom at night, estranged calls from bird to bird, the mynah and one of the parrots repeating the catch phrases of Aldo Wooters.

She surrounded what was once their bed (now solely hers, he believed, at least at that time) with her paintings and doll collection, but mostly the perches and cages. Each morning, a little after sunrise, the apartment awakened to a shrill chorus of parakeets. But by that time Mickey was usually out of the house, making sure he caught the early bus to the university. No matter how much the clutter and cramped quarters of his carrel reminded him of the corner into which he'd painted himself, it was quiet and it was his clutter by choice, asylum from the growing problems at home.

***

Mickey was safer in the carrel, in a secluded corner of the library's fourth floor, and in the clutter he would be able to let Bulwer's tape quietly disappear, absorbed by trivialities. He laid it atop a pile of ungraded papers, descended the stairs, then walked across the quad to the classroom where he taught "Perspectives on European Modernism," which he hoped was not as dull now and then as its title proclaimed.

But today was not that occasion: as they began discussion of Joyce's *Ulysses*, the class was silent, their eyes on laptops and smart phones. Mickey knew that if he stepped out among them, stole glances at their screens, he would see they were checking email, texting, visiting social media—a pandemonium of image and word that had nothing to do with Joyce, nothing with their assigned reading. In desperation, he asked them how the book was based upon the famous myth, and when they looked up, gazes mostly blank and annoyed at his interruption, it became clear that they had no answers.

"Ulysses," he prodded. "Now who is Ulysses?"

"The main character in the novel?" one student offered.

Mickey had no idea how to respond without coming across as obsolete and boring, neither of which he could be and keep the class's attention for the hour. Reluctantly, he nodded toward the raised hand of Diana Chen, the only student who did the reading and thought about it. Pretty in her black Bob Dylan T-shirt, black jeans and black knit cap, the only flash of color her bright green hair, she could be counted on for good answers and good talk, the sole escape hatch in a desolation of students. Mickey feared the day she might be absent, knowing the class would dissolve, falling from its fragile dialogue between one professor and one gifted student into a stark and embarrassed silence.

But Diana knew about Ulysses, knew the outline of the story. Was beginning to see how Joyce was using old stories to make new ones. For now, Mickey was grateful, even more so when Diana flashed him a breathtaking smile and a wave as she left the classroom with a brace of friends.

Eager for his carrel, Mickey walked briskly over the west side of the campus. For a moment he caught a glimpse of Diana crossing the quad, linking arms with a young man and resting her head against his shoulder, half-hug and half-bump.

Mickey tightened his grip on his satchel and turned in the opposite direction toward the bus stop, past the high-rise parking garage and the low-rise library. There, leaning against the library wall, lay a pair of books he first suspected had fallen from the night deposit. Naturally, he picked them up. The library was open, so he headed for the door and the circulation desk before noticing that these books were not from the library. That they were about chess openings, of all things, and apparently books for experts, it seemed, as he skimmed the murky notations of one introduction. It felt like something you'd find in an old modernist novel, something dropped by magic before a sober German at the onset of a midlife crisis in which he would wander Weimar streets, meet hard-drinking flappers and feminine, vaguely Orientalized magicians.

It would have been a perfect omen, had the day been cooler and Mickey not so lazy and willful. Instead, he opted for the air conditioning, taking the library elevator up to his carrel, avoiding the stairway because the brief jaunt through the lower

Midwest summer had drained him. He tossed the chess books on the floor, atop review copies and a sweatshirt he'd discarded a while back, when March had become too warm.

Bulwer's cassette had not vanished of its own accord. Cassette players were outdated, even in the usually backward I.T. Center, Mickey told himself, and who needed to mount an expedition simply in order to play the damned thing? He was right in the first place: this whole undertaking could lead toward an enormous squandering of time.

A stack of papers on *Nosferatu* lay on his desk, essays that Mickey figured would be little more than plot summaries despite his insistence on looking more deeply, on seeing connections. Beside them lay a book he was supposed to review for some marginalized academic press, and a doctoral dissertation for which he was the third or fourth reader, which he had set aside in jealousy upon realizing that it was drunk with critical theory and therefore at least in part over his head.

All this work made the tape somehow more tempting, but Bulwer's use of cassettes was retro, previous century, and playing it would demand of Mickey a quest of his own. Dutiful inquiry to the university IT Center indeed uncovered a player, which they loaned out to him after he trudged back across the sweltering campus and signed in triplicate beneath the stare of an administrative assistant who was no doubt wondering whether a thirty-dollar device could be entrusted to term faculty. Alone in his carrel between his last two classes, he slipped the cassette into the player, hearing Bulwer's voice, recognizable but distanced and estranged by electronics.

TO

Briscoe. T. Tommy. Seventy years at the last equinox. Born in little Yorktown, south end of the state. Foothills of Appalachia, not quite in it, not quite out. Those are the facts, camerado. Facts are the mortar of history, there to hold up and hold together the substance of things.

I love that you have asked me to talk here in your store, among all the stories. I dreamt over places such as this when I was a child, and to find it a place of my refuge now that I am grown into a man. It is the country of heroes, and all I have to do is look around me to find them there.

I am a man of independent resources. Of late I have dollars in hand, but always I have been in possession of veiled cleverness, of doggedness, of flat-out luck—the things that have kept me among you for all these years, far past the life expectancies of your garden-variety vagrant. I am the wounded poetry of this town, our scapegoat and rebuke. And I chose this this neighborhood, not long after I fell into it by paternal accident, and I have learned to live here among its ghosts.

I used to haunt the library here in town when my mamma returned and come to work there, a ghost myself among the shelves of books. But here Daddy Chrome arranges this place by inscrutable logic: fantasy down the dark aisle with the hole in the floor. The books on religion side by side with psychology by the window, like brothers who barely speak. The rows of vinyl, from Miles to Koko Taylor to Tom Waits and the good Leonard Cohen—the ones before he quit cocaine. Had I known this was sacred ground I would of come here earlier, but I thought there was a cover charge.

And now you want my story among all of these.

***

The cereal aisle in Hutchins Market was like this. A bright arrangement of color and words and enticement, and the very first thing I remember, the first scene of the story. My first memory was of words—words stacked up and beautiful on the shelves of a grocery store.

Daddy had left us to live in the city by then, and Mamma had moved into the upstairs of Aunt Coral's house outside of Yorktown. It was just the four of us there when you added on my Uncle Med, but he was usually working so my early home was ruled by women.

Aunt Coral's place was what we called the old farmhouse and its few acres, handed down by my grandfather as the shared property of his three children—all of them daughters—held collectively because Pappaw didn't want it passing to another man. The middle girl, Aunt Topaz, was always sickly and died before I was born, and neither Uncle Med nor my daddy was the farming type. So it become what they call a matriarchy or a gynocracy up in there.

Our upstairs was four rooms off a short, wide hallway. One was mine and one was Aunt Coral's and Uncle Med's. One they kept empty in case my mother returned. One had belonged to Aunt Topaz, and it was filled with clutter and storage on account of she had died in it and nobody wanted to go in there.

Every kid has a room—or maybe a whole house—that he imagines is haunted. When I come to the city I lived only a few blocks north of here, and every Victorian townhouse within half a mile claimed to have a ghost in it. Not too long ago there were a couple *of histories that come out about the ghost stories of the neighborhood. I used to not believe in them, but now I'm not so sure. Skepticism is a brittle thing. It's a place to hide the ghosts.*

Aunt Coral's house was haunted at least by suggestion, and my mother's room was probably the most haunted of all. I know Aunt Topaz died down the hall, but my mother plain vanished. She was part of that first memory—that memory in Hutchins Market—and then she was gone from sight. So much that she no longer existed until years later.

But I'll get to that.

People have told me it was impossible for me to remember so far back, that a child's memory usually don't commence before three years old and that I wasn't three just yet. But then it is also held that memory can begin when you put words around things, and since my first memory was of words, then I think it was possible, that it might of happened exactly the way I recall it.

Hutchins was the name of our grocery when I was growing up in Yorktown, like I said. It wasn't big enough for you to call it a supermarket—more like the Winn-Dixies and Kwik Cheks I saw up around the city before the day of Kroger. Ten short aisles, the floors always sticky and that faint smell of meat turning or about to turn underneath the bleach or the Pine-Sol.

Of course I must of been learning my smells and colors back then, back when this happened. But I could almost swear it was in the cereal aisle at Hutchins, though what I remember about the store is almost all from years later, and this memory is spotted and blurred, like ideas stacked on each other.

I remember my mother pushing the bas-kart—that's what they still call them here in the city. I remember my legs dangling out of the child seat. My knees were bare, so I expect it was summer, and the light was glaring, and I was riding slowly down the cereal aisle looking at the bright colors, the animals on the front of the cereal boxes where they had turned them face out as a display. All of a sudden the lines above the picture of the baseball player took shape and sense and direction, like colors took shape as they fell into words and I understood the word "Wheaties" above the man

I would recognize a few years later as Hank Greenberg. It must of been like that Frenchman felt when he was looking at the Rosetta Stone and the hieroglyphics suddenly dropped out of pictures into language. Because the whole world opened up, the colors casting circles on circles until they were creating patterns I would not again see the likes of until I dropped acid up in the city when I was in college. I remember pointing to the Raisin Bran box and reading the name aloud, and my mother gasping as she stopped the cart, and then pointing to the Rice Krispies and saying "rice".

I turned around in the seat then, looking for her, after her agreement or approval. But over my shoulder I saw her rush down the aisle and turn, and she went away. I swear it happened. And happened like that. And I know I must sound like a character in a book or an old story, whose adventure starts when he can scarcely walk. But there are many times that a story takes very little shifting to fit a book—as many times as when you have to twist it into some shape to make a story.

Later on, Aunt Coral told me that Mamma was simply scared how a two-year-old could do that. That she was afraid to think of where that left her, Daddy run off and her grass-widowed with a boy wonder on her hands. They told me Coral cleaned up after Mamma that day, as Coral always did back then: someone at Hutchins who knew Mamma and me called my aunt, who got a ride from a neighbor and come to the rescue.

Coral said she had the neighbor leave the car running, thinking she'd be only a minute picking me up. Said she found me in there happy as a clam, reading labels for the Hutchins workers. Kraft Cheese. Fritos. Ritz Crackers. While they waited for Aunt Coral they had tested me, and when I could read the names they had started writing down others on paper so I would not look at the picture and pretend to recognize the words, but Aunt Coral said later that I had read most of them, which was better than most of the grownups who shopped at Hutchins could do, and she said she kind of understood Mamma's fear and running away.

So that's a story mothers tell, I heard later. An urban legend that fixes itself to smart children or boastful parents, and there's a child in every school that is supposed to have this moment in his history. So believe it or not, but consider this: the one true result of my moment in the grocery store was that my mother vanished. She would call now and then, and she always sent presents on birthdays and Christmas and sometimes for no special reason. But she had gone away, pretty much, and I was raised by Aunt Coral and Uncle Med, who pushed things back in the shadows, underneath the bed and around the old boxes and trunks.

✳✳✳

We had no attic to speak of, and the cellar was give over to the furnace and to Aunt Coral's washing room. Sounds come from below when the coal heavers arrived, and the hand crank creaked on the laundry wringer. I didn't go down there much because of the hatchet stuck in the wood over the stairway, which I was afraid to pass underneath.

But the room where Aunt Topaz died had the door open always, and you could walk by and see things half in light and half in shadow, so they weren't forgotten, but regathered. It was physical: you took it in with all your senses. It was hot in summer and in the winter, the drafts would slip through the walls and brush against you as you walked by. One time a rat got in the room through the walls, and even before Uncle Med got rid of it you could smell it in the boxes. You know they have that smell that's like soured metal. That room was solid and certain, while it gave off emanations.

Mamma's bedroom was kept as she left it. Aunt Coral and me would go in there to dust, but we rearranged nothing, so even in the time I lived there, as the house passed from the '40s into the '50s, this one room remained the same. There was a time—I must of been four or even five, because it was before Becky Thatcher appeared, and I was lonely and looking for a place to hide—I hid in Mamma's closet to draw away from the world.

It was a little curtained alcove off her bedroom, all these clothes from the thirties hanging in it, and when I returned there after Aunt Coral had gone downstairs I found out that it went back a ways into a depth of the house I didn't even know was there. It was like that book where the children step into the wardrobe: I'd just read through it at the time, so maybe I was hoping one of our closets would have recesses, too, so maybe this is out of that book, and I only imagined what I am about to tell you.

At first I was scared to go back in there, but the cave you fear to enter holds the treasure you seek, and I knew that by instinct. So I crawled into the depths and into the light, because alongside her movie magazines, Mamma had collected buttons and costume jewelry, and there was a small ceramic bowl filled with multi-colored stones that caught the light behind me and glittered like treasure in a Technicolor cartoon. I sat down on the *Photoplays* and *Movie Mirrors* and looked them over, turning them in my hand like available gems. Even at five I knew none of the stones were valuable, but the light was caught in their colors and it seemed to set that dark closet all aspangle, like sometimes stained glass does when the sun shines through it into a dark church. And it was like I could read the light like I read the boxes way back in my earliest memory.

So by the borrowed glow of the costume jewelry I looked at the magazines I was sitting on, and I read through them all the way back to my mother. I didn't know some of the words, but I could make out the names under the photos, some circled on the page years ago by pen or eyebrow pencil. Barbara Stanwyck, Joan Crawford, Olivia de Havilland, and Helen Mack—the girl in *She*, you remember? I put on one of Mamma's turbans, it was black rayon velvet, and when you pushed back the netted veil, you looked like a prince in the Arabian Nights, you could explore caverns and find jewels and become a character in a large and wonderful story just about to begin. It was like Mamma yearned for that kind of thing, like just maybe when she left me in the cereal aisle she was heading out to find some purpose and undertaking.

Then the tape settled on dead air, and Mickey thought it was over. But it was only halfway through the reel. Bulwer had divided the interview into short sessions that lasted for about twenty to thirty minutes each. The tape reeled silently as Mickey took stock of Tommy's account, refusing to believe much of it at all.

It stood against most cognitive science that a child could remember in such detail. The tape was a tall tale, a drunk's story. Yes, Tommy was more grammatical than some, his reminiscences a little out of the ordinary, but it was a fable. It would have been more interesting to come at the story through its grit and sorrow.

He could barely imagine what life was like adrift in the city. Granted, it was more temperate than up east, less relentless than down south, but the middle ground seemed hard to maintain without a roof over you.

It was violent here: Mickey knew that much. Half the city concealed and carried, and between opioids and meth the vagrants were asleep in alcoves or atwitch on the street corners. The city was the dirtiest he'd ever lived in, but he'd heard of the north-south rule—that the litter piled up more in Nashville and Birmingham and New Orleans, so perhaps the lowest point in the Midwest was cleaner than elsewhere.

And the city hid layers of peril. Only this summer, university employees had been warned about a series of maulings west of the campus, the forensics of which baffled belief, suggesting a big cat or obscure Native American weaponry. Drownings became more frequent as the seasons changed, and early July was the Time of Floaters, when unidentified corpses drifted to the southern banks of the river, borne on the current sometimes for weeks, then disgorged in the red mud as though vomited from the stomach of a snake. And Mickey's own neighborhood was a suicide quarter, where hangings and guns to the head shook the community biweekly through the summer heat, as though residents decided to give up when the power failed.

Things could be worse, that was for sure. Mickey counted his scavenged blessings when Ed Merz intoned the daily list of the dead—a redneck truck overturned along the freeway that circled the town, a brother shooting yet another brother in the summer-baked projects.

And now the drowning of a homeless man and the confession of his murderers, a story arc that ended abruptly, barely having begun, and with such predictable drama that Mickey could not turn his thoughts easily to the past, seeing all of Tommy's life through the lens of its undoing, and wondering how much meaning even a good storyteller could fashion from the mess.

And he wasn't that good a storyteller, he decided. His novel resisted shape, and his scholarship headed nowhere. He didn't have the time for true crime. Mickey checked his email, opened a return message from Salvages:

> Re: Briscoe Project
> No, you don't sound ready. Wish you were.
> JB

As he deleted the mail, there was a knock at his carrel door.

Desperately he looked toward the desk light, the true giveaway that he was in. Though he had papered over the carrel's solitary window, you could still see the light in the room, and at these moments, cornered in a remote spot in the library, all he could do was move away from the door and keep silent, hoping the intruder would go away.

The last time it had been Athena Bumpas, department chair, wandering far from her spacious office to check on him, "poke her head in the door" to ask him how his researched fared. *Fine* he had told her: *the manuscript is being considered for publication*, when in fact the reader's guide proposal had just been turned down by the tenth academic press, and the only *consideration for publication* was Mickey's own wondering whether it would ever happen. This time, at least, a kindly editor had urged him to "go back to writing your own fiction, as literary criticism is hardly your strong suit," and the rejection had felt like encouragement. So Mickey told his persistent but uninterested department head that the general opinion was that it was *rough to transition from fiction to scholarship*, that the book would find a home after he had *shored up some necessary research*.

Bumpas did not believe him, of course, but it was a step in the long game Mickey could continue through another semester of ducking colleagues in the hall and hiding in his carrel.

This, too, would pass, as would the intrusive knocking in the quiet of the library upper floor. Or so Mickey suspected until the cassette tape lurched into the second recording, and Bulwer's voice rumbled into the carrel, re-introducing Tommy, who would again go on about his life story and the house and a cousin dead and deeply mourned.

"Professor Walsh? Is that you?"

An unfamiliar voice—not Bumpas, not any of the cadre of tenured pettifoggers who called themselves "core faculty", because none of them would have called him Professor. He opened the door cautiously to discover Diana Chen, holding an essay and looking up at him, irresistibly startled.

***

Naturally, she had done her essay early, eager for Mickey's feedback and no doubt hoping for a chance to revise before next week's deadline and the two weeks that followed, when her classmates' papers straggled in, rushed and unconsidered.

Mickey invited her in. But she paused at the doorway, smiled and handed him her paper, then tucked a silky strand of green hair into her cap. She stretched, braced her hands against the frame of the carrel door, her narrow hips leaning to one side. Then she turned around, and glancing back over her shoulder, told him she was *eager to hear his comments.*

That was all. The eagerness touched him like a faint perfume, lacing through the dreamy smell of mold and paper. He watched her walk through the stacks: she turned once again briefly, no more than a quick pirouette before she vanished behind a shelf, and all the while Tommy's voice continued on the player behind him. Mickey's hand shook a little as he rewound, having lost track of everything that was said during this brief and disarming interlude.

Bulwer began this part of the conversation. A husky smoker's cough gave way to a flat declaration of time and place, and then to a kind of prompt to Tommy, something that made Mickey believe that Tommy's memory, even after the space of several days, was in need of a tactical jog.

"Picking up the conversation with Tommy Briscoe," Bulwer began, "about where we left off on Friday. You were talking about your childhood at your Aunt Coral's. About the house and the farm."

VI

I've been telling you a lot about the house. There was Aunt Coral and Uncle Med, and there was Cousin Dilly for a while, a big old gangly teenager who was their only son. He was killed in Korea in '52: I must of been not quite five when it happened. I don't remember much about Dilly except Aunt Coral took to her bed for a week when she got the news from the army. That, and that he liked to sculpture things. There were the clay men no bigger than your finger, set in marching order in the dead boy's room, and there were the scarecrows out in the garden. Those were the statues I remembered.

Dilly made the scarecrows out of crossed tobacco sticks and torn shirts. Stuffed them with straw like in The Wizard of Oz, and set them up when spring approached, getting a head start on the birds. He put up two of them—one at the gate and the other at the far fence—and at night You could see the one by the gate, leaning over the fence like it was trying to unfasten the lock and come into the house. Some nights I would stand sentry by my bedroom window and watch them, figuring that if they come through the gate I would have time to wake up Uncle Med, or even Dilly himself, because if you knew the secret of how to make a scarecrow you surely knew how to unmake one, and knowing the men were in the house made me

31

feel safer, but not completely secure.

The clay men were different. There was a Chinese emperor who had an army of terra cotta soldiers lined up on duty underground, guarding all of his tombs and chambers, which I think of now when I remember Dilly's sculptures. But back then, they were fascinating and temptations: Aunt Coral wouldn't let me touch them, and they were even more hands off once Dilly was killed in Korea and his corner of the room became a kind of shrine.

After Dilly's death, the whole house kind of turned over. He was Aunt Coral's and Uncle Med's only child, and it must of been like the rooms of the house contracted when they got the telegram. Uncle Med only spoke of it once to me, telling me that the bond of father and son was like nothing else in the world, that it anchored both of you in your place and your manhood, that someday I might be lucky enough to know that bond. It was a strange thought, and I dwelt on it now and then until I come to understand it years later in the city.

Aunt Coral set out to make the whole farmhouse a shrine to the longed-for dead. The place piled up with ghosts, then, what with Dilly's corner and the whole room devoted to dear dead Aunt Topaz, and the grinding sound of the wringer washer in the basement when Aunt Coral did the laundry, and Mamma's absence. I have spent my life with ghosts and I can tell you they are a needful people.

Because of that need, and because of simply growing up, I found myself getting out of the house more and more. Early on it was my Aunt Coral who took me places. Mainly the library and Milton's Dime Store and the radio station, because Yorktown had its own call letters and the songs that they played—"Jambalaya," "White Lightning," all of Kitty Wells and Ray Price—everything that become a huge wheel that would center on Elvis when I was seven or eight.

I didn't have many friends. Aunt Coral would surely of told you that there was something eerie in a four-year-old boy who read books in an upstairs bedroom, lit by flashlight even in the daytime, sheets over his head and an electric fan blowing on him in all seasons. The times that she and my uncle tried to bring me together with other *children were times that did not go well. I can remember coming back to the house in Uncle Med's pickup, starting to breathe again as I clutched my* Edith Hamilton Mythology *as the truck climbed the red dirt driveway where Aunt Coral's car would be parked in the exact spot to block everything. And from that place in the road you could look up toward my bedroom window, and if it wasn't too late in the day I thought I could see the clay men casting shadows from the light on the desk, like shades standing by the window awaiting some boy's return.*

✳✳✳

Becky started like a shimmer over scorched blacktop. She appeared on a hot summer day as I tried to mold soldiers out of the red clay bank at roadside by the mailbox. She rose out of light, way over where the paving met the distance, and since I had seen mirages before, I did not regard her at first, but went back to the clay. When I looked up, the pocket of dark space was nearer upon me, and I watched it approach. It shambled up until it wasn't far from me at all, standing in the middle of the road and taking solid shape, until it was the doughy form of a girl about my size, standing on one leg and looking at me, eyes and nose and blonde hair appearing out of the half-solid shape of her, sinking again into pasty whiteness, like her face was surfacing out of the water, then going under, then rising once again.

Usually you blink at those things and they vanish, and the road was clear and definite around her as she seemed to simmer up into being, and she moved like foam on the river, and at first I could not make sense of her. I wiped my red hands on my shorts and scrambled up the bank to the house, where I sat guard on the glider and waited for something to draw near. After an hour or so, the sunlight past the trees in Uncle Med's yard began to tilt away from me and fade, so I headed upstairs.

And she was waiting in my room. Sitting at the table by Dilly's clay men, stretching out her watery hand and touching one of them, and I started to shout that it was against the rules, but I held back because I didn't know whether she was real. She turned to me and smiled, still fixing to touch the little statue. I stared her down and she drew her hand back, and the visits and the friendship started.

✳✳✳

I have read since about the astral body. When I was in the city I was in the library a long time, and the second floor shelves housed shadows and impressions. I found the writings of turn-of-the-century theosophists and mystics, and they spoke about the cloud of thought that hangs about you when you dwell on things, the vibrations and forms that are your emanations. It was there in that big-city library that I first begun to understand what Becky was, how she no doubt grew out of my longing for company.

But back then I figured her a ghost or some kind of resident spirit, and I would ask Uncle Med if he knew of anyone who died in the house. He would tell me Topaz, of course, but I had seen her pictures, and Becky was something of a different element, a strange creature between my thoughts and dreams.

By the time I turned six, she had color and full appearance. She followed me from room to room, and Aunt Coral, who always indulged me after Dilly's death, took to setting a place at the kitchen table for 'Tommy's imaginary friend.' Becky spoke to me first at that table, her lips moving and her utterance rising at last to a whisper, and by the time she had been talking to me about a month I began to understand her, to translate the little whispers and bird calls into speech. She would talk about air and water, about the woods to the east of Uncle Med's farm and the consolations and safety they offered with their shadows and sun, and the little Arethusa Creek that run through them.

She would talk about her mother as well. Thusa was in the woods, Becky told me, and Thusa was the woods. You could see her when the sunlight tumbled down through the leaves, or the creek caught the moonlight later in the day. Sometimes she was a reflection, and other times a blue heron standing in the water. I wanted to believe Becky, but I was already sinking into nature, so at *the time I thought that she told stories.*

Though Becky followed me at first, there come a time when the rules changed. On a hot sunny afternoon in the summer when I was seven, she rose from her chair at the table on which the clay men sat, descended the steps and passed across the eastern fields headed toward the woods, turning now and then to beckon me to follow. I could see the pear trees through her blue transparency, shimmering and wavering like you would see them through the rain. But the ground was dry beneath them, and as I followed her into the woods, I looked down at the wasps and the bees, drunken on their backs from the turned nectar of fallen pears.

I stepped into the shadows, and it was like the woods swallowed sound.

It happens in the city sometimes, when you step into one of those Victorian walking courts like the ones south of the park, and the street sounds get muffled by the close houses. But here in the woods there was an energy, like when you put a nail right at the edge of a magnet's pull and it tilts a little on the table, then settles as its weight struggles against the attraction. Something pulled me inward, and Becky vanished into the shade entirely, and left me to follow the draw at the heart of the woods.

I took off my shoes and waded through Thusa Creek, and the slow current broke muddy over my ankles because it was August and the water was low. I climbed to the far bank, leaned against a water maple, and started to put my shoes back on. Out at midstream the current sparkled over the rocks until they looked like a submerged treasure, like hidden gold. Then the flow of the creek seemed to stop and the waters to settle. I noticed I was at the center of something, that I had sat down in complete silence, and all nature and movement had stilled except for me slipping the shoes back on my feet.

I looked up, then, and a blue heron was standing in the glow above the underwater stones, balanced on one leg, regarding me sidewise, her gray neck and head coiled lazily over the flowing water. Something in me settled, and I knew I was home, and it was dark before I remembered where I was and started back to Aunt Coral's house.

But I carved a sign in the bark of the maple. Something that I could find when I decided to return.

When I got back home, Becky was waiting for me. She had filled a bowl with corn shucks and soaked them in water, wrapping them skillfully with her cloudy hands. She looked up to me and smiled, because I knew what she was doing, had learned the craft some time ago from my Aunt Coral, who had told me that corn shuck dolls were girls' work, but work it would not hurt me to learn.

While the shucks were soaking, Becky peeled a strand from one of them and tied it on my ring finger, then built the doll in the half-light of my bedroom as I watched her work and my fingers twitched. It was a far better job than I could of done, and when she was finished she held it up to me and smiled again and said it was ours. And I was drawn to it, and at the same time embarrassed, because we were standing at the threshold, her and me, of something very private and bridal.

It's our family, she whispered, and the curtains fluttered to the meddling wind. 'Our baby and your little son.'

And despite of the prospect of laughter and ridicule, that corn shuck doll would make a trip with me in the days to come. It would sit on a dozen windowsills, eyeless and dry and smooth, and be my companion in the city.

VII

Dry Salvages had changed since the first time Mickey dropped in a few years back. Back then, college students mingled with *poètes maudits*, wannabe blues singers with painters who would often surface later at Tamar's shows.

But nowadays Bulwer's following was dwindling. Tonight it was the skeleton crew of hipsters: Apache Downs and Billy Shepard, Max Winter and his girlfriend Ellen Vitale, who looked irresistible in a sun dress despite the glossy discoloration of the burns on her arm and leg. Daddy Chrome was in the back at his constant, obsessive task of shelving inventory, Alan Stack was up front, thumbing through a copy of the old Farina novel, and John was at the counter, leaning across and smoking, going on about baseball to a largely skeptical audience.

"I think it's generational," Apache was insisting. "Like our MMA up against your boxing. It's just moved on, and we can study baseball but we can't live in it."

"Oh, yes you can," Bulwer said, beckoning to Mickey. "A defined space that hints at an infinity. Other sports may hint at mythology, but that's what baseball *is*."

Max rolled his eyes, suggesting he'd heard this all before.

He got up from the counter-side chair to give Mickey a space, and thirty years his senior, Mickey sat down, a little grateful for the courtesy. Some things were generational indeed.

"Baseball," Bulwer went on, "is mythology because each game is a story that contains the prospect of eternity."

Max wrapped his arm around Ellen's waist and she leaned into him, her blonde hair light on his shoulder. "'Prospect of eternity' is right, John," he said. "It's the one sport that feels like it lasts forever."

Everyone laughed, and Billy Shepherd caught Mickey's eye and bowed, his hands folded, Buddha nature to Buddha nature. Mickey supposed that it meant someone was still reading his novel.

"Hey, now!" Alan chimed in, up to now a precinct nobody'd heard from. "If it's generational, the gods have departed. What's the Cavafy line, Johnny?"

"There are several Cavafy lines, Sergeant," John answered with a grin. "You know the one you're looking for."

"Oh, I do," the old barkeep replied. " *'Say goodbye to her, to the Alexandria you are losing.'*"

The kids regarding him with puzzlement, Stack rhapsodized about Crosley Field and County Stadium, lamented that now you had to go to Wrigley or Fenway to see the ruins of old sacred space. He recited the names of the ghosts—Furillo, Robinson, Spahn, Musial—like a litany of gods, and you could almost see the eyes of the young ones glaze over, heirs to a generation of 'roided millionaires in whatever sport they followed or didn't follow, or for that matter heirs to the staged performances of wrestlers and rock stars and charismatic politicians. Stack was in the right church, but the wrong pew: everyone in the room was in search of that world he was describing, but they simply couldn't read his map.

Then Bulwer took over, went on for a few minutes about how a baseball game could last forever, how the diamond was a kind of mandala which held the tension between movement and repose, east and west, offense and defense. How the angle of the foul lines made the whole world the playing field. It was poetic stuff and a little nonsensical, but he stopped it when Mickey pushed the cassette across the counter to him.

"Sorry you couldn't work with me on this," Bulwer said, turning the tape like a book he was pricing, then slipping it into a drawer beneath his antiquated PC. "But be honest: what do you think of it?"

"'Becky Thatcher'? Really? I'd have come up with something original instead of nicking *Tom Sawyer*."

Bulwer laughed. "'Emma Bovary,' maybe? Or who was that one in *Misery*?"

"Annie Wilkes," Mickey replied. "I'm going to look through the shelves."

Bulwer had a gift for needling. Mickey knew from long experience that there was no malice in it, but it was a kind of humor that unsettled, that lanced a guarded wound and drew out infection. So Mickey thought about the email, how he'd signed off on the project like some self-absorbed full professor, and wondered if Bulwer had taken offense at the dismissal. But Bulwer no more read malice than dispensed it: his ironies were gentle and selfless. So Mickey wandered shriven through the shelves near the back, around the hole in the floor where the light barely reached, and up by the back window, half-boarded against intruders but a place where a little sunlight crept along the spines of the mythology books.

Most of these, of course, were Greek stories retold, with some more scholarly works interspersed. They stuck to the shelf when you tilted them, but the pattern of dust indicated that Daddy Chrome had moved them recently. All the interesting stuff was bunched together and cornered: even in the last year, Mickey could see a great change in Salvages' inventory. The time would come, he figured, when these books were replaced by paranormal romances with impossibly beautiful models on the covers and stories impossibly plain on the pages.

Then a discovery derailed his self-pitying thoughts about the Decline of the West. There, between two young adult novels was a copy of Campbell's big book on the hero. Hardbound, in great shape. No doubt a fairly recent printing, or Daddy Chrome would have placed it on the collectors' shelf. Mickey opened the front cover to find its price a surprising $3.95: Salvages was always reasonable, but seldom rock-bottom.

The locomotive drawn abruptly, almost childishly on the back cover was no doubt the reason. The light back here was slanted, deceptive, but it seemed to be drawn in the same indelible black he had seen on the linen duster in the amphitheater.

He carried the book to the front, where Daddy Chrome was huddled with Bulwer on some matter of pricing.

"It's a good reading copy," Bulwer said. "Hardbound at that price is a deal, too. Sorry about the train."

Still a little annoyed by the earlier teasing, Mickey smiled nonetheless to seem more gracious than he was. Daddy Chrome looked at the drawing and said, "Synchronicity, gentlemen. That's Tommy's handiwork."

Bulwer turned the book to regard the drawing. "Why a train?"

"Not sure," was Chrome's response. "It's a hobo sign for 'catch out here.' You know, departing trains and whatever. Tommy liked the Hobo Code. 'Hoboglyphics,' the scholars call 'em. But what's it doing on a perfectly decent copy of Campbell? I'd be switched if I could tell you."

Then Mickey drew him the sign he'd seen on the linen duster.

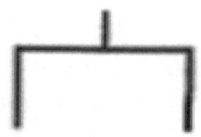

Here is the place, it meant evidently, and Daddy Chrome was not surprised to find it at the theater stage. Though he had no idea who might have put the duster there, he had little doubt that the hoboglyph was Tommy's, too.

It made sense to Bulwer. The stage was Tommy's center of operations, he said. The omphalos, his radial point. But why he had taken to defacing merchandise—if indeed he had—was more a mystery.

"Do we have your attention now, eminent Mickey?" he asked. "Are you prepared to undertake?"

Mickey allowed that his interest was piqued, but let on that he still had priorities and a schedule.

"What do you think the sign on the book is there for?" he asked Daddy Chrome. "Your best guess…"

He scratched his head, the broad "I'm thinking" gesture of a bad actor. "Usually 'catch out here' meant a point of departure. Where you could pick up the train for parts elsewhere. Why it's on a book is another matter. Maybe it's another kind of departure point. Maybe if you can read it, it's for you."

Mickey fought the temptation to pick up the project and run with it. Tommy's mystery was more and more inveigling—a scholar-gypsy coding the neighborhood with signs and wonders.

"I wish you'd do it," Bulwer pled softly, dropping the soft irony for something a little more compelling. "I owe Tommy, after all."

✳✳✳

Mickey knew the story from Max Winter, shared with a joint outside Salvages one night right after Bulwer had locked the store down. And even without the cannabis it was hard not to laugh at it, imagining Tommy scuttling all heavy and hairy into the crawl space in search of copper piping, which was valuable currency in the underground economy of the neighborhood, the untraceable tangible asset of crackhead and wino.

It was a time when the neighborhood had been plagued by a

number of burglaries in empty properties—newel posts from the Victorian houses along the western part of the precinct, leaded glass from the windows and period tile from the fireplace hearths, all fenced through Honest Herman's Antiques and Curiosities up on the eastern end of Broadway by the cemetery.

In an act of protective paranoia, Bulwer brought a shotgun to the store—an old 12 gauge—and some heavy field loads he emptied of shot and filled with rock salt. It pained him to remember it now, it mortified him and unraveled his *ahimsa*, his Buddhist non-violence, but there you are. And when he arrived early on a Sunday and, unlocking the front door of Salvages, heard the scuttling of something underneath the flooring, his response was quick and thoughtless.

Now the truth of the matter, Max explained, is that rock salt is pretty much harmless unless you shoot someone at close range. It so happened that Tommy had gotten about ten feet into the crawl space and become spooked by the dark and the oppressively close quarters. At least that was what he told Max later in the theater. So Bulwer came up behind him, six or seven feet away, and blasted a round into his ass.

Bulwer said Tommy's pants shredded like someone had blown off fireworks in his back pockets. Said he roared and scrambled sideways into the shadows, that you could see the soles of his shoes catch the light and dig into the earth of the crawl space. That there was a rattle and a moan and all of a sudden he pulled himself up into light through the hole in the back shelves of the store. It was rough going for Bulwer to back his way out of the crawl space, and by the time he did, Tommy was well gone, moving like a ragman through the parking lot of the abandoned grocery store, past the laundry and into a space between houses. Not that Bulwer planned on chasing him down.

Later Bulwer would hear about the miracle at the Shangri-La Movie Theatre down on Fourth Street—the healing ministrations of Dr. Caligari.

Tommy, it seemed, had sought refuge in the balcony of the Shangri-La midway through a benefit showing of the silent classic, *The Cabinet of Dr. Caligari*, the arty German horror film about the mad doctor who sends out a sleepwalker on a killing spree. Tommy would claim later—and Max was a witness to his testimony, working at the Shangri-La during the last six months before what he called "the Tarantino Fire"—that Caligari had healed Tommy, or so he claimed, with a stare from the screen into the shadows of the theater, a stare meant for him alone. Max also claimed that, though his pants were shredded, Tommy's backside was sound, if dirty.

Bulwer and Tommy would reconcile outside Huntington's Diner less than a month later, but the shooting lingered in Bulwer's memories and regrets, and unlike the good Buddhist he tried to be, he dwelt with his violence until, like the lapsed Presbyterian he was, he reckoned that an act of charity and homage would clean the slate.

Yes, Mickey understood the penance. He felt Bulwer's pain, if not T. Tommy Briscoe's. He just didn't want to devote a year of writing to the cause of atonement.

The cassettes contained a tall tale, and the tale grew in height at the prospect of several more recordings. Which was why Mickey surprised even himself when, joined by Alan Stack, he followed Bulwer into the back office, accepting an invitation to hear yet another tape. What interested him at the moment was less the story Tommy was telling than Bulwer's response to it, his need for it. And for that matter, Daddy Chrome's and Max's needs as well, and apparently Alan Stack's, for some reason, because he joined Bulwer and Mickey in Bulwer's inner sanctum to listen to the next recorded stage of Tommy's exploits and deeds:

७१११

School was a lonely place for me, and it was a good thing that Aunt Coral taught second grade there or I would of had no friends.

Yorktown Elementary was built by the WPA ten years before I was born, and by the time I went there, it still had a kind of new-building glisten, like a castle decked out for a banquet. The floors were waxed and the gym was still spanking new, on account of it was outsized for grade-school children, who would rather play outside the school. At the time it was the cleanest and the brightest place I ever seen, but there was a sadness there in wandering the halls alone.

Something in me knew that York Elementary was no place for Becky Thatcher. Early on I had figured her as insubstantial, hazy and translucent for a childhood friend. She come to school with me the first few days and stood in the back of the classroom. You could see the door of the supply closet through her blue dress and pale arms, and she was always scowling at me in a manner that made me wonder whether I should ignore the teacher and focus on her instead, make sure she was happy and settled in our new surroundings, or if I shouldn't be there at all, should be back at the farmhouse among important things rather than sitting in a circle and reading when I could do that already.

For a while I pretended to struggle with the reading, because I didn't want to stand out, and the young teacher was pretty and I liked her attentions. But at home I was already halfway through a children's version of The Odyssey, all filled up with great adventures, with monsters and magic and natural hazards, and next to its wonders Dick and Jane and Baby Sally seemed trifling and dull. But there were moments in these books where the words ran against a picture, because we were not yet supposed to recognize "squirrel" or "candy". It was like a reward in the midst of your reading, like hieroglyphics for the young, and I would look up from the page and rejoice silently, knowing that while my classmates knew the picture only, I was in on the greater mystery, knowing the connection between the picture and the word that gave it meaning, and only a small step away from knowing, as I would by the end of the year, that there was a mystery that connected the picture to the thing it represented. For a while, I thought all of those connections were my own extraordinary secret: I told only Becky Thatcher, because there was nobody else I trusted with such knowledge, not even Aunt Coral. Things and the pictures of things and the words about them, all connected. And the word and the picture, I told myself, were not really the squirrel and the candy they stood for.

It would take me a while, though, to understand that the same unreality held true for the creature in the tree and the sweets in my mouth. And when I figured that part out, I would be prepared for the rest that would come to pass in Yorktown.

To be honest, so little came to pass there, and for so long. The sameness of its days was at first a solace, but it was not long before I knew I was trapped in red dirt and Appalachian foothills, between the dust from the quarry and the hot smell of tar from where they were laying the roads out of town. All creatures of greatness—the ones who rose above their surroundings—were politicians or preachers, and early on I discovered I lacked the appeal of either, and I figured it meant I was headed nowhere.

I wanted to love school because Aunt Coral loved it so. At least I could ride home with her in that 1950 Plymouth P-18 Deluxe that seemed to stretch halfway from the town to the farm. I would stand in the back seat and hop on the upholstery as I told her how the day had gone, making up half of it but sticking to the facts of the story only enough to spare Aunt Coral my loneliness and gloom.

Sometimes we would head to town after the school day, to Hilton's Dime and Notion Store, to Brake's Drugs, and the courthouse.

The courthouse was the second version of the building. The first was relatively new in 1864 when Confederate guerrillas come through recruiting and, finding all the young men hidden, burned the old building to the ground. Another version rose from its ashes in the early 1870s—this time to become a haven of peace, encircled by old men playing checkers, whittling, and telling impossible stories.

The Tattered Men, I come to call them. Comfortable scarecrows, clay men on the shelves of my childhood. They had stories, and I was now of an age to listen. I sat by the benches and checkerboards, the pungent smell of Red Man and smuggled whiskey dense in the air, as they would go on about their adventures.

Fett Pruitt told me he had been a Confederate general, a claim I trusted until I was old enough to do the math. Even then, I assumed he could be long-lived, like the patriarchs in Genesis. But when his son, Little Fett, claimed to of been a Confederate colonel in his own right, I was too savvy to believe him, but something in me still shifted the numbers, still wanted to believe.

George Bannister recognized me as the nephew of Medgar Downes, and told me how once he had been fishing in Thusa Creek, about where it divided our farm from the Guthries'. There he was momentarily swallowed by the most enormous catfish to ever roam the waters of the state. He figured it had found its way upstream from the Mississippi Delta, muscling up against the water's resistance, always upstream, gathering strength and size until it followed the bend of the Ohio north and east, then the Cumberland south and more eastern still, always the harder direction until it squeezed itself between the banks of little Thusa, its wide mouth raking the red mud until it caught up a young boy fishing midstream, swallowed him, *bore him along through Medgar Downes' woods, past the Guthrie cemetery and all the way up to that point where the creek narrowed past the clearing where Stephan Downes shot the wolf that cold winter, and he asked if I knew that spot and I nodded, though I was not sure I knew it at all, just swept up by his telling.*

It was there, George said, that the fish could swim no further, that it wedged betwixt the muddy banks, its gills flogging the current for air, and then it spewed up the boy ten yards upstream, and he should know because he, George Bannister, was that boy, and just look at this scar on his forearm where the catfish finned him as he spurted out to safety.

I heard the whole tale, but begun to doubt it about the time the fish took a turn up the Ohio. Or begun to doubt the facts of it, though I continued to believe the tide of the story to its very end, swept up in it like the fish and George Bannister, adrift in the adventure of the tale.

Then Ben Koger would tell me how when he was a boy the water witch in my uncle's woods had cured him of lying forever. Not like some, he would tell me, nodding at Old Man Bannister and winking. But Mr. Koger's stories seemed as embroidered and strange as Bannister's fish tales, though he assured me they were cleansed, because of the granny witch who haunted Thusa Creek back when he was a boy.

He saw her on the banks, he said, not far from where the catfish got lodged. Said you couldn't tell the difference between her and a regular woman except for the way the sunlight shone through her skin. And she looked straight at Ben Koger and announced what everyone in hearing knew—that he was fixing to tell a lie.

He told the granny witch that lying was what he was used to, that it was the solution to problems and sometimes the key to pleasures, but he said she wasn't having any of it, that if he kept on lying it would come back to plague him: eventually, she said, he would start to believe himself, and then the things he said would lose their power. Lying would sour his breath and rot out his teeth, and that he kept on doing it he would spend the last of his years alone.

Well, Mr. Ben said this scared him some, and he asked the

granny witch if there was anything—anything at all—he could do to stop his lying. 'Like drives out like,' she told him. 'Look around you. Everything you see, hear, take hold of with any of your senses? What if it is a lie? Even you?'

Of course that made Mr. Ben think some. What, indeed, if he was a lie? And he said he looked at his hands, watched his reflection hold steady in a calm pool by the creek bank, only to vanish when a current of water turned it again into an eddy, a flow. It was like the world was falling apart in front of his eyes: he couldn't put a word to the creek or the woods or himself, because those things could dissolve at a moment's notice, into mud and water, wood and leaf, skin and flesh and organ. Even the moment was a memory, Mr. Ben assured me, everything you think: because the second you pin a thought on something it is no longer there. When you understand things, he told me, you are making things up when you think you understand. It's all a story, he told me, and stories are the ways we make sense of things even when things don't make sense. Something in that calmed me, though it would take me years to find peace in it, and when at last I did, the peace was not in Mr. Ben's story but in coming to know that a story is a lie and a truth at the same time.

Back then such speculation made my head hurt, and when I told Ben Koger that, he laughed and said he understood, because here he sat by the courthouse, alone in his last days, with bad breath and rotting teeth and a game of checkers which was the same few patterns put together differently.

I don't remember whether it was the same day or one earlier or later in which Simeon Bandy, who usually played the black to Ben Koger's red at the checkerboard, spoke up at last after never having joined in the stories. He would drop in at the courthouse occasionally, emerging from mystery and bound for mystery, with only an hour's stay at the boards, where I never saw him lose. I don't know whether he talked to me first on the day Ben Koger told me about the granny witch and lying, or whether those occasions were days or weeks apart, but I suspect it was the same summer, that it had to be—right before the autumn when Nicholas Mays come to visit, which I will tell you about later—but it was some afternoon all humid and sunstruck, with Sim Bandy in a black wool suit way too warm for the climate, and me hunkered by his chair as he stopped the game with Ben Koger and looked off toward the hills and the rock quarry and the haze up there, and said, 'Boy, the time was when I knowed both your parents.'

IX

"So when did you know him first?" John Bulwer asked, when the tape reeled into silence and the three of them—John and Stack and Mickey—sat in its aftermath. Mickey understood that it had passed the time for fanboy stories of sleeping hobos in bus stops.

"You first," Mickey said. "The both of you."

It turned out John had met Tommy before the incident of the crawl space, had seen him a number of times near the CVS across from the store, had taken up conversation with him and found him harmless and far-fetched. Had even seen him in full Elvis headed south down Fourth Street before the midnight choir one time, on an overcast night in early July that boded rain and lightning. Bulwer had followed Tommy that evening, down to the park and the theatre, where Bulwer said he heard the Brischords for the very first time.

It was a revelation, apparently. Multi-racial, multi-aged, multi-gender, more than what America was supposed to look like and more of what weird America was bound to bring to the table. Tommy in full lamé and pompadoured like a goombah, the background singers Falcon Holly (alto), Daddy Chrome (baritone), and Magnolia Street (transvestite), with DJ Mel Burruss playing karaoke cassettes off a boom box. It was a time before the kids had joined in—the now-dead De Chevre boy and the nerd kings Apache Downs and Billy Shepard—and Bulwer claimed there was something to the sound back then, not pure but cleansed of some impurity. It was a kind of jubilant innocence, he said, from the least innocent of sources, because there wasn't a one of them in that vagrant quintet who hadn't been damaged by the way the world rushed on around them. The confusion and the tumult of the music was a shadow, then, contained and given meaning by the circle of the park.

Bulwer said that the night he followed them to the amphitheatre, he stopped at the mulberry trees near Sixth Street and watched the lights from the theatre stage—mostly moonlight, he said, but a ring of candles and lanterns the girls had produced from somewhere, so that the flames caught the glitter on Tommy's lamé and not much else, the others moving in shadows as the singing continued. John Lennon's "Instant Karma," Bulwer said. Other loopy '60s songs—Donovan's "Hurdy Gurdy Man" and "Atlantis," Zep's "Ramble On," all done with strange Jordanaire background vocals. The Stones' "Gimme Shelter," which was Tommy's signature song in his street-corner summer concerts, but also the bizarre "In Another Land"—it was as though they were all embedded in Bulwer's memory, which was no doubt part of why he was so sorry when he filled Tommy's backside with rock salt later on.

But he said the last song they sang was Leonard Cohen's "Hallelujah," that broken and melancholy and exultant song that apparently Tommy was singing before it became a standard on all those karaoke television reality shows. Bulwer was still standing at a distance, plucking mulberries from the tree he was under and eating them slowly, pacing himself because too many of them aren't good for you. He said when the song began, either he drew nearer or the circle of candles widened to take him in, because the park gently filled with light, lamps and votives all around him all the way back to Sixth Street, and as Tommy was singing the last verse, the one about an uncertain God and nobody seeing the light, the radiance faded suddenly and winked out at last, and all that was left was the tight little circle of candles around the stage, and the Brischords singing that long chorus of hallelujahs. It was emotional to hear Bulwer tell it, with the yearning in his voice, and when he was done he lit a Marlboro and confessed that on that night he had been smoking weed and that it all might have been that, just a buzz from the reefer.

Bulwer regretted that he had gone full 2nd Amendment on Tommy Briscoe's ass not a year later. At the time, he claimed, there had been a number of break-ins on the block, the usual chaos at 4th and Fellini expanding over several blocks, and Alan Stack had arrived at the Wilde one Monday morning to find a back window broken and a case of vodka abducted.

Bulwer confessed it was a time when his dharma warred with his patriotism and lost the battle. He had bought a shotgun two months earlier, telling himself he would wave it at intruders and hope for the best, but if the best didn't turn out he had loaded the shells with rock salt, unaware that you pretty much had to be point blank to the target before they would do damage. And it turned out, that afternoon in the crawl space underneath Dry Salvages, that he was close enough and then some, tearing a hole in the unidentified and shadowed bottom that happened to be attached to Tommy Briscoe, and the rest became mildly and locally historic.

Mickey had heard a version of this story from Max Winter, who was an usher and menial at the Shangri-La Cinema north of Broadway. Max claimed that Tommy crashed the benefit showing of *The Cabinet of Dr. Caligari*, sneaked to the balcony of the Shangri-La, and cried out early in the film. When Max and another employee rushed toward the balcony to see what had happened, they found the old reprobate cured remarkably of what he claimed had ailed him, at least to hear him tell it. Tommy claimed that the good Dr. Caligari himself had reached through the screen and healed his wounds, and sure enough there was no evidence of the shooting on the old man's semi-bare rear end, though the seat of the pants had been through trials.

After a pause, Alan Stack spoke up, saying he had heard the shooting story as well. That his first meeting with Tommy was when he almost threw him out of the Wilde one rainy Thursday night a week later to the day. Tommy had staggered in a little late apparently, when the bar had shifted its clientele for the evening. He had that boiled raisin and urine smell of persistent bad wine upon him, and he was a little too much local color for the older gentlemen who just wanted privacy and safety among the likeminded.

Stack had guided him to the door, where for a moment they stood and Tommy assured him that it was only refuge from the rain he sought, neither alcohol nor companionship. Thanh was there, fortunately, and reminded his partner that this was a neighborhood establishment, so Stack relented and Tommy stayed, telling stories as a kind of admission to the group. First he told of his miraculous healing, then of his electrification on a balcony over at the university. By closing time the regulars had circled around him to hear the stories that kept coming, stories of the town and their collective youth.

Stack, it seemed, had introduced Tommy to Bulwer's evenings of storytelling, and for over a year had listened as the neighborhood's favorite mendicant Elvis had told stories of Yorktown downstate, of being lightning-struck and tornado-swept in the big city, elf-shot and saint-addled in this particular neighborhood. Stack confessed to being proud to have reeled in a local celebrity, and confessed as well to giving Tommy the occasional drink on the house, against Thanh's better judgment and after the stories subsided. This kindness was what bothered Stack the most, for he had come to think of it as an impurity— less charity and more a way to bring back the entertainment. Now, in the aftermath of the week's tragedy, he was certain he was the last of the friends to see Tommy alive, and fairly certain he had given out one for the road on that fateful night when Tommy did not need one more. So he was atoning, too.

It was why they had enlisted Mickey. He had less of a dog in the fight, they claimed. He could write the story, because the way Tommy told it was more like a novel than a history or memoir. And again Mickey begged off, excusing himself because of too much work, too many obligations, but now they tag-teamed him there in the back office of the book store. Under the ironic stare of the two older men, he was asked, then asked again, about his own first meeting with T. Tommy Briscoe, and, no, glimpsing him asleep on a bus stop bench did not count at all.

So it fell to his turn, and Mickey told Bulwer and Stack about the time he saw Tommy at Cave Hill Cemetery, the funerary landmark at the edge of town, a week or so after burying his mother.

Madeleine Walsh was not the forgiving sort. Her waning years were the first of Mickey's marriage, and she and Tamar, each of whom cordially hated the other, were at least allies in their disappointment over him. Madeleine would hover in her parlor, standing with the aid of a walker, her limbs aquiver with suppressed rage as she dismissed Mickey's novel, his position and salary at the university. The door was closing, she told him: after fifty, it was too late for a man to become serious.

She did not live to save the date. Dying when her son was forty-nine, Madeleine insisted on being buried in the city's most historical and prestigious cemetery. She planned her own funeral, and when Mickey suggested that she might want to be buried beside his father in Vermont, Mother claimed that Cave Hill was fine by her, and that he wasn't Mickey's father, anyway—a preposterous claim, since Mickey looked just like the old man. Ultimately, she got what she wanted: a lavish funeral and "a tombstone with birds atop it—surely even you can manage the birds, Mickey." And since he was in the same town, what she wanted extended beyond the mortal coil, for he felt obliged at first to go to the cemetery for regular visits.

Of course, Tamar never accompanied him. So on Sunday afternoons, his routine consisted of going or not going to Mass, but always ending up at Cave Hill before they closed the gates at sunset, standing before the grave with reluctant relief, wishing he had mourned or could have mourned. He had taken charge of the birds on the tombstone, as she requested. But he had chosen herons, having read somewhere that they devoured the weak or ailing among their young. They were his memorial atop hers, a story from the inside, writ subtly in stone from its every angle.

Mickey tried not to judge as he stood before the marker, the herons facing one another stupidly across the marble, the grave in a spot that lost light by noon so that by this time of Sunday it usually lay in shadows. So when a darker shadow crossed the grave while he was standing there, first he took it as a trick of light until he heard Tommy speak behind him.

"Gate's about to close, young fella," Tommy said, and no longer being used to being called *young fella,* Mickey was flattered and turned, expecting a kindly old man, but getting instead the heavy, hairy article, complete in lamé, pompadour and sideburns. Mickey knew him instantly, and when asked whom he was visiting, gave him the short version. Tommy admired the birds atop the tombstone and said something about *honoring our mothers no matter what,* and when Mickey asked him what brought him here, he said that it was a place you could sleep safely, was all, and he wished Mickey well and ushered him out, and it was a first conversation of surfaces, fraught with meanings Mickey would understand only as the project began, as he began to research, to talk to the neighbors.

Because Mickey took the project, of course. On a handshake and nothing more. In that little side office of Bulwer's decrepit store, he accepted yet another of the tapes. It was almost superstitious to tell Bulwer that maybe the project was a good idea, so Mickey said that this tall tale about magic in a Southern small town had changed his opinion a little, though in fact what he had heard was not as convincing as the worries over what he was going to do if he didn't take up some new work, and take it up right away.

He thought about the apartment filled with birds and paintings and resentment, about a university carrel filled with the clutter of rough drafts and failure, about hiding places and unattended matters.

It was early evening when Mickey left the book store, walking through the park on the way back home. The production of *King Lear* was afoot at the amphitheater stage, rumbling over the scene on the heath. The king himself is homeless, and the disinherited son of the Duke of Gloucester, Edgar, is playing at crazy, disguised as a madman named Tom.

And of course there was little reason not to stop and watch. The king sat on the stage, surrounded by the last remnants of his following, and the storm rose up on the heath. Mickey could see the drummer rolling against the tympani backstage, for the acting company billed itself as using original effects—*the ones they used in Shakespeare's time,* Bulwer had announced ironically, *right down to the PA system and the electric lighting.*

The actors gestured broadly, and the drums rolled again as Edgar ranted above the tumult, the famous speech about the wandering madman eating rats and cow dung and warding off seismic demons. And even though Mickey could see the artifice, he was swept into the story like he always was with Shakespeare, and a rumble in the distance, a real one of approaching thunder, rolled across the river and the western neighborhoods of the city.

The first drops of rain fell as the scene ended, and the lights went up, and the announcer proclaimed that the play would undergo a rain delay. As the audience rose from their seats, picking up the blankets and newspapers they sat on, gathering their popcorn and sodas and heading for the cover of the promenade, Mickey made for home. After all, the story didn't end well.

The rain rose as he walked through the court past the central fountain where the goddess rose from the water, which spilled over the half dozen or so little godlings that crouched below her at the surface of the pool. Some neighborhood smartass had dressed her in a wool hat, and the lamplight caught her in a half turn, green little breasts shining with new rain. As Mickey reached his door, the sky broke open, and he thought about poor homeless Lear's confession in his own staged deluge on an imagined heath:

> *Poor naked wretches, whereso'er you are,*
> *That bide the pelting of this pitiless storm,*
> *How shall your houseless heads and unfed sides,*
> *Your loop'd and window'd raggedness, defend you*
> *From seasons such as these? O, I have ta'en*
> *Too little care of this!*

It was the only passage of the play he had ever committed to memory. And now the reason he had memorized it fell into place at last, as he took the first steps of a journey mapped out for him. Because Mickey had *ta'en too little care* of Tommy and his kind, just like all of them had done. And while Bulwer's and Stack's sins against Tommy were those of commission, his was, perhaps, that of omission, having guessed what was right and decent all along, but having neither the gumption nor the energy to do it.

The apartment was still except for the plaintive chipping of one of the birds, still hopping about in its covered cage. Tamar wasn't in yet, so Mickey sat at the kitchen table and listened to the next of the tapes.

X

Sim Bandy didn't tell me much about my mother that I didn't already know.

She was the spoiled one of the brood, the pampered youngest child of Alma and Daniel "Redcap" Stockton. She followed Aunt Coral to college, and by the time Mother got there, Redcap had saved enough from tobacco farming and teaching and odd jobs to foot the bill for at least one girl. She had made a teacher, like Aunt Coral had done through hard work and waiting tables, but instead my mother turned toward drama, spending her first year studying to be Barbara Stanwyck.

When she come back to Yorktown, she had taught there for a respectable decade. Then she had pushed into spinsterhood, thirty and unmarried at a time and in a county where twenty was held to be too late. At last, in the fallout of an awful scandal, she took up with a boy named Ace Briscoe. There were other secrets as well— secrets kept from me that I would only find out later—but the young couple settled at Aunt Coral's in a kind of unspoken shame, my mamma continuing to teach and my daddy working the quarry for a while, but soon out of work, leaving Mamma to support a man twelve years her junior.

When Mamma turned up pregnant with me, it gave the scandal new life. She was old to have a first child by county standards, and of course the story returned about how she 'robbed the cradle and drew an ace from the deck.' Somehow, if she had not been put in a family way, the town did not have to think of conceptions, but of course it made it rougher on her to teach, Aunt Coral said. The school year come to an end about the time my mother started showing, and at midsummer Ace took off on a business matter, leaving her at Aunt Coral's and promising to be back by evening. Mamma told him to pick up a gallon of milk at Hutchins', told him she wouldn't need it until the next day.

He didn't come back. At least not while Mamma was in Yorktown. So Pearl Stockton Briscoe (she kept the "Briscoe" on account of dropping it would make it sound like I was a bastard or most likely that she was the mother of a bastard) didn't return to the school, didn't settle into a job, just stayed at Aunt Coral's and got bigger and sadder. When I was born she set up my crib in Aunt Coral's bedroom, where it stayed until I grew out of it a few months after she had left me in the cereal aisle.

All of this I know, from what my aunt told me. I slowly gathered the rest like a nosy child gathers rumors and half whispers. But it was Sim Bandy who first told me more about my daddy, about his skills and demeanor.

Ace was a picaro, as I learned that term in college. A rogue, like the wandering heroes of old Spanish novels. Simeon Bandy had heard tell of my father's further exploits, of him making his living from shoplifting in the smallest towns to street and roadside peddling, all the way to bigger dodges in Nashville and Memphis, in Birmingham and Louisville, on account of he traveled a lot in his ventures. Department stores were Ace's frequent target, the simple old changing-room scam, and he had more elaborate car and apartment stings that I could tell you about as well, but his major sources of income were tactical and solitary. Pool and chess sharking—Sim had no idea how to play chess, being a checkers man, but he said that Ace's pool hustle was artistry, a long dance of push and pull. I knew nothing about such things back then, least of all that they would become my source of income through my growing years, when my father drove into my life after his long absence.

I saw Ace Briscoe for the first time when he appeared at Aunt Coral's door the day before my tenth birthday. It was a Sunday morning after Thanksgiving, and he pulled up in a brand new Montclair Phaeton sedan. I recognized him from the pictures, but I felt more for the car than I done for him—it was red and white, its body streamlined like lightning had carved it from the metal. It wasn't scary but it was dangerous enough to reckon with.

I recognized him from the Polaroids. He seemed kind of ageless, though, much younger than I had imagined for my mother's husband, and I think it was then I begun to realize what had scandalized the neighbors, though I could not put words around it then. He was right about thirty, olive-skinned, his black hair shiny in a D.A. so that he looked like a delinquent in a movie. I nodded stupidly from the porch when he asked if my aunt was at home, and he stopped at the door and looked back, asking me if I could talk or if I was just plain impeded. I found my voice and told him to go on in, and in a minute I heard voices raised inside, his and Aunt Coral's, then Uncle Med's eventually.

Wasn't long before Ace come out the door and sized me up, telling me to get in the car, because we were headed to the city. Uncle Med followed him out and nodded to me, and I was off on my first adventure out of Yorktown. We were headed up the old Dixie Highway to the city, where Ace promised me we would see a show at the Armory and have us a Co'Cola. I warmed to him considerably for the offer, for the trip and for missing Sunday school. It was about three hours driving from Yorktown to town and to the Armory, and all the way Ace told me stories about life on the road, about his tour with the Army against Hitler (and how it had been him who killed the Fuhrer in a knife fight, no matter what they told me at school). By that time I had learned my lesson regarding war stories from "General" Fett Pruitt, I could do the math enough to know Ace would of had to be outlandishly young when he seen service in Europe. And this time the numbers made it possible, however stretched, so when he said, 'I skewered the Fuhrer,' the bad rhyme made us both laugh, and me in part because it was perhaps true. It was the first laugh we shared with one another, and we stopped for lunch in a diner shaped like an enormous Indian teepee, and by the time the fries and the greasy burger had somewhat settled I had somewhat bonded with him.

We passed through the small towns, circling three or four courthouses. Only once did Mother come up, and Ace said only that she was a good woman and a good teacher—a knowledge that I trusted would somehow mean more when I could gather up other pieces later. Then the roads before us become four-lane instead of two, and we were approaching the city.

A railway overpass spanned the parkway heading north to town. It's still there, though every month or so a trucker wedges his rig underneath it trying to take a short cut through that part of town, and the traffic is diverted for hours. But the first time I ever saw it was that Sunday morning. Signs and portents painted on its abutment, high school nicknames and slogans I can no longer remember. I used to think the King's name was blazoned there already, although I might be confusing it with later graffiti—the things they wrote after his passing. And after all, at ten years old I was not yet skilled in reading the mystic signs.

But I felt the air crackle about me, like when you pass through static electricity, and even the hair on your shoulders and the back of your neck seems to bristle. We must of driven by the park and past the library and up past Broadway, because the next thing I saw was department stores on both sides of the streets, and restaurants and a lineup of theaters—the Ohio, the Dodd, the Rialto, the Shangri-La and the Bijou. For me they were names out of the Arabian Nights, and it seemed like I had arrived in a land of marquis signs and awaiting lights.

Ace parked the car in a big surface lot on what was Walnut Street back then, and he opened the trunk and produces this Radio Flyer wagon. It was an amusement too young for me at ten, but its false bottom—a board spread over the wagon bed, a wide gap in its middle—caught my interest, because I was coming to a fascination with secret compartments and illusions, like the closet in my mamma's room. He ordered me to sit inside the wagon, to slip my legs between the board and the cold metal bed it covered. Then he spread an old army blanket over the wagon, so it looked as though my person ceased at my waist, as though my body was halfway there.

Ace hauled me to about a block from the Armory and set me on a street corner with an empty coffee can near the handle of the wagon. He told me to sit there, to not fidget, and to look pitiful. And the passersby started making it rain like they say in Seventh Heaven and the other clubs down near Berry Avenue, but these folks were donating for the crippled child, quarters and half dollars and even a patch of green in the can, and Ace staring me down from a distance so that I said nothing. By the time the show began at the Armory there was thirty dollars in the can, and that was 1950s money. Ace had a gift for the mystique, had placed me at the right corner at the right time. He told me a while later it was all position and angle, like a game of chess.

He talked about the chessboard to me as we sat like kings in the high seats of the Armory, overlooking the stage but away from recognition. It was back then I learned that the last tier in the arena was the vantage point, the best view of all in a complicated house, that the cheap seats give a body philosophical remove. Ace told me that when you were in doubt during a chess match, it helped to stand and step away from the board, because at a distance all geometries looked different, took on clarity and slipped into their design. He had enough foresight to know, he told me, that chess is a better game when stripped down to mathematics, when the pieces rise into diagrams, diagonals and verticals and angles above the wood or plastic of bishop or pawn. It was like they left their bodies, he told me. Like they rose and converged on a plane where they become energy, where they were purified of the carved horses and the castles and the mitres that constrained them. In the air they became clean and abstract, and Ace told me that at that level of the game, it took a wizard to do the numbers.

And I saw what he was saying. From the time we had gone beneath that underpass, the city had commenced to show me new forms, new intersections. When we had passed the park and the theater where years later I would set up my kingdom, I had seen people on the stage even though it was late morning and they never show that early, transparent actors borne aloft by wire and cable, the faint noise of lines rehearsed in accents as we sped by in the Phaeton. And the mysteries had not let up: when the money rained into the can, I felt my legs vanish for a moment and I almost cried at their loss until my father emerged from an alley and restored them and lifted me to my feet.

And it was all leading up to this. After a spell, the lights dimmed in the Armory, and we waited after that until the band come out and the first song began. Then the god come on stage from behind the drum kit, his jacket buttoned and slick as sharkskin, and halfway through "Heartbreak Hotel" I understood, on a level underneath knowing, why Ace Briscoe had brought me to this place.

It was the first and last time I saw the King incarnate. There were other times, in dream and in acid, the time in the tornado, but here he was in a time of his greatest beauty, right after the second album (which I bought two days later) and over a year before he joined the Army. That night he was radiant, agent of visions, and I swear I saw another behind him as he played and sang and danced, an avatar of swirling gems and light, and I wanted to ask Ace if he saw it, but I was afraid to turn away, afraid that it would be gone when I looked again. It could not of been a shadow or reflection, because it moved in a different manner, behind him and then absorbed by him, then covering him and receding. It had a separate life and glamor, it expanded and gestured like a judoka through "Don't Be Cruel" and "Love Me Tender", while the drummer and bassist seemed not to notice.

He ended the set with "Hound Dog," and as the applause swept over the Armory the glittering figure behind him continued to dance as he took his bow and passed through it into the shadow. Ace nodded to me and we left by the side door, passed through the alley to the Phaeton and headed back the road we'd come up. As the U.S. highway branched into state roads we talked about the show, and Ace gave me five dollars on the haul I'd made.

He promised we would do this more often and in other cities, and at ten I could believe him until well after Christmas. But that evening everything seemed possible even when the tank of Yorktown's water tower came into view and we turned on the gravel road to Aunt Coral's. I had no idea that it would be midsummer before I saw him again.

I got the first album for my birthday from Aunt Coral and Uncle Med, the second for Christmas along with five dollars I spent on a plastic chess set and a book to try and learn the game. When it come spring and the old men were on the courthouse square, I took the chess set up to see if any of them knew how to play, but none of them did. And Sim Bandy had passed in the cold of January, taking with him the possible stories of my parents. So the chessmen sat on the shelf by Cousin Dilly's clay men, and spring turned toward summer and the month of my great and surprising change.

Years later I would read the story in 'News of Today' about the archaeologist who unearthed the bust of Elvis on the shores of the Aegean Sea.

It was near the town of Commagene, a city ringed by walls next to an ancient port, or so the news article said. The archaeologist, a man named Giuseppe Tucci, had uncovered the stone bust, and it took some people in his crew to recognize the resemblance. The News wrote this as proof of reincarnation, and when I seen the face, reading the tabloid as I sat on a park bench behind the theater, I could see the resemblance, but I wondered if it proved anything all that spiritual. Statues, I knew by then, were commemorations: they set spirits in the memory, so that when the eye rests on bronze or stone, on wood or clay, the heart remembers how spirit breathes into inanimate things, and that maybe because of that, the whole world is alive, at least in places particular and attuned.

I knew my Uncle Med's farm was alive, was a breathing patch of land. That rock and red dirt and the spare forest of hickory and water maple all housed resident spirits, some of them lively and loud like Becky Thatcher, while others waited silently for approaches and changes.

In this time of waiting I fashioned a bust of the King and set it among Cousin Dilly's clay men on the sacred memorial shelf that Aunt Coral had marked off in a room full of ghosts. I moistened Dilly's long-dried clay with tap water and spit, let it set for a weekend until it was once more pulsing and workable.

Clay itself is alive, I am told. It houses organisms that respond to the pressure of your hand and fingers. And maybe that was what they meant in Genesis, when God sculpted Adam out of earth and at the last step, breathed a soul into him—a breath that was part of the breather like blood or seed or jism.

The clay head resembled the King somewhat, and partially my father in its hollow cheeks and poker face. I sculpted the eyes shut at first, but when the summer broke and the first October rains swept over the southern half of the state, I dipped my hands in rainwater that had pooled on my windowsill, then moistened the face again until I rubbed the eyes open.

It was then that I saw the clay figures and the shelf, the house and the farm and the woods beyond as expectant, breathing and whispering me out from there and away.

***

There are places that subtract the world. I suspect they are like Ace's geometries, like the countries where chessmen go to die. But they are powerful places, and I have been in maybe a dozen of them during my time. It is like all commotion moves away from them in centrifugal force, like when I would drop a stone at the center of Uncle Med's pond, and a body could ride a band of energy away from them, through concentric circles until finally that energy comes to a stop, in the farthest circle where forms walk, glittering or shadowy, enlarged and moving on their own like the one behind the King on that long-ago November night. But at the heart of the wheels within wheels there is a stillness, people. And if you find that once in your days, you count yourself blessed, and I have found it maybe a dozen times, so many times that I figure I am one of God's dowsing rods, that there are places where I have walked that underwater springs have risen up to follow me.

In the woods I found the first of those places, that winter and spring after I had seen my daddy and turned ten. Over the paling fence and into a field that sloped down to the frog pond, where the drone and rattle of the wild choruses fell silent when you drew near. But that was not the secret center, the heart of the wheel, because you could still hear the rush of the creek off in the woods, and following the sound would take you into shadow and into a stillness that hid all kinds of vibrating life.

Uncle Med gave me freedom of the woods, except for one area I was forbidden to go. That was where the Guthrie farm bordered our own, and I was not supposed to venture onto their land.

It wasn't that the Guthries were hostile. I had met several of the family up in town when I was with Aunt Coral, and I was always greeted pleasantly and Velma Guthrie would make small talk to Aunt Coral, all the while keeping her hands tightly on her little twin sons, Donald and Ronald, like if they slipped from her sight the world would end. It made me glad, to see her attentions, her mother-hen hover, but something in it made me sad as well, so I would wander over to the courthouse or to Hilton's Store while she spoke to Aunt Coral.

Velma might of thought I was standoffish or peculiar, but I was simply drawn away from the Guthries when they clung to each other, like it was something I wasn't supposed to see, a mystery. After all, Uncle Med had told me that the Guthries kept to themselves, in a kind of territory between distance and mystery. It wasn't a forbidding place, but you kept away out of respect.

Which was like the Guthrie graveyard, which lay near the fence on the edge of their side of the woods. A path led up to the fence and stopped, and you could look across and see the headstones. I asked Aunt Coral how far the dates on the stones went back, and she told me the Guthries had been there before the Stocktons, probably over a hundred years, but that the stones were not my business.

Sometimes I went with Becky to that spot in the woods. When we did she would melt into the light between the trees and become insubstantial, she would distill into a voice in my head tempting me onward, and I'd look over the fence and try and read the stones, but they all faced east toward the Guthrie house, so you could only guess that the big ones were the heads of the family and the smallest the babies. And then Becky would come stand by me at the fence, all watery and translucent, sometimes just a blue ripple against a backdrop of trees, and she would coax and goad me to climb the fence and wander the cemetery.

I never done it, though, until the summer after I saw the King in the city, in the fullness of August when I was ten, right before Nick Mays come to Uncle Med's place, offering me a summer job.

Until then I had been mostly a studious sort, already helping Uncle Med with some of the lighter farm chores, talking to Becky at the edge of the woods or out my window at night as she sat on the roof, hanging between mist and some kind of smoke congealed and doughy in the air of the hot night. And we would talk about the books I read, and sometimes I would imitate the King for her, singing "Love Me Tender" until I no longer wondered nor cared whether I had the voice for it.

By then the fence seemed lower, the trail up to the graveyard seemed at last too short, and Becky's voice had soaked through me until it was both inside me and outside, and I had no way of telling the difference. It was the first time I crossed a threshold, I suppose, and I landed softly on the other side of the fence where the ground felt different and it seemed like the whole woods was listening.

Becky said 'Come on,' and her words were as soft as thought, and we took hands and walked through the scattered stones. The mounds beside the graves were all grassed over, like it had been a long time since the Guthries lost someone, and it made me think about Aunt Topaz who I didn't remember, not to mention my mother, who was only a faint recollection of a lap, of arms about me, of an uncertain voice singing bye oh baby bunting. I had to sit for a minute by the grave of Corrina Guthrie 1877-1898 and I imagined her lying deep in the ground, her hands folded, awaiting an astonishing change.

Arethusa's voice sounded at first like Becky's. From the other end of the graveyard she called me, and I looked up to see her astride a white mule near the fence row, the sunlight shining through her watery skin and through the hide of her horse, the fence posts' shadows you could see behind his withers. Oh, and she was beautiful, so pretty I figured I could not of imagined her out of the air, and she beckoned to me.

The mule walked slowly in the creek bed, and you could see the red course of the water through his flanks as Thusa Creek seemed to follow us, keeping pace with the mule's gait, stopping when he became willful and bent to drink at the muddy stream. Arethusa wrapped her arms about me, leaving me to guide the mule, and I coaxed him along with tongue clicks and whistles, like Uncle Med did.

Looking down on his back was suddenly all dizziness, like watching a tide from a high place. The fear of falling down mixed with desire—that pull of the ground and gravity that scares the hell out of you when you realize you are fixing to give in to it. I pressed against Arethusa, felt the breasts of the water witch against my back and the inside of her thighs against my haunches, and I could not decide whether I wanted her to sing me to sleep, or whether I wanted something else.

And Arethusa tells me not to look, to look ahead of us instead. And she says 'See the roads, True Thomas?' and it was like she said them into being—three trails branching off in different directions, one of them wide and straight ahead, another beset with thorns and briars that turned out of the woods back toward Aunt Coral's house, and then the third one, the one we took, that wound around a ferny hill I did not remember ever seeing in the woods, but the mule beneath us turned slowly through the green quiet. Then ahead of us was the Guthrie plot again, and we had come full circle like we had wandered nowhere by moving.

The mule stopped by Corinna's grave, and the dates on the stone had gone away since I last looked. And there beside the stone was a fresh mound of earth, and all of a sudden this choir of cicadas ratcheting up around the graveyard, so you noticed at last how quiet it had been when the silence broke. Arethusa leaned over me and gave me kisses three, one on each cheek and one the first kiss on the mouth I ever remember. She tells me 'You will have to go now,' tells me 'them kisses will have to last you, True Thomas,' and I started crying in spite of myself. It was like the whole woods faded around me, and I was kneeling in the mud on the banks of the pond, and it had not been cicadas at all but the frogs singing, and up the hill Nick Mays's car was pulling up alongside the house.

IX

It seemed that Nick Mays would have more history to him.

From what Tommy said, he was a celebrity of sorts, a kind of Evangelical circuit rider who showed up through the mid-South over a span of thirty years in increasingly strange incarnations. A quick internet search turned up nothing but a birth year (1927) and a death year subject to question marks (1974—swept away during a tornado? 1978—hanged in a jail cell? 1981—swallowed by the earth?). 1974 seemed least plausible, since a Rev. Nick Mays had confessed to the murder of Elvis Presley in early 1978, but of course there could be two, even three preachers by the same name.

In all three accounts, the Mays in question was born in 1927, which would have put him at thirty when he visited the Downes farm. Why Tommy had reacted so immediately (and so unfavorably) to an itinerant man of God was a mystery, but the recordings Mickey was hearing made it clear he did: as Tommy said early on, looking at Mays was like looking down the stairs into a dark cellar that you knew was rat-infested.

And yet when Mickey went to the public library to search the local and state records, he found more about Nicholas Mays and discovered that not a few who remembered him claimed that he was unbearably handsome. "Beautiful" was a word that came up—seldom a description for a man among folks religious and Southern, but when it was, often used with suspicion and a little distaste.

It seemed there was a Mays who was preaching south of Yorktown in the mid-1930s. Also named Nicholas and noted for a kind of backwoods charisma. So of course Mickey imagined this to be the father of the Nicholas in question, until Mickey read in a brief, passing comment about how *the Holy Spirit had rained gifts upon this child* and it was clear that Mays was seven or eight when this was written about him.

The visit. Tommy's return to the woods. The flight to the city.

All of these incidents were alluring, of course, but the lines they cast out ended nowhere, as though Mays had vanished from history, the only accounts bearing witness the drink- and drug-addled reminiscences of a derelict in his seventies. And yet, subject to his own fantasies, alone in his cramped and ill-lit carrel, Mickey found himself imagining…

The close quarters of a country shack, smelling of kerosene heat and vinyl on its insides, the only book in the house a King James Authorized, no liquor on the premises by the dictates of a grandmother, and a boy at the window, imagining complex worlds on the other side of the glass. Nicholas Mays was already taking shape in imagination, and so Mickey needed to be especially wary.

There was not much he could tell Bulwer or Stack, but he had to tell them. Mickey knew that he was on fictive grounds, spinning out of scant yarn, and that the "real" Nicholas Mays— the adversary who died three times—was no doubt past recall. And yet he knew that Tommy's story had to have an antagonist, an opponent to the hero, and Mays was as close to the item to be found so far.

***

The Fourth Street bus line went south from the library past the park and amphitheater, all the way to the familiar sights of Fourth and Fellini, the CVS pharmacy and the cornered bank, and closer to Fifth Street Salvages and the Oscar Wilde and the abandoned building between them. So much of Tommy's story was confined to this narrow place: next to the expanses of the farm and the woods and the long highway from Yorktown to the city, a small grid of streets and one longer thoroughfare seemed like a cramped arena.

Mickey made that point to Alan Stack as he stopped for a whiskey before walking the last blocks home. Stack nodded sagely like the good bartender, letting Mickey go on and on imagining Mays, imagining Tommy's downward journey into the city. It was later that Mickey would recognize his own speculations as very little more than rephrasing a worn truth, his own truth: how we often start with ambitions and huge prospects, only to find them dwindling into a small space as the years and our own limitations pile on board and the ship sags on the current. It was not only Tommy who had taken a trip from large and magnanimous grounds to the cramped spaces where people ended up, no matter what road they took from here to there.

Stack had never heard of Nick Mays beyond what he knew from the tapes. He assured Mickey that he hadn't heard the last of the jackleg preacher, that Tommy would speak more on the subject. Stack was impressed, though, that early on Mickey had plucked a villain from the crowd of stories. Yet he wondered if the story needed a villain. After all, Titus and Humphrey had come into the story late, killed Tommy, and confessed to the murder. To Stack, these were the obvious villains. Mays, on the other hand, was foxfire, a dodging and deceptive light amid Tommy's long series of wanderings and setbacks.

"So Tommy wanted to be a thrice-dead evangelist?" Mickey asked.

Stack shook his head. Then interpreted the phenomenon of Nicholas Mays as the afternoon sun reflected through the front window and the glass door over the shelves of bottles, lending a bejeweled light to the main room of the tavern, until the Wilde glowed like the inside of a temple or cathedral. And it struck Mickey, as Stack talked quietly, leaning over the bar, white shirt particolored by the reflection from the bottles, that in a way the Wilde was a temple. It was a thought he pushed down because it brought up Tamar's insistence that her husband sought the wrong churches, and he hated when her insistence carried even a grain of truth. He did know, however, that there were times when the only antidote to her lectures about whiskey was whiskey itself, and he toasted her before the first tall swallow.

Mickey attended many churches, and the priest of this temple was speaking. Something about the neighborhood and something to do with hungry ghosts. No doubt Stack had picked that up from Thanh, and maybe become half-Buddhist himself over the years of living with his Vietnamese partner. Mickey knew that the Buddhists believed in dissatisfied spirits, narrow-throated and swollen-bellied, who spend centuries in unsatisfied hunger, consumed by desires while living, and now inhabit a spectral country where nothing they eat is enough. Stack claimed that Mays was one among many that you saw in the blocks surrounding—ghosts of the living and the dead.

"There are ghosts that have peopled this neighborhood since before I came here," he announced quietly, pouring himself a neat scotch since nobody but Mickey was about. "A black saxophonist who hanged himself for love over on Floral Terrace back in the 'thirties. Ten years before, it was an industrialist who was shot to death by a prostitute he had stalked for months, the bullet passing through a sheaf of poems he had written to her and secreted in the breast pocket of his shirt, trying to muster the courage to give them to her at last. A Confederate veteran who taped together grocery bags to make his shirt while hiding seven million dollars' worth of Union gold in the floorboards of his house. And the real hungry ghosts themselves: Thanh still swears he saw his dead mother behind the theater down at the park."

"Do you believe him, Alan? Do you believe any of the stories?"

"I don't believe in ghosts, Professor. But they're there. Living ghosts as well."

And Stack maintained we were all hungry ghosts, all of us chasing nourishment we could not grasp or swallow or digest. There were stories he had seen full on and those he had glimpsed from a side street: the crack whore's desperate gaze, straight into his eyes, as she sat curled and trembling under the CVS sign down at the corner, the quieter drama of two Jehovah's witnesses saving a 6'5" transvestite at the entrance of that same drug store. The woman who claimed to be Jesus at the next bus stop south, and the teenaged boy who collided with Stack in the parking lot of the now-defunct Red Giraffe, dropping a plastic bag filled with gay pornographic videos, blushing and muttering as Stack helped him pick them up. The bicycle traffic of middle-aged black men that always swelled in bad economic times, and the cluster of younger men at the gate to what was once a flourishing walking court, all of them regarding passersby with apprehension and menace.

"I have my own ghosts, too, Professor," Stack announced softly and strangely. "Things from the war, yes, and things from a past I set aside. But one of them is a simple guilt that clings to me, and I read somewhere that every ghost story is about guilt, about unfinished business. Is that right?"

Mickey allowed it was one way of looking at it, and urged him to continue.

"You see, I poured Tommy Briscoe a last whiskey the night he died. He came into the bar, already a little bit buzzed, I fear. He had another story to tell, but it was the height of the midnight traffic and I was too busy with orders to linger and listen. I suppose it was a way of brushing him off. Homeless drunk pacified by whiskey. But it might have slowed him. Might have untuned him at a moment when attention mattered. I had other things to attend to, even if it was only a Wednesday night. But what I did was set Tommy aside, and for that I blame myself and carry regrets. I'm a ghost as well, I suppose, hungering for what might have been. And that's a stomach you can't fill, a craving nothing can satisfy."

Mickey thought of his third novel, the one that would not emerge after the first moderately successful book and the second one that was a trip to the woodshed. Thought of the scholarly work he was supposed to do in order to keep on at the university, now a series of dodges and masquerades, of trips to the library to borrow books he would not read, of using them to block his carrel door as he hid among them. And of course he thought of Tamar, who had seemed all supportive and bright and funny while they were dating, now an austere presence in a self-fashioned aviary, and he figured that thinking of her last was part of that strange and ghostly hunger for what might have been.

And Nick Mays began to transform in his imagination, from the handsome ambition and the eloquence and the faith into someone who must have stalked through the mid-South, highly touted in childhood. As he grew into manhood, wondering how all that promise might flourish, at last wondering why he was bogged in the role of a Gospel child star, running the same rural circuit, and if God had called upon him to spin his wheels for the rest of his days and end up forgotten like the rest of them. It was like Mickey knew his story, like there was little doubt that the arc of Nick Mays's life tended exactly this way.

And what must he have thought when he heard of a child up in Yorktown, scarcely out of infancy, who could read all the signs at the Hutchins Market? Why was it that, when that child was ten Nicholas Mays made his way into Yorktown to discuss the boy's calling with his uncle and aunt.

It had Mickey going from the time he left the bar, weighted with three bourbons, and found his warm and indolent way back to the apartment, relieved that Tamar was out somewhere. He made a pot of coffee, trying to yank himself up into alertness, but the afternoon was too far gone.

The phone rang, but the caller hung up when he answered,

so Mickey sugared the second mug of coffee and wondered about Nick Mays, about Tommy.

Because the current tape contained mysteries. Tommy's reaction to the itinerant minister had come from a place beneath logic, almost visceral in that way that a baby or a dog reacts to the tremor of menace that slips by those more mature and reasonable.

Nick Mays figured in the rest of the episode, and later, at other junctures in the story, he would slip in and out of attention. If every story needs a villain, the good reverend was a likely candidate. But something in him slipped that noose, and he came to seem like all the others, tangled in their nets of desire and comeuppance.

XIV

There was a bit of the panther in Reverend Nicholas Mays. A bit of the pirate as well, so at first blush he was rakish, inviting, so that I hoped that adventure was afoot.

And the Reverend was relaxed and polite when I come in, perched on the sofa, balancing a saucer and a cup of decaf on his lap like it was a jittery baby. And Lord, he was a striking man: blue-eyed and built all muscular and lean, like a young Gene Kelly, brilliant in a red shirt and a black vest, his hair pompadoured and his jawline sideburned like the King, so you could see why Aunt Coral was charmed by him.

We shook hands, and it was the first time that someone done that with me like a grown man.

'I have been talking,' said the Reverend, and his voice was rough and musical. 'I have been talking to your auntie and uncle. And I have heard tell you are a remarkable boy. Reading the boxes at the grocery before you were two years old.'

He shook his head in wonderment, so I claimed not to remember, though I suspected I did and I know so now. I liked to hear the story rehearsed, done again for the benefits of others. It was a flash of celebrity in the midst of what I would soon understand as my path to being nothing all that special.

But Aunt Coral was not about to let me down, not from my first rescue at Hutchins, not through the singing of my praises to all who listened, never until I left Yorktown. She always had my back, was my admirer as though she thought that somehow Dilly's soul had taken wing and settled inside me as a kind of solace. So she bragged about my intelligence, my love of books, and the Reverend asked me, 'Thomas, what do you know of the greatest of all books?' I knew since he was a preacher that he meant the Bible, so I folded my hands on my lap, bowed my head a little like in church, and I said I liked the stories of Jacob and of Moses and of David, sneaking a glance up to make sure he was approving.

I saw Becky Thatcher standing behind him. She was pale, even more than usual, and something about her was translucent, for even if I could not see the frame of the window behind her, the summer sunlight come through it and lit up the surface of her skin, and then she was barely of substance, pretending to hold a cup of Aunt Coral's decaf, her pinky crooked with irony at my good behavior.

'I can't stand the proper Tommy Briscoe,' she whispered, though nobody heard her but me. I willed her out the door, but she would not budge this time, as the Reverend Mays talked about some great adventure he had in mind for the both of us. We would spread the gospel, he said, through the most benighted corners of the region.

'For your intelligence is from God, Thomas Briscoe,' he said, his grip a little too tight upon my shoulder. 'He has singled you out from among the multitudes. With such anointing always comes a great mission. You are not to hide your light under a bushel, no, for no man, when he hath lighted a candle, putteth it in a secret place, neither under a bushel, but on a candlestick, that they which come in may see the light.'

Aunt Coral and Uncle Med nodded. They were swept up by metaphors. But behind the Reverend Mays, Becky Thatcher made a face and stuck her finger in her ear. And Nicholas Mays went on about why he was here, about the circuit he wanted us to ride together, dispensing salvation and selling Bibles in what he called the Seven States, which you could see from atop a mountain he spoke *of, somewhere to the east and the south of us. We would travel the foothills of that mountain, he claimed, and the plains beyond the foothills, and I would be shown forth as lit by God's graceful light, as a vessel of His will.*

And Nick Mays told me that 'Verily there is no man that hath left house, or brethren, or sisters, or father, or mother, or wife, or children, or lands, for my sake, and the gospel's, But he shall receive an hundredfold now in this time, houses, and brethren, and sisters, and mothers, and children, and lands, with persecutions; and in the world to come eternal life.' It was what he said, and I was switched if I could understand him, but it sounded like fortune.

He looked at me with all kindness, and my aunt and uncle did, too, and there was only Becky behind them, shaking her head, glowing like a long-dead girl in your great-grandma's school picture. I wanted to believe my aunt and uncle, wanted to believe the minister because he was a minister and because he offered something that sounded splendid and plenteous, but Becky stuck her finger down her throat as if she was gagging herself, and she was right, I knew it, because the air tensed up and the light in the room surrounded her, making her all hazy and luminous.

Then my fancy cleared, and down in the hollow of the Reverend's blue eyes a darkness whirled about and beckoned me, and it was like looking into a dark cellar where you could smell the rats before you saw them. And I pulled back before he drew me in, and my mind raced over how to put off the journey and adventure he held before me.

It was hard, though, to stand against your elders, against Aunt Coral, the one who had plucked me from the cereal aisle and given me life and shelter and sustenance. And yet for all her reverence, and for all the blue-eyed charm of Nicholas Mays, perhaps by accident or instinct my Aunt Coral maneuvered to my side. I was in school, she reminded him, but the term had not yet begun. Barely past midsummer, and I would have six weeks to see if this might be my calling. She insisted that she and Uncle Med would talk things over, then talk to me the next morning, and among the three of us, we would decide.

I had the night to sleep on it, because it seemed quite genuine that she wanted me to have my say on the matter. Alone in my room, lying in bed and looking to the open window where the moonlight shone on Cousin Dilly's clay tattered men, I worried myself toward the edge of sleep, when I felt the mattress dip and sag beside me.

Becky Thatcher was lying with me, and though it was a hot July night she brought with her a chill, and she covered us both with the thin blanket we kept at the foot of my bed.

'You know you shouldn't go,' she whispered to me, her cold body nestling against my back as she wrapped a luminous arm around my chest. But I knew of no such thing, and the fear I felt over the Reverend Mays begun to fade, as the prospect of a long trip by car, seeing sights I had not seen before under the guidance of someone older and wiser and more glamorous was stretching before me like the wonderful adventure of the previous fall, when Ace and I had gone to the city to see the King.

And 'it ain't the same,' she whispered, and snuggled next to me, and there was something exciting and improper about her being here, in my room, in the middle of the night before I was to set out on this great decision. 'It ain't the same,' she said again, and I felt her coldness seeping into my back until I was breathing out mist into the bedroom air, and I remembered the frightening deeps of Nick Mays's eyes .

And I said no, no it ain't. I stirred under the blanket and turned to Becky for warmth, but there was none. We lay there, and I knew it was late and that she was right, but I was pressed to know what to do about it.

'Pack up and return,' she told me at last, her lips moving breathlessly at my ear. Take what you need and leave the most behind. 'Find your way back to Mother, back to 'Thusa. She is the one who understands.'

I agreed with her, because I remembered the warmth of 'Thusa's arms as she and I sat atop the white mule. But still it was mysterious, Becky's advice, for a ten-year-old boy is unsure what he needs for an adventure. The journey Ace had taken me on was a day trip, and I had required no packing. And I could not wake Coral and Med in the hours of the morning, tell them I was running away, and ask them what I should take along.

It ended up that I took half a loaf of Rainbo and a jar of pimiento cheese, which I wrapped in a bandana intending to tie to a stick and tote over my shoulder, like I had seen runaways do in the picture books. Finding no stick, I tied it to my belt, then stretched it open so I could slip in the two record albums of the King that were my gifts, though I didn't think far enough ahead to know how I would play them again. And tiptoeing into my mother's deserted room, I looked into her closet among the Photoplays and found the bowl of costume jewelry, which glinted but a little through the moonlight in Mamma's room.

All being collected, I headed quietly out the back door, through the garden and across the field toward Uncle Med's woods and Thusa Creek that flowed through the trees. Becky followed me for a spell, then walked beside me: at one point she stopped and shielded her eyes against the moon, and I watched the high dry grass wave through her body and I remembered where she had come from, and suddenly felt lonely in the summer night.

✳✳✳

When I entered the woods, the air clung to my face and crackled, and my first response was that half-panic you feel when you walk into an unseen web. I waved my hands about, warding off spiders who were not there.

I had crossed into something entirely new, I was certain. I was nearly as certain that there was no returning from this.

The woods looked different at that time of night or morning. Sitting there in the middle of a small circle of trees, I could look through the undergrowth up toward the Guthrie property, and it was not long before I could see the faint glimpse of summer sunrise, the woods layering with colors of light—red farthest to the east, then yellows over the farmyard trailing into shadow blue-green that circled the trees where I sat. I must of gone to sleep as I watched the rise and spread of light, because I woke up strangely cold in the afternoon, my clothes soaked with a rain that had fallen while I slept, the country around the woods glowing bright like it had been refreshed and recovered. My bandana was open, the pimiento and bread half-eaten and a buzz of flies over the leavings, the record albums lying on the cloth, their jackets soggy, the picture of the King washed into the cardboard by the rain.

There is no telling how long I had slept. But fresh awakened, it dawned on me that what I saw about me, just for a moment at dawn, had been circles of light, circles in circles. Looking down into the bowl I had carried, I noticed that Mamma's costume jewelry had arranged itself as I moved to this spot in the center of the woods. Barely out of sight but not out of hearing, the Thusa was rushing over the rocks on the creek bed, no longer dry but filled by a rain I did not see coming.

The clearing in the woods felt like the heart of the web I had come into late at night, running from the house and the Reverend Mays. It was like I sat in its center, and it tugged me gently in all directions like it was weaving itself around me. I tried to stand up but was held down, and after only a little struggle I gave up again, and again fell asleep, waking up in the dark as the whole day had passed me by.

I wondered about Aunt Coral and Uncle Med, if they were all right and why they hadn't come looking for me. Neither Becky nor her mother had come by either, and I would of despaired except that I was so sleepy, and the clearing was the coolest spot in the summer woods. Before I knew it, I was nodding off again, and I can remember thinking it was like stories I had heard of young people passed out in faraway places, doomed to sleep years before they returned to find their home, their town, their stomping grounds forever changed. It was a sad and lonely thought, but one I could not keep steady, and I was heading back to sleep when a noise stirred me and I looked up to see a figure framed in light just outside the ring of trees.

It was my father, who had come to search for me over the miles. And I thought, still half asleep and suddenly uncomfortably cold again, that he was there to take me away from Yorktown. And whether it was kidnapping, like some said it was later, or whether it was a rescue, like he told me it was and like I believed for so long, by dawn we drove beneath the underpass I had seen that November, past the Confederate monument and among these elegant brick houses you see about us now, back then unrestored and seedy, and the air snapped and sputtered around us, our destination my new city home.

Seven

By accident in a world where the accidental was losing, Mickey took the wrong bus to the University.

Two lines ran south from the stop near his apartment, and the bus he boarded was making its way into the south end of the city by the time he startled out of his dream of Tommy's retreat into the forest and subsequent rescue. He looked up, and the houses were shotgun and single-storied, aluminum-sided or roman brick ranch, and it was obvious the bus was crossing into the suburbs.

Mickey swore at himself as he disembarked at the next stop. Already the morning was sweltering, and unless he stumbled across a windfall of luck, he would be late to his morning lecture. Of course, a world without accident is also a world without luck, and by the time he caught the Second Street bus headed north along the broad parkway, he was dripping sweat and fifteen minutes away from the time that class was supposed to begin.

Mickey told himself that he was still in charge of the show, and that students could wait for what he thought about Hermann Hesse. He knew, however, that they wouldn't wait long: college mythology still held to an unconfirmed rumor that students are required to wait ten minutes for a grad assistant, fifteen for a non-tenured professor, and longer and longer as the rank rises, so that if your teacher is a full professor and dies on the way to class, you are obligated to sit in the lecture hall until you die as well.

By calculation and urban legend, Mickey figured he had until 10:15 at the best. That window was still open, though, when the bus approached the underpass at the edge of the campus. He was breathing more easily now, reviewing lecture notes in his head, until he noticed the jagged slogan on the side of the underpass, the "ELIVS" written in spray paint against the gray stone of the abutment. Then he thought he felt the air bend and crackle as the bus dipped under the structure and onto the university campus.

It was the very overpass under which Ace Briscoe must have guided his car nearly sixty years before. The same bridge he navigated again months later, when he brought his rescued son to the city. A horizontal line lay beside the inscription—an accident of stain or weather, perhaps, but Mickey had become the interpreter of every message and glyph the city uncovered, as though it was mapping him an itinerary he did not know how to follow yet.

The bus let him out at the next stop, the one by the Engineering School. He retraced the route on foot, passing beneath the bridge into shadows that smelled of piss and diesel fuel, until he stood by the graffiti on the abutment.

The story went that Tommy had seen such an inscription—a broadly sprayed and misspelled "ELIVS" on a bridge overpass the week Elvis Presley died. That it had been the event that sparked him to don the lamé and begin his underground career of impersonation, the midnight choirs and impromptu concerts he had made famous for almost four decades in the oldest part of the city. The paint on the concrete appeared fresher than Mickey suspected it should be—the horizontal bar fresher still—but he figured his forensic skills were pretty much untried. If it wasn't Tommy's original sign, perhaps someone had refreshed the paint much later, or more improbably, someone had seen the original and copied it here, for reasons Mickey could hardly imagine.

And yet, with the mystery still opaque in front of him, there was a sense of being in the right spot at the right time. The heat and delay of a botched bus route had led him here, and his walk back beneath the overpass, skirting the litter and repair scaffolding, felt as though he had found an appointed path, a route of his own among the perplexing shadows. For a moment copying the graffiti seemed almost understandable, as though someone else—a kid, no doubt, saggy-panted and facile—had painted his way into the story Mickey was still trying to grasp, making things uncertain on the path that he could only hope would end at a definite spot.

The sunlight was intense, almost unbearable, on the other side of the passage. The old buildings of the south campus edged against the intersection, and it struck Mickey that almost all of them were a century old, that this would have been roughly what Tommy Briscoe had seen from the passenger seat of his father's Montclair Phaeton. Mickey crossed the intersection and slipped between two of the science buildings, headed toward his office with still enough time to drop off his briefcase and make it to the classroom.

He looked down at his watch— 9:53—but when he looked up again, it seemed as though the world had shifted entirely. It wasn't his end of campus, but the roundabout and the parking lot didn't seem new, and Mickey couldn't imagine having forgotten them. Beyond the roofs of the IT Center he looked for landmarks that, to his alarm, were no longer there. It was as though the pieces on the board had been surreptitiously moved, and you were a newcomer to the game again, pressed to sit down and improvise at a moment's notice.

Well, at seven minutes' notice. No, five now. No time to get to the office.

He picked up the pace, his breathing ragged in the heat. He slipped off his jacket as he walked, loosened his tie, the hair on his nape already stringy with sweat as he passed the IT building into a little shady alcove he did not remember at all, where he stopped, leaned against the wall, and gathered his breath. A poetically just ending for a term professor, he thought darkly: dropping dead of a heat stroke on his way to class.

The tower bell was ringing the ten o'clock hour when, in a last surge of energy, Mickey rounded the corner of a building he did not know and saw the familiar side steps of Gottschalk Hall and the Humanities Building beyond it. It was as though some large and inscrutable movement—or, more likely, a trick of eyesight—had shifted both buildings so that it appeared he had circled them and now approached them from the north.

When he climbed the stairs toward the classroom, heaving his satchel and gasping gratefully in the air-conditioned hall, Mickey had forgotten the subject of the lecture, much less the particulars. Fumbling through his briefcase, bypassing a clipboard and ungraded papers, he found the copy of *Demian*, opened it, looked at his scrawled marginal notes, and thanked an inscrutable Power that it was Hesse he was lecturing on, not Lawrence or, God forbid, Joyce again—books he was finding it harder to navigate. At the doorway he paused, thumbed through the first few chapters, and scavenged enough ideas to begin the lecture and the day.

***

Right after the class, Mickey scuttled back to the library and mounted the stairs to his carrel. It had taken less than fifteen minutes to glaze over the students' eyes, to make less wondrous the book he had looked forward to teaching but had scrambled in heat and confusion. His gaze and thoughts had drifted out the window, and it was with a quiet but mutual sigh of relief that his students and he had packed up notes and left the classroom. Now, drumming his pencil on the sheaf of essays he had yet to read, he thought back over Tommy's story. How the boy had simply packed his belongings—a sandwich and some Elvis records—and ventured into the woods and into a new life, just like a fairytale hero, the figure in the legend.

And here Mickey sat, holed up in a cramped office, still sweating and puffing after wandering the campus for all of two disorienting blocks. There was no place to go but out of the woods. But even so, there on the edge of his own adventure, he paused for a final misgiving. Why wasn't Bulwer writing this himself? He'd been around books for half a century, knew his way among words. For a moment it darted through Mickey's thoughts that this might be a setup, the motive for which he had yet to discover. But turning it over in his mind revealed no ulteriors, nothing to stop him from proceeding on good faith.

And after all, perhaps nobody would read this anyway. Or Bulwer and Stack and Mickey himself would be decades dead before some survivor—Bulwer had a daughter, Mickey understood, and Stack as well, surprisingly—would pick up the manuscript, thumb through it, and give it a last dutiful read before setting it out on the curb.

Inspired by the bravery of a ten-year-old in all his rashness, by his talk of ghostly companions, circles of light, and sinister ministers, Mickey stepped forth into the journey. To be honest, it was more exasperation than courage. A point in a long string of events where at last you find yourself in a story. One with plot and character and, if you are good at it, headed through heat and sunlight toward a place of meaning.

XIV

I have seldom since left the neighborhood.

I have wandered out to its margins and felt its borders stretch around me before they gave way and I was barely outside my stomping grounds, where the air smelled more like diesel and I could hardly breathe it. But still my encampment was in sight, always over my better shoulder, the turn-of-century houses, the gable and brick.

The old drunks and junkies, the stoners and especially the acid heads tell you that the street map always changes. You go onto one of the numbered avenues and find that a house you remembered a night before is gone now like it was razed or demolished, but where it stood is no foundation, like it had never been. Until you see it on a side street, planted in a lot that had always been vacant, wedged between two old town houses like an intruder, or rippled in the summer air like you are seeing it through water. Sometimes the lights in the windows will change color at night, like there has been an accord or conspiracy among the people who lived there to cover the glass with the same color of shades, and the neighborhood is a warren of energies, where a step out the door of the library can land you backstage at the theater in the Park, or by the Witches' Tree, or in the strange shelving of Mr. Bulwer's book store.

I noticed this soon after I started school in the city, that the chemically estranged were right and the normal folks wrong: the Old City was and is wheels in the middle of wheels. It took intoxicants to first follow the paths, but I was ten and sober at the time I come to the city, so everything around me bristled in a kind of slow confusion.

Later I often wondered why Aunt Coral and Uncle Med never sent after me, and it was almost four years before I learned the truth. Ace Briscoe's truth, however, become easier to read: though had I thought back on Thusa Creek that he was coming to my rescue, it turned out that his plans for me were pretty much the same as those Nicholas Mays had been brewing when he come to visit back in Yorktown.

Within a week we were working the city with me as a boy preacher, my shirt and tie purloined from the Men 'n' Boys Store by slipping them on in the dressing room under Ace's outsize shirt which I had worn onto the premises. Presentable now, and putting on sincere like another layer of raiment, I was standing atop an orange crate and bearing witness to small multitudes, and hell-fire and end-of-days brought in the spare change as the summer worked toward autumn in the town heat.

Ace taught me how to hack when I preached, which went down well in the west end of the city where they were mostly black, and down to the south where they were mostly transplanted hillbillies like ourselves. Downtown I was supposed to be more unadventurous, and we never went east in the county, because they were all Episcopal, Ace said, and averse to tongues and signs.

And so we fared in the early times, until September come and the beginnings of school. By that time we had lived on Floral Court for two months, right across from the place Doctor Turner hanged himself over lost love and lottery tickets, and I was beginning my growth among the company of ghosts.

We moved either six or seven times over four years, never more than a couple of blocks from the previous address, but sometimes into a place that was suspiciously like the house we had just left. My daddy would skip the premises when the police would inquire, and it seemed as though every house we settled in was haunted by something. We would move, I would become acquainted with new ghosts, and almost like a change of seasons we would uproot and I would leave old friends for new ectoplasm.

The day after we arrived in our fourth apartment, I saw a shadow through the apartment window and dismissed it as a branch against the glass, an encroachment of topiary as the house slid soundlessly into the vacant lot next door. Soon after, though, the milk carton was emptier in the icebox, and the box of vanilla wafers—one I had picked up at the new Winn-Dixie when Daddy had sent me with five dollars' worth of hustle to stock the house—was opened and half cleaned out. When the corn shuck doll was taken off the shelf and put on my bed for two nights running, I suspected we had a squatter, but I did not know who it was until my first month had passed at the school over on Second Street.

My school was a block from where we had ended up in August, so close to the high school that its big gothic tower cast a shadow across our desks in the very early hours of the school day. Outside the cars and City Transit buses rushed by up Second or east and west upon Lee Street, so the classroom was noisy and I had to concentrate to focus on the work.

Not that it was hard learning. I still read better than my classmates, and the one thing I had learned outside of books was that the Reverend Mays was wrong about hiding some lights under some bushels, that when you were quicker than the others you were supposed to hide that light so as not to offend or anger them. I pretended to struggle with reading again, but I learned a new lesson: that here in the city the lower reading groups mixed the quiet and frightened among the hardened bullies or felons. So I quickly appeared to catch on, rising in the ranks in a matter of weeks, and though I escaped assault and battery thereby, I made no friends. I remained a lonely country boy with a swindler father, alone with a paper bag lunch reading my Boys' Odyssey during recess.

It was then I begun to realize that like Ulysses I was a wanderer, too. A boy of many resources, an invader of cities. Our new surroundings seemed more and more like islands of dusty hardwood floors, stops in a journey headed somewhere I could not figure until much later on the top floor of another tower, over at Gottschalk south of here. But for now I thought I saw a pattern at last, and I followed the map of the venture.

It had turned October, and the Halloween decorations were going up in the halls of the school, when I stepped out into the afternoon and the air pressed around me, broke over me with a rustle of wind and leaves. The sky was autumn bright, the shadows of the buildings as clear and defined as though somebody had painted them across the sidewalks and the streets. It seemed like all the city was anticipating something, and as I was turning toward home I saw Becky Thatcher in the shadows up Hill Street. By now I had guessed that the ghostly squatter was none other than my old friend, and when the shade beneath a cluster of front-yard oaks took form and swirled into a gray-white shape like a curl of smoke, I recognized her at once.

She was wearing the same blue dress, as button-nosed and blonde as ever, but there was something watery and dark in her blue eyes, like she had just risen from the river and dried herself off. She held out her hand, and when I refused it, slipped her arm through mine and walked me up the street, her whispers loud enough to drown the city sounds.

Becky knew nothing about Aunt Coral nor Uncle Med. She had left Yorktown, she said, the day after me, and it had taken near a week to get her bearings and to find my whereabouts. She had waited for a month at the window, in the yard.

'It was cold out there on the terrace,' she whispered. 'Like winter, though it was July. And when your daddy up and moved you, I had to find you again, even though you was only a block away. It was sorrow and following, and the building moved more than the Briscoes, and at night I would climb up in the tree by your each new house, where I would nest and take counsel with the owls.'

I wondered how much of Becky was really there to feel sorry for, and how much of that suffering would just go away the moment I stopped thinking about it.

She tugged at me and said, 'I have a quest for you...'

I asked her what it was, and she told me about the treasure of *the old Confederate lieutenant.*

∗∗∗

Bennett Young was from the Bluegrass, but he resettled in the city in the years following the Civil War. As a young officer in Morgan's cavalry, he was famous for courage and recklessness. He broke from the army after Gettysburg, traveling north through New York and into Vermont and New Hampshire, the story goes. There, with a band of less than a dozen men, he had waylaid a Federal supply train loaded with arms for the battlefront and with gold for Mr. Lincoln's Washington. He had fled across the border into Canada, the rumors had it, and appeared five years after Appomattox at the doorstep of his friend Tom Lark, unrecognizable for his rags and beard, but ready to stay and to build an enormous house just two blocks south of Fourth and Fellini. By that time all the rebels had been restored, and Young would become a judge of some renown, but there was always a rumor that he built his house on stolen Yankee gold.

So it was a pirate's quest that Becky invited me on. Now my future lay plain before me, and glowing with great and excessive splendor. My name would fill the world, and I would plow the dancing seas and make people shudder.

The Young House was on the narrow street that bordered the north side of the park. I passed under the street lights crossing Fourth. Becky was beside me, and as usual we made but one shadow on the road. I stopped in the middle of the street and listened to the night sounds of the park. There was voices rising from over at the theater. It was too late in the year for the summer Shakespeare festival, but it was the Shakespeare voices, all in rhythm and putting on English accents that sounded pretty good to a ten-year-old's ears. I stood at the corner of Park and Fourth and took some steps down toward the theater before Becky hissed me back. I had got close enough, though, to get a glimpse of the stage.

If I had been older I would of recognized Midsummer Night's Dream, because now I must of seen it a dozen times in my sixty summers of roaming the park. But the first time was the strangest, the Queen of the Fairies and her troupe all lying on stage like they were preparing for sleep. All of them were covered in a dull green light, which made it seem like I was seeing it all through sunglasses or a Coke bottle.

The Queen of the Fairies was naked, as far as I could tell, except for a wool cap, but she was decent enough, a blanket draped over her chest and thighs like she was a French model. All around her the fairies slept, winged boys dripping with dew, each of them naked, and green as old bronze. All of them stirred and stared my way, all drowsy and from a distance, so that I could not tell if they were looking at me or if I was lost in the off-stage shadows. Then Becky hissed at me and beckoned, and I turned away from them, feeling their gaze tug at my shoulders and arms as I made for the house at the corner where Lieutenant Young had spent his last years.

It was the oldest trick in the burglary book, to open the coal chute door and slide into the cellar, especially since so few of the houses now used coal in the city. Becky had decided that the treasure lay in the cellar anyway, in a strongbox under the dirt floor. I slid through the window and to the ground, and for a moment I hunkered down in complete dark, groped around me, feeling that panic that you feel when you can't see anything and all you know is that you are on foreign ground. I was Pinocchio down in the belly of the whale, scared and alone with no cricket to console me.

You could hear footsteps above, the floorboards creaking. I scratched a mark on the cellar wall above where we figured the treasure lay, and I vowed to return to it later.

Then a latch turned in the far high corner of the cellar, and a door opened, and the room was creased with light.

All around me was wine up to the rafters. Whoever owned this place had jerrybuilt a wine cellar in the basement, and when the bottles in the hanging racks caught the glow from the upstairs room, it was like I was in the middle of a kaleidoscope—green and yellow and the deep red of blood or burgundy. I would not see colors like this until the acid nine years later.

Up on the landing stood a boy several years younger than me, framed in lamplight or sun, I could not tell. He looked down into the cellar and drew a sharp breath, crouching and shielding his eyes to see what was at the bottom of the stairs. Oh Mamma, he whispered, and I was standing among jewels and gold, all of it made of light and without substance, so that my feet and hands passed through it without holding on to it. Then I started to cry for no reason I could understand, and I must of been hypnotized by it all, because I woke up in bed with only pieces of the night left in my memory.

I lay there getting my bearings, my eyes still closed. The room smelled like hay and forgetfulness, and I dreamed my way through a desolate tunnel, full of cameras and dollies and deeper still and dreamily through a tunnel toward a receding arch, the wreckage of a carnival and of Roman ruins all about me in the spangled night, and the smell and slow breathing of something cold and coiled...

And I thought, help me, Jesus, out of this...

and when I opened my eyes, for a minute I thought I saw a symbol drawn on a shadowy wall, then Dilly's clay men in formation on a table by a window, and I thought of Aunt Coral. Then the room settled, the clay men vanished, a bus exhaled on the street outside, and I thought Ace hollered at me from the other room to get up and go fetch us breakfast.

I crawled through a cellar window and found myself on the court, blocks from where I had descended. The moonlight was pale and tilting back toward summer, the traffic sighed, and I looked up the sheer walls of Conrad's Folly, the city's first "skyscraper"—built in 1897, top three floors burned away by a 1913 fire, home to its own inscrutable ghosts. It was still hours before breakfast.

Ace was blocks away.

Time had buckled in on itself and I had passed through centuries and back, bearing the promise of wine and jewels through befuddled space.

XV

My daddy was a fly-by-night. He was a card shark and a mimic. Once made a house disappear on River Street just with the power of suggestion. I had seen him drop an eight ball too soon and seem to lose the game, but on close inspection the patsy would discover the eight was still on the table and a different ball entire in the pocket.

He was a master of quick change and chaos.

Oh, yes, he fell off in his latter days. Getting caught repurposing teddy bears off children's graves was his low point, until his defense that he sold them for only five dollars apiece come to show that he had lost the borders of his scruples.

But there's a high tide for the shell game, just as there is for any art. There is a point where you're at the peak of your earthly powers and so blinded by your own glamor, you do not see that the next step is fixing to take you down. You are headed for decline, though at the time it might seem otherwise. I reached that step for myself when I was nineteen or twenty, but Ace hung on without visible decay until up in his forties. After which, it was not long until he left this world.

It remained a mystery to me just why Ace rescued or abducted me in the first place. It was all legal after Mamma's abandonment, but it never seemed in character for my father to take on ballast, and even at ten or eleven I was quick to see. After all, he lugged me from house to house in the neighborhood, employed me in the shifts and sleights of his livelihood. It might of seemed that I was being used as some kind of winsome apparatus, but I believed that the bond between us was magical and strong, like a boy in some hog farm waiting years for his father's return.

I got up courage to ask him at last, right after the Bay of Pigs Invasion. The news out of Cuba was scary and dim, and the river where Ace and I were walking was cloudy and cold as well. The stink was high on the river banks, and we slogged through the spring mud looking for shored flotsam. I had begun to question Ace's wisdom and to see our ventures in the city as circular and pointless. But Ace was all about the next thing, from how a $300 win ticket on Crozier for the Kentucky Derby was a sure thing because he knew a man, down to a game that would be more in his own hands, when the Russian boy wonder come through town in June.

On the other hand, I was tired of moving, tired of the three-card monte of daily living. I was wondering why I was here in the city, trolling the banks, instead of back in Yorktown on the farm.

At first Ace refused to answer me, or answered like you'd expect: the son belongs with his father and other things that neither of us believed. But after a while, wading knee-deep into the slurry of the river, he beckoned me out there with him. And beckoned with more drama when I said it was too cold in the water, see? that it was thickening up to ice.

He called me a mama's boy and drew me in deeper, where the water was to his waist and up to my chest. I felt something brush by me born on the flow of the river, and it crested downstream in a cracking of paper-thin ice, a big back above the water and gone again, scaring the daylights out of me.

But Ace didn't seem to notice. He was talking about Nick Mays, about the danger of that kind of man, and that Mays was a fanatic, and that something in me had sniffed it out if I would just be honest, that there was a smell to them of tomato soup gone bad, and of sweat and metal.

When I was chest-deep in the water, Ace put his hand to the

back of my head, and he looked into my eyes so long that I could not take it, and he asked me what Nick Mays could bring me that he and this city could not.

I said that Mays had spoken of the keys of the kingdom, the keys of Heaven, and that had I gone with him, maybe I would be on the right path, headed toward some kind of promised land, some kind of paradise or glory, and Ace looked at me long and hard, like he was looking at the heart and dimensions of my soul.

Then he pushed my face down into the water and held it there. I swallowed the current and choked, but he would not let me up, would not let me breathe. It was like oil in my throat, and I wrestled against him, but I was thirteen and he was Ace Briscoe.

It was a few seconds or minutes before I saw a light above me, and a blue opening in the surge of the water, and I thought I saw the bankside, the smooth rocks along the shore, and a woman riding a white mule framed by all that light. I stretched out my arms to her, but right then Ace yanked me up by the hair. And the warm light went away and we were knee-deep in the river.

He asks me what I was thinking about when he held me under the current, and I tried to answer but the water kept pouring out of me. When I could not get to the words, he pushed me closer to the river again, the tip of my nose cold and wet as the tide brushed against it. I coughed up the water, coughed up something else, and stretched out my arms trying to swim in the air, but he held me up.

And he said "air" then. Said that what I was thinking about was not paradise, was nobody's kingdom of heaven. That I was thinking about air. About just breathing. And that when I yearned for simple oxygen as much as I yearned for fairy tales and myths, well, it was then I would be on the right track, then I would be headed toward all in the world that a body was promised.

Because all we could hope for, he said, was the day we were in, the turn of the card and the money to spend. It was all that mattered, he told me. It was what I was yearning for, he said, there with my head underwater, only I was too high-minded to admit it, to him or to myself. It showed that Nick Mays or not, Sunday school had its monstrous hold on me and I was looking for paradise down river while all the glory was here on the banks, on the city streets and at the games my father ran for money and liquor and fame.

I wanted to tell him that he was wrong, but Ace would not brook disagreement. I wanted to tell him that it was not paradise at all where the water was taking me. That it was no fairy tale country, that it was not even air, because air was too easy. Instead it was the home I remembered, that the light on the water give me a glimpse of before it was winter and the city again around me, and once again the day by day survival at the side of Ace Briscoe.

We climbed back up the bank, and it was bleakly cold. It was a good eight city blocks to our part of the city, and I knew they'd shut the heat off in the apartment but since it was second floor we could ride the warmth of the place downstairs. Ace walked ahead of me and I tried to keep up, my thoughts on dry clothes and the old army blanket that had covered my legs that day outside the theater when the King was fixing to sing for us and everything in the world held promise.

But dry clothes and the blanket could not make me warm that night. I shivered in them, and dodged Ace in the apartment until he left at sundown to my great pleasure and relief. That night the bleakness come again, and I got out of bed and started over by the window because I was hungry for light and a street lamp would suffice. And there I seen Becky Thatcher hovering outside, her face pressed up against the edge of frost on the glass, her eyes like snowman coal in the freezing January. I put on my leather jacket against the cold in the room, and sang to her "Are You Lonesome Tonight." Then she beckoned me to the window, and when I brought my face next to it, she kissed my cheek through the glass, and though I could not hear her for the wind outside, I read her lips.

She told me she would never be the one to leave, never at all, for as long as I stayed in the care of my father.

✳✳✳

I would be in Ace's custody for several more years. I saw his rise, his excellence, and probably caught the first signs of his decline if I'd had the sense to read them. I believe, though, I was there for his absolute height, for his crescendo in brilliance and meanness, that day at the hotel when Arkady Volkov come to town.

Nobody remembers Arkady Volkov that much. One of them meteoric Soviet chess masters, little boys groomed for the game like they groomed their girls as gymnasts. Volkov vanished from sight around 1970 or so, but he was only about fourteen when I saw him back in the summer of 1962, a year younger than me and riding on ten times my promise.

It was outside the Brown Hotel off of Broadway—pretty posh quarters for a commie, said my father. But despite the accommodations, Volkov could not of been comfortable, under guard and restricted by a pair of burly apparatchiks or some such, who it seemed were the only ones to whom the boy was allowed to speak. I knew the look of discontent when I saw him step out of a cab at the hotel carriage porch. There wasn't much of a crowd—a few reporters present along with several old people in their church clothes, who looked like chess players do in the movies, like librarians with social wherewithal. Volkov shook hands with everybody except for one old boy, dressed in a suit as well, but with shiny spots on the trouser bottoms, who stood back and regarded things.

There were some introductions where some of the old people tried out their Russian, but Volkov wasn't really sociable, just shaking hands and nodding until his handlers hustled him through the revolving door into the hotel lobby. Two men in dark suits and sunglasses—weightlifter types even bigger than the apparatchiks— stepped out of the alley and folded their arms across their chests, almost daring anyone to pass into the lobby without their approval.

Ace said these last ones were probably KGB, and for the first time I had that term explained to me, and the whole adventure took on a whiff of secret agent intrigue, like it was a scene out of Dr. No, and I probably would of become Bond on the spot if From Russia With Love had already come out.

But there was no love from Russia in Arkady Volkov, nor love for Russia, I was guessing. He had cooped-up eyes, and at fourteen he had the bearing of a prison lifer. I would only see the eyes on the next day at the challenge, but the shoulders stooped and the shuffling gait, two steps out of the cab and then one step slow after the other, his head tilting side to side like something was coming, and the commissar's hand at the small of his back pushing like his handlers were steering him toward a final resting place where they would crown or canonize him. I could tell that this was daily, a circle he had repeated already to the point that he just wanted it to stop.

I thought about Arkady Volkov that night, and about Nicholas Mays. And Ace didn't seem so bad after all, even with his shell games and scams. I did not know at the time, though, that my father was fixing to up the ante, and the events of the next day would be the high tide of his triumph.

The next morning there was to be a simul in the lobby of the Brown. Arkady would take on a number of opponents in a kind of rapid-fire match, moving from table to table, holding each game in his memory or gathering it into his thoughts at once and reacting on instinct—I'm not sure quite how he done it. We overheard from the crowd that he was hard to beat in this kind of event, though every once in a while, one or two in the group had done so.

The lobby was glittering with sunlight flashing through the beveled windows and the glass on the revolving doors. The air was geometric, dust motes riding the wedges of light until the big room looked like a cathedral done by Dr. Caligari. Tables were set up in an open square, maybe twenty challengers in all, hopefuls up against the Russian grand master. I was not surprised to see Ace take a seat at one station, right between two Asian kids from out in the East End, boys younger than me that I knew I would never see again. And Ace had mussed up himself, his hair ruffled and his shirt buttoned wrong as camouflage, like a blanket over his legs in a Radio Flyer wagon.

Ace sent me to the back of the lobby when Volkov stepped into the square, guard-dogged by a pair of operatives in dark shiny suits, like he was a commissar himself. The dust motes in the lobby caught and rode the angles of light, and it was like the square was shot through with networks of waves and lines, as the boy moved from table to table, making his move in a matter of seconds. He stopped in front of one of the Asian boys, looking down at the board for most of a minute before he moved on to Ace.

Which is when Ace lit a Tareyton and blew smoke across the board. The Russkis crowded in on Volkov, like he was being threatened with combustion, and the hotel staff and the others in suits stepped in, and Ace was cautioned to put out the cigarette. But Volkov waved them away, his little hand stirring the smoke above the board. He looked down at Ace's opening, which was a pawn to knight three that evidently Volkov wasn't used to seeing in amateur openings but Ace had told me he was going to use for its bewilderment. 'Now Volkov will have to reckon whether I am a ringer or an idiot,' Ace had told me. 'And if he weren't a Russki he would just figure I am an idiot, but the Russkis are always looking under the rugs for spies.'

Whatever my father was planning, the boy fell for it, because Volkov rushed through the next five opponents and as he rounded the corner of tables headed toward Ace you could see him looking ahead, checking out my old man as he leaned back in his chair and smoked, and the light from the windows gathered dust and haze until it seemed like bright rafters had descended on the tables. It was all Volkov could do to step around the light and settle in across from Ace, and by the time he had done that Ace had slid the bishop over behind the pawn, and you could tell that the kid was nervous now, that he come to recognize that this was a bona fide chess opening, to suspect there might be a plant at the simul. So Volkov makes a quick move, then circles again to see that Ace is setting up to play a genuine match with the master, and in the course of an hour the boy's game falls apart on all fronts, Ace blowing smoke at him and whispering over the board as the boy sat down. Taunting Volkov, crushing out cigarettes on the table beside the board.

And the light in the room took on further angles, I swear. Like Ace had told me when we saw the King in the Armory. And this must of been the time when abstraction fell into gristle and blood and bulldozing, like Ace claimed it always did in the end, and beauty and geometry found its way down to survival.

I got up from where I sat and circled the lobby until I was behind my father, who looked more angular, less human in the doctored light, which spread over his shoulders and shadowed and reddened his hair and the chessboard. And it seemed as though bishops and rooks were hovering inches above the squares, and I could see them but I suspected nobody else could but Ace and Volkov. Volkov leaned forward and was fixing to move a piece, but his hand settled on light and he drew back, cupped his chin in his hands, and stayed in front of my father until he stayed too long and had forfeited the game to the left of Ace, until the handlers stirred him from the seat and herded him on to the next chair, and the one after, and the whole event became a cycle, each time resting in front of my father.

As you might of guessed, Volkov begun to resign from game after game until he was needing a victory over Ace to break even with his matches. He settled down at the board as Ace was lighting up another Tareyton, and the handlers flanked the boy, and he looked at the arrangement of the pieces with this look that was just asking who dealt this mess? And all the while Ace whispering things to him, and the light over the board buckling in smoke and Volkov sniffing, trying to concentrate.

Then Ace says something that sounds like nishnya, and he leans across the board and repeats it, and the boy blinks and nods and they both stand up from the table. Daddy had offered Volkov a draw, it seemed, and the commissars hustle the boy back up to his room, all of them muttering in Russian, and the fat man in the suit steps from the crowd of old people and hands Ace something that would turn out to be a hundred-dollar bill, and it turned out to be a public triumph that would also foot half our rent for the month.

I was never to learn who the man was, only that he gave Ace the money and sealed the deal on the moment of glory. And for a while I looked up to my father, at least into the summer when school let out and I was to become his gofer and factotum once again. But up into March of that same year I was proud of Ace, and we joked that he was the grand master, and he showed me parts of the city up close, like the amphitheater and the Witches' Tree barely more than a block from the stage.

***

He showed me the tree on March 28th, and the date is important on account of the story of the tree itself. It was on that day, Ace told me, that a big tornado had hit the city back in 1890, causing death and havoc in its path. During the storm lightning had struck the stump of a felled tree that stood on the very spot that this one stood. Being one who was not interested in tornados or lightning—at least not at that time, though it would change later—I ignored the story until he told me about the witches.

That first tree, Ace told me, had been felled by the city, but before it had come down, it had been the haunt and the haven for the witches and granny-witches, the warlocks and sibyls of the city. On the eve of its felling, someone in the sorcerous community had tacked a note on the trunk of it, a dire little poem that promised revenge if it was cut down. 'Revenge on the elevenmonth,' Ace had said, in his best carnival barker baritone, because he didn't believe it, but I was not sure enough to disbelieve it myself.

Sure enough, eleven months to the day after the poem was posted and the tree fell, that 1890 tornado struck the city. The pictures of its aftermath show a wide tunnel of damage up Market Street, the wooden buildings splintered like a bomb gone off, and the brick and stone all buckled and rubbled away. South of the downtown, though the tornado passed to their north, this neighborhood took on damage. High wind and lightning, a bolt of which struck the stump of the old tree, splitting the nitrogen out of the air and earthing it in the roots, where it lay for a generation, while things about it changed like an alien spirit had passed into the ground and embodied the wreckage.

The tree that grew in the place of the old Witches' Tree was gnarled and galled and knotted from its sapling days. Ace said that the witches recognized it as a child of their own, and graced it early with decorations—dream catchers and talismans and beads—and that unto this day on the great witching nights, Midsummer and Mayday and Halloween and others, the tree took on adornment. And I listened to the story and gave the tree a wide berth until the untimely hot Midsummer Night that year, a day momentous for my history.

***

I had been laying low when it come to Becky. Something about her seemed too green and familiar, and when she knocked on the window the time would come that I wrapped my pillow around my ears and fell asleep refusing to listen.

In time the knocking turned to scratching, and as spring moved into summer I grew used to the noise, until the heat rose in the summer and, early on a night in late June, I threw open the window because of the stifling air.

I woke not long after I had fallen asleep. Becky was standing by my bedside, trying in vain to stroke my shoulder and looking sorrowful because her fingers vanished as they touched my arm.

She told me to come with her, and for the first time in months I followed, drawn by her sadness and quiet. Out the window we crawled, then walked for several blocks in the close, steamy night until I heard the voices intone and figured we were near the theater.

I remembered the play from school, the witches and the ghost, and I recalled our teacher saying that it was bad luck to say 'Macbeth' when you worked on a production, so I didn't say it that night and didn't say the name aloud until fifty years later, when tragedy come to that DeChevre boy.

But that night we walked, Becky and me, along the lamplit street north of the park, and you could hear the play from there, and there on our right was the Witches' Tree, decked out with baubles and signs. I let go of Becky's hand and circled the old knotted trunk, and when I looked back she had vanished, leaving a waver above the sewer grate.

It would be years until I saw her again, but there was no way of knowing at the time, as I stepped onto one of the oak knots, just the right size to hoist myself into the lower branches, like the tree had grown a staircase just for my climbing. From the branches you could see the stage, and it had reached the part in the play where the trees

110

were moving. I swear I felt the Witches' Tree uproot beneath me, heard the scrape as it staggered across the pavement and toward the mulberries that lined the northern border of the park.

I could barely hang on now. It was getting late, and the summer night was smothering, even hotter than when I had climbed out of the window. Ahead other trees moved toward the stage, cardboard props held up by actors and apprentices, and the mulberries around me groaned and stretched their branches, and it was like a forest drawn toward the stage's heart of light. And they were breaking the news to the king that the woods was moving, and the Witches' Tree seemed to rustle across the sidewalk, and after that I could remember no more.

✳✳✳

I woke up in sunlight near the statues of the lions. How I got there I could never tell you but it was the first of a number of nights I did not and would never recollect. Of course I was startled to begin with, half afraid and half hoping that Ace would of missed me by now and gone angry, but the sun was not that high and I rushed toward the apartment, pretty sure that he wasn't awake yet.

Something about the streets had changed and shifted about. When I crossed Third Street I was lost. Some of the accustomed buildings were missing, like they had been swept off in a natural disaster. The infirmary at the corner of Oak Street was there as I remembered, but around it were buildings I had never seen before. All of this was in broad sunlight, and I wondered if I was dreaming this now and whether my night astride the Witches' Tree had been a waking time. But the infirmary had always been my landmark, and I could steer by its heights to a block away, to the apartment where we lived and where I thought that punishment would no doubt await me if my luck hadn't held.

The window to my room had been closed, though, so my spirits sank and I went to the front door. It was unlocked, and as I stepped into the foyer I smelled coffee and heard conversation coming from the kitchen. And it was the first time I had seen her since that day in

Hutchins Grocery. Her back was to me and she was smaller than I had imagined, but when she turned to face me, the light rushed into the room, and for a moment I thought I was rescued from something I could not name and given a task I could name even less.

'Tommy?' She said. 'It's Mamma. And haven't you grown so tall and handsome. And aren't you still my boy?'

XVI

Here Mickey turned off the tape. He had no idea how long Tommy had spoken, but his desk seemed narrower now, and for a moment he thought the carrel itself had contracted.

He knew the story about the drowning or almost drowning. It was a Zen parable he'd seen in a dozen forms—the old monk schooling the young monk about the urgency of God. Tommy probably had picked it up somewhere in conversation or the library stacks or seated in front of a library computer in between porn sites and Elvis web pages. And the Witches' Tree was already a legend in the city, and though the boy's happening to climb its branches just as Birnam Wood was moving to Dunsinane there within earshot of the stage seemed, to his novelist's eye, a bit hokey and contrived.

He'd never heard a version, though, of kissing an imagined girl through a wintry window pane. Nor of a boy stumbling in on his long-lost mother seated at a kitchen table, bathed in light. And when he thought of these parts of the story, something gave way in Mickey Walsh, and his eyes filled with tears and he gasped, calling himself a sentimental geezer, a doddering, senile drunk, then gasping again, a little surprised at the rage he had just turned upon himself.

Mickey realized that the whole Tommy story was taking hold of him. He tried to deflect it one last time: taking out his laptop, he tried a page on the novel, but the characters stood motionless and spoke in circles, creating text but no traction.

Text but no traction. His own words made him laugh, because immediately Mickey suspected that if this novel were ever published, some lazy reviewer would use it to describe the book as a whole, in that triumphant way that lazy reviewers have of using the writer's own words against him.

This, of course, provided that the book was published to begin with. All things were distracting Mickey from the task at hand, including the critical work that sat on the other end of the carrel desk, a half-empty water bottle from mid-March perched solidly on its pages. Suitably derailed by now from novel and scholarship, Tommy's reminiscences echoing in his head, he left the library and walked across campus to the bus stop.

✳✳✳

The bus let Mickey off just south of the park, and at once he was tempted to visit the Witches' Tree for himself. Countless times he had passed it in his walks up to the Wilde and to Salvages, and he had paid it some attention, had picked up its legends now and then from pamphlets at the Visitors Center and guides on neighborhood tours. Imagining Tommy in its branches and the tree slowly shuffling toward the amphitheater had given the old story new flesh and meaning, and for the first time he began to get his thoughts around the *lore* of Tommy Briscoe, how something in the recorded memoirs seemed to be taking shape, giving a muddled and nomadic childhood a meaning and direction.

Yes, Tommy was drug-addled and whiskey-bent, and years among the elements, where mere survival must have occupied all his thoughts rather than memory or contemplation—where angles of light were set aside for what Ace Briscoe had called *the gristle and blood and bulldozing of just getting by.* And yet the tapes were showing Tommy as a creature of reflection, capable of looking back on his life and seeing its poetry, its causes and connections.

And making things up when fact and memory failed.

The tatters in the life were mended with patchwork, Mickey reckoned.

And he was also coming to believe that he could supply the rest of the embroidery. Now, as he followed the sidewalk toward the promenade and the stone lions, the tiered amphitheater sunlit on his right, he began to feel that he owed Tommy something, and he knew it was not steeped in the same guilt that Bulwer and Stack had talked about when they entrusted him with the tapes—that it was more than a sense of things left undone, but all about things to do.

A tall woman dressed in yellow, almost splendid in an outlandish golden cape, stood on the stage balcony, carefully folding Tommy's old linen duster. Mickey stopped and regarded her, and she stirred with that sense that someone was watching until her eyes found his and the two of them watched each other in silence.

"What?" she said finally, her voice surprising, aggressive, second tenor. And Mickey's memory jogged, and he recognized it was Magnolia Street on stage.

***

"Magnolia Street" was born Johnnie Lee Ruffin, and came to the city from out in the state in the early '90s, when she was he and seventeen. Very soon she found her way to the drag clubs in town, most notably Confrères in west downtown, where she shared the stage with the two Militia Queens, Ruby Ridge and Blanche Davidian, her impersonations of Diana Ross, Tina Turner, and Whitney Houston lifting her rapidly to minor celebrity. She was "the D of C," the Diva of Confrères, and it was no accident that word of her reached Tommy Briscoe, who by that time had imitated Elvis so often that he was on the brink of becoming the

King. They hit it off immediately, Magnolia became Tommy's backup singer, one of his few confidants. Some rumors had them even closer, though John Bulwer and Alan Stack claimed no knowledge of that kind of connection.

Over the years as her looks waned, Magnolia had been seen less at Confrères, more in the old town where it was rumored that a rich man secretly paid for her apartment, that now of independent means, she spent her time with cocaine and gin and singing of occasion with the Brischords. Police had questioned her after Tommy's death, but as to what she had known or said, nobody was certain: drag queens, it seemed, were not always the most reliable source of information.

***

"Miss Street?" Mickey asked, his mind racing through the protocols of gender regarding drag queens, all thoughts heading finally toward a vanishing point of ignorance.

Magnolia tucked the duster under her arm. "Who wants to know?"

"My name's Walsh. Friends with John Bulwer and Alan Stark."

She wasn't having it. "Everybody friends with them two."

"I knew Tommy Briscoe a little, too." Mickey wasn't sure whether he was lying, but the statement got the job done. You could see Magnolia's shoulders slump, even beneath her magnificent cape. She leaned on the balcony railing and squinted.

"This is his jacket," she said, holding up the folded garment to plain sight.

"I saw it up there a couple days past," Mickey said. "Wonder why the crew hadn't taken it down already."

Magnolia brushed back her hair, a gesture so fluid that for a moment Mickey wondered whether she was natural or wearing a wig. Certainly she was nowhere near high drag, wearing a simple oxford shirt tied in the front. She came down the steps onto the stage, and now he could see her short denim cut-offs and the

116

surprisingly smooth and tapered legs he had admired once from a distance before being informed that Magnolia was Magnolia.

"They take it down ever afternoon," she said, posing winsomely in case she was being watched that way. "I been putting it up of a morning, but I'm afraid that sometime when they take it down they will throw it away, and I can't have that."

Mickey nodded.

Magnolia sat down on the stage, folding her legs beneath her. "Where you know Tommy? The store? The bar?"

"Both. Mainly the store. My bar time was earlier than his, I understand." Mickey was unsure why he made the distinction, but Magnolia read something into it and nodded.

"'This is the place'," she said, and when it was obvious that Mickey didn't understand, she added "What the sign say. On the jacket."

"Ah. So I have heard."

Magnolia beckoned to him. "Got a cigarette?"

It so happened that he had. Since the day that Bulwer shoved the pack of Marlboros across the counter in his direction, Mickey had been on sad decline. The next one he had bummed was "for the road." He had smoked it on a walk across the park, and in the spiraling decline of a day or two, had given up eventually and bought his own pack at the convenience store a block from the campus.

Now he was handing them out. He lit Magnolia's cigarette and she steadied his hand with a touch soft and a little confusing.

She asked him where he was headed, and offered to go along with him. Mickey figured he would be solicited or panhandled by the time they reached the Witches' Tree, but to his relief, Magnolia turned out to be good company—soft spoken and smart. On the way they talked about Tommy—her general and rinsed memories, he guessed, as they walked down the colonnade and passed the tennis courts, where middle-aged white people in visors and spandex watched them curiously.

When they reached the Witches' Tree, Magnolia stood at its base and looked up through the branches. "Tommy always said this tree moved," she muttered. "I never seen it anywhere but here, but he stuck with his story."

"Do you miss him?" Mickey asked.

Magnolia turned, the brown of her eyes almost swallowed in the widening dark vortex of the pupils. "What do *you* think, Mister Professor? I miss him something terrible."

Then she added, as Mickey averted his eyes, "But I don't think them boys should be lethal injected for something neither of them had a hand in."

Of course he tried to ask her about this. Suddenly, if there was any truth to what Magnolia said, the end of Tommy's story was changed, no longer a police procedural that clicked open and shut like a jewel box, but something muddied and resonant. But no matter how Mickey insinuated, came aslant at the issue, Magnolia was suddenly silent, as though any more said was a kind of betrayal.

So Mickey left Magnolia Street by the Witches' Tree, taking one last look at her from the colonnade across the park. Standing beside the tree, a golden shape at the edge of his sight, she lifted her cape and, for a moment, it became a pair of wings that spread from her shoulders to envelop her. She seemed to hug the gnarled trunk of the tree, though from this distance it was pretty hard to tell. So he turned and crossed the court near his apartment, where atop the fountain the goddess stood in a spray of water, her own bronze cloak glittering as she and Magnolia seemed suddenly like facing statues, paralleled but each beyond the sight of the other.

It all left Mickey wondering at the mystery of Tommy—at how, no matter how much of his life was revealed, things became more strange and enigmatic the further down the road you fared.

XVII

Mickey had urged Tamar to slow their pace. He dreaded being the first arrival at an Athena Bumpas dinner party. He knew that, alone with the department head, he would be subject to all kinds of questions about the progress of his work. Or even worse, he would confirm his suspicion that she didn't know one non-tenured faculty member from another.

Athena lived only a block away from Mickey Walsh, but it was miles when it came to social class, prestige and power. Her Victorian town house had burnished double doors: Tamar had told him that such thresholds were common during the period, since the families often held wakes and visitations at home, so the entrance had to be big enough to bring a coffin in and out. When Mickey wondered aloud how often Athena made use of this advantage, Tamar replied that statements like that were one of the many reasons he had never been promoted, why they were invited to the second shelf dinner instead of the first.

The "shelf dinners" were common knowledge among Mickey's department: in the middle of the summer, as the faculty geared up for the fall semester, Athena would have them all over. In shifts, of course—tenured faculty closer to the beginning of the semester so as not to pull them early from holiday, but non-tenured and graduate student instructors a month before that.

As they took the gas lit sidewalk on the pricey circle of Athena's historical court, Mickey looked north toward the park and the theatre. Faintly, muffled by distance and the sounds of passing cars, he caught a whisper of Shakespearean, knew that it was past seven since the play was underway. Which meant that, by the time they ascended the wide steps to Athena's house, they'd be late by fifteen minutes or so, enough that a flock of grad students, lured by the opportunities of food and attention and self-promotion and wine and more food, would be circled in the parlor, talking among themselves and wondering who this middle-aged Irishman was.

"Are you sure this wine is enough?" Tamar asked him.

Mickey shrugged, considered the price, and knocked on the door of Athena Bumpas, who greeted him with a broad, theatrical motion into the house, as though she were sweeping the two of them down the hallway.

✳✳✳

Author of a celebrated collection of short stories, *Late Night Thoughts on the Eroica*, Athena Bumpas came to the university in her mid-twenties and was tenured in a powerful rush when she persuaded all the powers of the academy that hers was a star on the rise.

Mickey had read the volume, initially disappointed to have misread *Eroica* as *Erotica* in the title, then feeling guilty and obligated to see it through. Smart and schooled, Athena Bumpas was variously gifted.

Her real gifts, however, lay in a kind of highbrow self-marketing. She was ten years in finishing her novel, a six-hundred page stream of consciousness monologue delivered by a nineteenth-century governess unable to leave the house where she was employed. The book came out to initially glowing reviews, which waned in enthusiasm when the reviewers actually started to read *My Own Visitant*.

Mickey was with the later reviewers. In an attempt at professional graciousness, he had started to read *My Own Visitant*, but he balked in its opening pages. The novel seemed both self-consciously lyrical and completely free of traction. After a third attempt, he gave up altogether, marveling at the online reviews that praised what he had found to be pretty hard going, like stirring wet sand.

He asked Bulwer, who had read more than any of his university colleagues, whether it was fair to drop *My Own Visitant* at the threshold and Bulwer admitted he was pressed to point out a threshold in the big rambling tome, saying the house just went on behind the door and you didn't want to be trapped in it like some tiresome governess.

Mickey had said at the time, thinking of his own third novel, that ten years seemed a long time to take in finishing a thing. That maybe Athena had worried the story into tangles. And he remembered Bulwer's wheezing laughter, remembered the old man's succinct judgment.

It took her nine of those years to unhinge her jaw and devour the competition.

✳✳✳

Here was Athena in all her particolored splendor, layered in sweater and vest and blouse as though it wasn't July outside, looking for all Mickey could imagine like a Tarot fool standing at the edge of a bluff. With her customary Louisiana politeness, she guided Tamar and Mickey into the dining room where other guests were already seated.

The graduate students looked up at his arrival. Mickey was surprised to see his student, Diana Chen, seated among the youngsters beside a young man who seemed familiar—no doubt the boy Mickey had seen squiring her across the quad a few days back. Timidly she waved, but she was the only one: seeing that it was just Dr. Walsh, the grad students turned back to each other and the wine, as Athena showed Mickey and Tamar to their seats among three familiar faces—Ken Weir, Dan Waite, and Michael Williams.

These were the three other term faculty of the department. The four of them had last names beginning with "W", which made it easier for Athena to confuse them constantly, though Ken was a wry, squirrely goblin, Dan a serious hulker, and Williams simply old and faded. Mickey scavenged his memory for their areas of scholarly expertise, coming up blank. As the wine was passed, however, Waite, seated to Mickey's left, made some sort of Eucharist joke, and Mickey thought he remembered that Waite had written articles on medieval liturgy, having lost a tenured job when some seminary had reeled even more radically toward fundamentalism.

At least he was drinking, Mickey observed to himself, giving himself a more generous pour and passing the wine to Tamar, who frowned at the fullness of her husband's glass.

"That's three quarters full," she whispered, enough that Ken Weir, sitting to her right, must have overheard.

Mickey shook his head. "One quarter empty," he replied a little too loudly. "I'm always the pessimist when it comes to alcohol."

Meanwhile, Weir was doing his best to charm Tamar, while his wife squinted over her spectacles at the table setting. Weir and Tamar had met at this event last year, so she was in familiar hands, and Mickey was a little relieved that his wife's glare would be deflected for most of the evening.

"Don, won't you be a dear," Athena drawled, "and open another bottle of the pinot noir?"

To which Waite rose from table and dutifully stalked into the kitchen, not bothering to remind the boss that his first name was Dan, after all. Mickey followed his colleague with his eyes, hoping to see whiskey or at least cognac on the bar cart. It seemed, though, that Athena was holding the hard stuff in abeyance for the tenured faculty later in the summer, if there was any in the house to begin with.

To Mickey's right, Tamar and Weir were talking about Henry James, of whom Tamar knew nothing—though she could fake her way through any conversation by sheer quick-wittedness—and Weir knew far too much. Mickey took in the décor of the dining room: dark wood offset by burgundy macramé wall hangings, as though some designer from forty years back had renovated a hunting lodge. Athena had done well for herself by finding the right place at the right time: he'd be damned if he could figure the pathway of her success, but she had found it early and stuck to it well.

At the other end of the table, the grad students were talking about *Twilight* and *The Hunger Games*, both of which were now legitimate doctoral subjects. Williams was keeping up with them marginally, trying with little success, Mickey reckoned, to come off as hip.

Sighing, Mickey took the freshly opened bottle from the passing Waite, refreshed his glass and set it before him, anticipating a long evening. He poured again in the midst of Ken Weir's lackluster little lecture on *Turn of the Screw*. "Nothing new there that Athena didn't rewrite at five times the length," Mickey muttered, his lips on the glass, and Tamar kneed him under the table. Meanwhile, Athena was hosting her dinner, moving from chair to chair, talking to Williams as a pair of dutiful graduate students placed bowls of vegetable stew in front of the guests.

Mickey was well into his third ample glass when Athena leaned over between him and Tamar, asking his wife how she had been keeping over the past year. Mickey grabbed the wrist of a hand that had reached in to pick up the wine bottle, only to find that it was the hostess herself. Graciously, Athena dislodged herself from his grip, and his ears warm with pinot noir or embarrassment, Mickey topped off his glass and returned to drinking as Tamar's account of her paintings and birds receded into alcohol static when he turned away his attention.

"And Mickey?" Athena asked, her voice genteel and distant like someone on public radio.

He took an enormous gulp of the wine, waited until the

room stopped tilting, and turned to join the conversation. "Pardon?" he asked much too loudly.

"Your work. Still the modernist book? And the novel?" Athena's eyes had already turned away, looking toward Ken Weir who was eagerly thinking through his sales pitch.

Mickey took a breath and crossed the threshold. "No, Athena. Something new. There was this homeless man who stayed across the park. Tommy Briscoe. You might have seen him over by the theater. Well, he was killed a couple of months back under circumstances that seemed dubious at first, then cut and dried, but dubious again given what I heard from a drag queen over by the Witches' Tree."

Tamar's stare could have melted metal, but Mickey was in for the duration. "I've made a deal with the owners of Dry Salvages and the Oscar Wilde that I would write his biography, because he's just intriguing enough to make a good story, or at least I hope. But it's not even as simple as that, Athena."

He took another long sip of the wine, then stared directly into Athena's wide eyes. "I'm beginning to think Tommy Briscoe was not of this world. And if that's the case, we have news on our hands."

Tamar dropped her napkin on the table and stood. "I'm sorry, Dr, Bumpas," she said quietly. "I'm not feeling well. I think I'll head home before it's too..."

Athena's hand on her shoulder was all sympathy, and Mickey remembered that the department head had been married three times and could tell you a thing or two about impossible men. "I surely hate to see you both go," she fretted, averting her eyes, but Tamar was quick to respond.

"Oh, I think Mickey should stay a little longer. No trouble on my account."

Athena was all bustle and good hostess, urging Mickey to accompany Tamar, that it was dark outside and even if the neighborhood was relatively safe...

All the while, Mickey refused to budge, his eyes fixed longingly on the bottle that had moved to the other side of Dan

Waite.

At last one of the graduate students—apparently Diana Chen's presumed boyfriend, though the room was now blurred and shadowy—offered to escort Tamar home. And they left, the glares of all the grad students affixed to the drunk and sullen Mickey, who stayed seated and minded his purple reflection in the glass.

✳✳✳

His behavior had stopped all conversation. Slowly, Athena's party crowd dwindled until, with a perfunctory nod, Williams left with a wife who was too lovely for him to deserve, and only Mickey and the Waites remained. To his irritation, Mickey could hear Janice Waite's hissed insistence to her husband that he was *the last man left here*, that he *ought to do something*. To spare Dan Waite any more responsibility, and no doubt himself an ass-kicking, Mickey wrangled to his feet and lurched out into the humid city air, not bothering to say goodbye to anyone.

The gas light on the court was charming and retro. For a moment Mickey felt himself transported back to when this neighborhood was new and the nineteenth century was turning into the twentieth. Rail money and distillery magnates had settled this street: Athena's house was first owned by a tobacco executive, though a number of semi-famous painters and writers had landed as well at these addresses. But now it housed apartments and the consciously picturesque dwellings of the arty rich. Only a few steps from a *fin de siècle* fountain, barely a block from summer Shakespeare, it was a gaslit Arcadia back then, and a mixture of gentrification and absentee rental today.

The Shakespeare was over for the evening. "I am a very foolish fond old man," Mickey groaned, sitting at the curb, listening to the rush of the water from the center of the courtyard. From this distance and under the flood of alcohol it looked as though the statue had vanished from atop the fountain.

"You all right, Walsh?"

It seemed that the Williamses had lingered on the court, Mrs. Williams taking in architecture while her husband paced the sidewalk, probably clearing his head. Though Michael Williams wasn't one of Mickey's favorite people at work, the older man had managed to avoid being offensive, and, like Mickey, was another of the second-shelf novelists who had gravitated to this university, this city. Mickey had heard that Williams' books were "poor man's Tolkien," but since nobody in the department read each other's work, the judgment had been made from glimpses of book covers and the resulting rumors. Williams taught Modern European Fiction as well, though his language skills were supposedly no better than Mickey's own.

They could have been kindred minds thirty years ago. But the climate had changed, the arts departmentalized and compartmentalizing until people like them were on the way out. It was no country for old men, with each dog guarding a collapsing manger.

All of this Mickey thought, his mind dismantling the man and the well-intentioned comment before he replied that yes, he was all right, that he just needed a little air before he walked home.

Williams nodded. "Live in walking distance?"

"Just over on the next block," Mickey answered, wondering how to cut the conversation short.

But Williams was lingering. "Actually, Walsh. What I overheard about your project? Sounded good. I'd read it."

"Thanks. Nothing earth-shattering, I guess."

Williams laughed. "I lost the ambition to shatter earth years back, though I'm older than you and sinking into senility. Sometimes now I wonder if all those dreams of artistry didn't make a half-assed teacher. If I missed what I should have done all along. Or at least missed doing it the best I could."

Mickey was losing patience. Moaning, self-absorbed old coot. Made him wish he'd taken a bottle with him, slipped it out under his shirt while Bumpas was inattentive. 'I guess,' he began, figuring Williams expected some kind of answer, that there'd been a confession that called for politeness in what he'd say next. "I guess a lot of people come to that crossroads."

"You're probably right," Williams said. He signaled his wife up the block, who seemed ready to go. "I grew up here. Then lived away for much of my life. Returned because I thought the calm of the past was here, that everything stopped until I stepped back in the stream. Well, what was it your Jimmy Joyce said about Ireland? *The old sow that eats her farrow?*"

"That's what he said, all right," Walsh replied, even more eager now to be rid of the intruder. "But I'm not sure what that has to do with either of us."

"For me," Williams said, "it's pretty simple. Turns out I'm not the hero I imagined I'd be. But I might be something else."

With that he stalked away, waving at Mickey, long strides taking in the pavement.

✳✳✳

By now, Mickey's head had cleared a little, though not entirely.

Upon closer look, the bronze girl was still there, standing in the lamplit spray. Supposedly Venus, if Mickey recalled it correctly. She stood atop the spray of water, her veils flowing under the arch of her raised right arm. Trumpeting little sea-cherubs circled the base of the statue, their horns spouting water like forgotten music.

There was no way he could go home tonight.

Reaching over the lip of the fountain, Mickey dipped his hands in the water and splashed it onto his face, drenching his shirt collar and the tie Tamar had insisted he wear. He wondered if she was too angry to sleep, then realized he was far more concerned with avoiding an argument than he was with anything resembling his wife's well-being.

"Galatea," someone pronounced behind him. Diana Chen was sitting on a park bench facing the fountain, her knees drawn up beneath her as though she was strangely cold on this summer night. "And not Pygmalion's Galatea."

"I thought she was Venus," Mickey breathed. Then said it again, this time louder.

"Lots of people think that," Diana said. "But the original statue first appeared in Chicago in the 1890s. Things get mysterious after that, and this is one of several copies. It's Galatea, all right."

She stretched and yawned, curving her arm over her head. Her tee shirt hiked ever so slightly up her belly, and Mickey watched for a long, unfettered second before decency drew his eyes away.

"Galatea?" he sputtered. "The...Pygmalion's Galatea? "

Diana grinned. "Nope. There's more than one Galatea. Like these statues. She was a sea nymph. You know the Cyclops in the Odyssey, right? Well, he fell in love with *this* Galatea, and she wasn't having any of it, so he kills her boyfriend. Steps on him, if I remember right."

Mickey grinned. "Ouch. Forgot you were an Art History major, Diana. You're so good at novels."

"Thanks, Dr. Walsh." Diana lay back on the bench and looked up into the clear summer sky. "I'm only here until Jordan gets back."

"Your boyfriend?"

She shrugged. "Guess so. He's supposed to be walking your wife home. You in trouble?"

Mickey nodded. "Pretty much always. So this is another Galatea?"

"Actually," Diana drawled, stretching out the word and folding her arms across her chest, "the sea nymph is the only sure Galatea. Someone else gave the name to Pygmalion's statue, and that was years after the story was written. She went a long time before she had a name, which is not surprising."

Mickey leaned against the basin of the fountain. The water licked against his hands and he tried to recover balance, to see things straight, closing first one eye and then the other until the world tilted back into order. He wasn't going to answer Diana's *not surprising*: it seemed thickheaded to comment on it, thickheaded and somehow uncomfortably intimate, so he resisted that professorial part of himself that had to have the last word on everything.

"How far do you live from here, anyway?" Diana asked, and for a second Mickey wondered himself.

"About a block. Your Jordan should be back soon."

"Oh. Well then he'll know the way to your place if you want us to walk you back."

For some reason he felt his vanity bruised. "Nah, nah," he said, a little too loudly. "You two can go on then. I'll just wait here until he returns."

***

He awakened the next morning by the fountain, lying on the park bench Diana had occupied during whatever part of their conversation he remembered. The sun was already full over the horizon, and church bells rang from somewhere several blocks north.

Carefully, Mickey smoothed his jacket, his mouth cottony and the familiar, insufferable headache rising to meet him. He had no idea what time it was. And he had no intent of going home before he went to the university and met his class. The prospects of that bird-loud apartment and his wife's antagonism were much worse than standing rumpled and fetid in front of the student body.

The bus driver's watch gave him two hours before the class began, so Mickey rode the few blocks in silence, his head leaning against the window, his hair matting from the condensation. It was a hot walk to the library as well, and he was puffing by the time he reached his carrel on the fourth floor.

Hysterica passio, down, thou climbing sorrow, he whispered. *King Lear* vivid in his head, the old man courting a heart attack out on the heath. Once again, it seemed that he had botched things thoroughly, although it still might be a step toward freedom.

As he entered the carrel, he noticed a folded note on the floor, no doubt slipped under the door this morning. It was from Diana, asking if he was OK.

No...really and truly OK?

He slipped the note into his jacket pocket and sat with a groan at his desk. Was tempted to light a cigarette, though no other infraction could get him evicted more quickly from the library.

I guess a lot of people come to that crossroads. Yes, he had said that, removed and dismissive, when the old guy was just trying to be kind.

What little else he remembered from what Williams had said seemed to boil down to *get out of town*. Or, more gently, perhaps, *don't look for home at home*. It made Mickey sad to think that so many things had turned beyond recall, and so soon, and all at the same time. He pushed the button on the cassette player for the next entry in Tommy's saga.

XVIII

I would not see Ace Briscoe much again.

*From that day in the kitchen on, he become a ghostly presence.
I sighted him now and then in the vicinity of the old neighborhood,
but his nets spread wider than my own, so instead I would mostly
hear things.*

*There was a steamboat that they brought up from way down
south when I was about fourteen—an old craft in pretty bad shape,
that the governing powers had restored and put back on the water for
annual races against another, better-kept steamer from up the river.
Despite the fact that their boat was better than our boat, it turned
out ours could win like clockwork on the odd-numbered years while
the upriver boat won on the even.*

*You know the saying about boat races, and it only took about
four years for suspicious people to catch the pattern. Rumor had it
that a sly, red-haired man from the southern part of the state had
proposed it to folks in the city, helped make the race official, and
walked away with quick money before people recognized that the
whole operation was foreordained.*

*It was like that with Ace, who was scarce but visible at the edge
of your suspicions. I thought I saw him once or twice, and always*

in a crowded place. So that by the time I swam through the crowd to get to his spot, he had either vanished or turned out to be someone else entirely.

And yet I had this dream about a fox. Or rather a fox man, some kind of creature that split the difference between human and animal. He was red-headed like my daddy, and spindly and a little stooped over like nothing I had ever seen. Sometimes he seemed handsome, like the Reverend Nick Mays, and oftentimes when I dreamt of him I would start out believing I was talking to the preacher, then his form would change again, and he would become the fox or daddy, or something composed of branches and shadow.

And this dream come back again and again, and each time I would run into the creature—sometimes in the woods beside Thusa Creek, sometimes in the park where the theater was, but more and more in the old city. He would peek out of the narrow space between houses, too narrow to even pass for an alley, and he would confront me, and each time it was the same.

It always started with me asking him who he was. And the reply was always the same, and once he answered, it was like we would repeat the words on script for as long as I dreamt the dream.

And the fox man would tell me how he was a dweller in dreams, and stuck there until I stopped dreaming him. On account of once he had a dream, years ago when he was but a boy my age, and in it he saw a wise old woman, maybe a deaconess or a granny witch, and she had asked him if a saved man was subject to the laws of cause and effect. And the fox man was sly and foxy, so he thinks that, no, he had the good sense to step around cause and find his way to effect, and when he said this to the woman, she vanished and he was stuck in the dream instead.

And each time he would ask me why it was wrong for him to say that he was too smart for cause and effect. And I would always answer if that was wrong, then he must be subject to cause and effect. To just confess and get out of the dream. And he would look at me and vanish in the shadows.

Each time I had the dream, down until the last time, it would be the same. But each time it was different, because the world of the dream was more and more the city, and the fox man was more and more the fox.

✳✳✳

In dreams and in waking, I begun the mapping of my haunts and environs.

To the south is the long stretch of highway, lined back then with the desolation of auto shops and fast food restaurants. Most of your immigrants come up this way, seeking their fortune in the city instead of in the mines or on the dirt farms. This was the road lined and guarded by statuary—Confederate soldiers and goat boys and goddesses. They may not be home to the spirits they stand for, but I have heard tell that they are often dreamt into being by the thoughts of those who ponder them, so that on some nights all of them take on life and movement, and it is best for you never to meet their eyes, and to the north...

...there are serpents. Or a single serpent, muscling its broad green back against the border or the state, all-sentient, all-knowing, like Thusa Creek back home, lifting you from the banks and dropping you miles to the west, further south and back a time zone, the brille over its slotted eyeballs glittering like the eastern fire to the west as it looks for you and looks out for you, riding the current and becoming the current, form indistinguishable from vehicle, while to the west...

...the animal energy splits and mingles. Leopard and fox patrol the double-digited streets of the city's ghettoes, of the projects and the decaying neighborhoods of the riverside, the ruins of Fontaine Ferry and the desolate, abandoned tracts where old people and children are stalked and taken down by creatures half sinew, half wind, coursing between houses, scattering leaves and litter, vanishing when light is thrown upon them, gathering substance in the gathering shade, and to the east...

...nothing but a wall of fiery light that keeps you from leaving the town, reflecting you with irresistible swift pressure back toward the city's center and heart. Along its surface forgotten forms dance, shadows mingling memories with light, barring your migration, *burdening you with memories and hungry ghosts.*

So you remain here, menaced and herded in on all sides. The towers to the north are mirrored by the rebels to the south, the westward shadows of animals corralled and vanishing in the prohibiting light from the east. The city is beautiful from a distance, and you forget that it smothers its occupants, devours its young. It fails its artists and starves its scholars, depending on where in the great and secretly mapped urban ground they are born and grow up: from its south end would-be novelists to the actors born outside the city, to the singers and musicians that haunt its westernmost streets to the painter just north of the river, whose images mold and crumble in neglected basements. It is where they all go to die in separate, desperate careening across the wheels within wheels that move just under the surface of the city like clockwork grinding down and away.

Unless you find the park at the city center. Green thought in a green shade. Here stone and light and water and wind become poetry, and ordinary things pass into something else and something more.

I have begun to mark the spots. To set forth in code and glyph the pattern of the town, so those who know the mysteries may read and navigate. Those who come after me may map the city as a whole, from smokestack to river and from river to light: I will not be here long enough to finish.

Though I have mapped its ins and outs, the points on its perfect compass. I have mapped its circuit and I will map its road home.

✳✳✳

Life with Mamma was different from life with Ace. It was much more proper: it put me in school daily and improved my grades, because I was left with nothing better to do.

Ace was a memory, then a fox in my dreams, then at last he was a fiction. Like Mamma said he would be. And instead of making father-son stories out of venture and shiftiness, I listened to her autobiography, to why she had left and why she had returned.

Mamma claimed no real recollection of that afternoon in Hutchins when we first parted company, but she did remember the long series of wrongs she had suffered during that absence. She'd gone south, she said, and she had picked up some gumption along the way. Went to a library science program for a year, then hopped around among various schools, concealing that she never got certification nor even a degree. Was married once again, toured with a theater company for a year, then took up as a librarian, because it was the South and she had discovered you could make up credentials and get by.

She always hated Ace. She still does. And she buckled down on my schooling as the best chance that I wouldn't be like him, she told me. It wasn't long, though, before the idea come to me that I was her understudy, that she was priming me to do things that Yorktown and my arrival had somehow kept her from doing.

She got a job at the Free Public Library, right by the statues of Lincoln and Prentice, and she moved us to a place that was steadier. Now we were on one of the courts, in a little clean apartment within eyeshot of the big houses on Fourth Street, and though it was now a bus ride to my old school, it was a short walk for me to the park where my adventures in the city had pretty much first begun. It was a move full circle in a country of circles, and I would of loved the location if my freedoms had not been restricted. There was no wandering after school. No Becky Thatcher, no Witches' Tree, no Shakespeare in the Park, no friends to speak of for a while, though I still got along with my classmates.

It was like being swallowed whole. Mamma was always on to the neighbors about how good she treated me. But I had few friends back then, and would go straight home from school to study or to her workplace in the library, and when my homework was finished, I would diagram sentences for what she called fun.

Now I never found it so fun, seated at that kitchen table where I had said goodbye to my father, a sentence chosen from one of her favorite books in front of me, and pencil and ruler for the diagramming but as I look back on it, perhaps it is the one thing she showed me for which I am most grateful. Under her guidance I *saw that things connected by words, that the contradictions of life get resolved when you tell a story about them.*

In my captivity my studies prospered. But they all were geared toward the old Boy Scout virtues, which Mamma had read somewhere and vowed to raise a boy by. We would sit in the kitchen and I would recite them: I would be trustworthy, loyal, helpful, friendly, courteous, kind, obedient, cheerful, thrifty, brave, clean, and reverent. And there was enough of my father in me that I knew how to pretend an interest, but I suppose at that time I performed no virtue the way that Mamma understood them, for almost always I ended up confined to the house for my own good.

***

We couldn't keep many books in such close quarters, so I would go up to the Free Public Library where Mamma worked the desk and there I would continue to read. It was my main allowance of freedom in my early teens: Mamma saw this as leading to my improvement, and she was right, though by coming late she never knew me well enough to recognize that I could find mutiny and misdemeanor in a calm place.

To get into the library, you go by a tall bronze statue of Lincoln, then up to the steps past the statue of George Prentice, that other native son who hated Catholics and foreigners and Yankees and done his best back in Lincoln's time to thwart and stifle them. Prentice stared out at the Unitarian church, his white hands clutching the arms of his marble chair, and I always passed him by in a rush, because by that time, I was coming to sense the tremors in solid things—the way concrete and bronze and marble put out a frequency, and how the inanimate and the animate spoke to each other by wrinkles in the air. It was the geometry of Ace's chess game given shape in stone. And by the library, the sheer mineral energy would sputter and raise the hair on the back of your neck as you climbed the stairs.

Inside it was safe and shadowy, smelling of almonds and dust and mold and vanilla from the moment you stepped through the revolving door. To your left was the children's room of the library, where my adventures had started when I first come here while living with Ace. And still sometimes I would seek solace there, reading the children's book about Ulysses and looking at the Viewmaster slides of the old city. I loved the Dewey Decimal System back then, and soon figured out the map of it, and began to find the things I loved—the poetry and the novels and the mythology.

One day, bored with the Viewmaster and marking time Mamma's workday ended and we headed home, I climbed the stairs to where they kept the newspapers and magazines. It was brighter in the room, the windows filled with late afternoon light and the ceiling lower, the fluorescent bulbs flickering and sputtering but casting more light on the fine print. It was all adults in the room, and I took note of that, being fifteen: it was like a rite of passage when you moved from fiction into grownup things, so I sat down at a table and thumbed over the back issues of the Courier and the Times.

I had no idea what to study in these premises. So I went to back issues of the papers, discovered archives and microfilm, and found myself looking down a corridor of history—of the little things in the town that reporters had noted but that had slipped from attention in a month or a week. I found Volkov's visit on microfilm, but nothing of Ace in the article. There was something to do with an Asian boy who had beaten the grand master, and something about a minister from south in the state, but nothing of my father's triumph in the hotel lobby and his heroism against the Red Menace.

I admit I was disappointed. Even though I lived with Mamma now and was being groomed toward respectability, I still rooted for Ace from a distance, and it would of been almost like celebrity by connection to think of him receiving praise in the papers.

Late that afternoon I rushed down the library steps, for the first time too close to that Prentice statue that I had avoided in my many visits. My leg brushed against the pedestal and it was like pressing against dry ice, the burn and the freeze and the sting of it right above my knee so that I cried out, and looked up at the statue like you would when someone had hit you from behind.

And the arms of Prentice's chair of state had vanished, and his hands were on his knees as though he was fixing to rise up. He looked down with white eyes and for a minute in the evening sun it looked like he was smiling, a big grin spreading from sideburn to sideburn.

XIX

The scholarship letter was supposed to change things. Tuition and room and board at a university that was fixing to go public to save itself from financial ruin.

Mamma told her neighbors how she had sacrificed to send me through the local university, majoring on the fact that it was private and expensive, until even I was coming to believe that she was footing the bill and that I had better pay her back by going to medical school.

Now for the first time she opened the blackout curtains in the apartment, gave me sunlight for reading, encouraged me in bringing home the books because the glory reflected back on the genes she had give me, and on the Stockton family in general.

I saw it as a windfall, too, a ticket away from home that didn't involve the army, because it was 1966, and a boy could leave the house and end up in a firefight in the Ia Drang Valley before he knew what hit him or was fixing to hit him. Already many of the boys at school were talking of enlisting or resisting, but I was asleep in a pipe dream of college, of parties and girls and friends and draft deferments, because I was a peaceable sort.

So by June of that year, I had my papers in order, and by August

I found myself on the top floor of a town house on Third Street, my furniture a mattress and book shelves made from planks and cinder blocks, the view out my southern window taking in the Confederate Monument, the art museum, and the grid of classroom buildings that stretched all the way to the overpass and Eastern Parkway.

Back then I thought it was my schooling, not my living quarters, that was preparing me for a life to come. So as the first day of school approached I found myself excited and anticipatory. Headed down past the monument on over to a new life filled with prospect and promise on a sweltery day where clouds were gathering off over the river, headed east toward the campus and toward me, bearing lightning and the rumble of a summer storm.

✳✳✳

I come to navigate the university in patches. It was south of my stomping grounds, and I hadn't gone far outside the old city except back in the early days along with Ace. What lay before me was a road of trails, little alleys between buildings like the landscape of my dreams in which I had seen the fox man.

My science classes were the farthest off, in big slippery buildings at the parkway's edge. Getting to class was easy if you woke up early, but I was inclined to oversleep, and usually rushed across the campus hoping I wouldn't get lost on the way.

The campus was a uncommon series of alleys and circles and connections. I had seen aerial photographs in the library, and from high above it made a kind of sense, but up close among the brick and stone it made me nervous until I oriented myself by the playhouse, a converted chapel from when the university was an orphanage. Perhaps it was the comfort of the pointed arch on the windows or of finding out it was built to save the orphans' souls and being an orphan myself with two living parents, or maybe it was just the white frame like a safe spot in a story. Because the university was large and loud and indifferent, and soon I was treading water in the sciences and passing only in my literature and religion classes. It was the library all over again, finding my way through the numbers back to places in my passion.

I knew I was out of my league when it come to my fellow students. They were better dressed and some drove cars to campus, but it was more their polish and good grace that set them apart. For a while I regretted not having hit the books like you should if you are on scholarship, but there was no mending and so I continued, pushed on by the fates of my own laziness.

Only John Bulwer believes I have read my share of books. It must be the lamé jumpsuit, which has its own detractors. But at one time I had read many—James Joyce and Thomas Mann and Pound and Eliot—all about fragments and fables, and it was a puzzle to me to connect one story to another, like I tried to do with the buildings when I looked at the aerial shots of the campus. First term was a road of trials, but slowly I got better, and I begun to gather friends along the way.

There was Buddy Drake, a year my senior, who all of you know as Daddy Chrome so much that he has transformed to fit the name, becoming all shiny and paternal in the passage of years and reluctant to remember the handle he used to go by. He was the one who helped me steer through Ezra Pound, but that day we met in the third floor seminar room up in Gottschalk was a convergence of place and time and person, Buddy sitting on a windowsill, with the sun behind him and outlined like some ragged hero. He was tall and gangly and furry with '60s hair, and I liked him at once.

Buddy come from proper family and the East End, so he was a little more posh and upmarket than a country boy who was schooled downtown. It was the first time I found myself in the presence of scholarship, and I begun to notice the thing that Buddy kept saying, that every student in a college literature class would rather be a writer than a reader. It made sense to me then, even if Buddy was strongly against it. He kept putting books in my hands—modern books that took place inside people's heads, or in fragments, or that tribulated your sense of time until you didn't know what event followed what. But with Buddy's help and the charity of professors I managed a steady C plus in my work, though by the spring of '68 my grades were straining my scholarship, and I started looking into work at the

Kroger in case I could not navigate my studies.

We had finished the first of our tests that May, and I had no idea whether I had failed or passed, when Buddy decided we should go on an adventure. Down at the end of Market Street there was this old amusement park—fun houses and roller coasters, a swimming pool and a night club called Gypsy Village, where a band called Zuice was playing. They were supposedly headed somewhere in local music, like the Monarchs or the Carnations or the Trendells, and Zuice's lead singer had star potential for a high school kid, if you asked Buddy.

I didn't want to head west that night: it was too cold for shirtsleeves and too warm for my leather jacket. I was tired, and I knew that to get to Gypsy Village you had to pass through Negro neighborhoods, and that was one of the things that still scared me about the city, especially since the last few days in that part of town had fallen into racial restlessness. But Buddy was all for it, and my eyes were blurred from reading, and I figured a trip on the 15 bus might give me time to pump Buddy's brains on Lord of the Rings, which I loved dearly but he had never warmed to. It was dark by the time we reached the end of Market Street and stepped off near the Village, slipping in with the rest of the crowd even though neither of us was of age.

But then neither was the band. They were a cover group from somewhere down in the South End, and they were midway into their first set by the time we got there. Aron Hunter was the front man, probably sixteen or seventeen, and it was the last I would ever see of him, though the story goes that he bounced around in music through the early seventies and either got sick or got addicted, depending on the story you heard. But he was at his prime that night, lean and blonde and lovely and wicked on the Stratocaster, though at the time it was music I did not care for—strange George Harrison Hindu songs and druggy anthems—and yet the people were dancing, jerk and watusi and swim to tunes undanceable.

The band stopped for a break not five minutes after we come in, and the crowd milled around, the girls in their high hair, the boys still pompadoured and sideburned, even if the hippie days had begun in the rest of the country. It was a stay in time, that club: I had heard that the amusement park next door was integrated, but the club sure wasn't that night, wall to wall white and mostly of age, though Buddy and I leaned against the far wall out of the lights, so that if anyone carded, we could lie low or leave.

I don't know who started the flask around, but some might say it was the first step in my downfall. I took a swallow of fire, felt it slide down and burn in my chest, and wondered how anyone could make it a practice, though I would certainly catch on in the coming years. Yorktown was in a dry county, you see, where Methodists and Baptists had joined hands against the city and for the profits of the bootleggers among their congregations, and I had grown up without liquor in the house and just never had got around to it in the city, but this night was the start of my making up for lost time.

I took a second swig from the flask, and the boy standing in front of me protested, so I passed it up to him, and around me the talk had begun about riots, riots in the city just east of here, how the coloreds was mad at something again. And it might of been the whiskey, but I clearly remember thinking at the time that it had been only about two months since someone had killed Dr. King, and my next thought was that I was far from home.

Then Zuice was back on stage, Aron Dennis piping out something about songs for the journey, and then the band done "Magic Carpet Ride," "You Can't Do That," "Hurdy Gurdy Man," and the people in the club would dance or try to dance and fail or just stand and listen, and the night seemed ready to fall into discord. The days of dance music were changing right on the floor here, and a third and fourth swallow of that passing whiskey got me giddy, and I figured I was standing on the border of new prospects.

Buddy tried to hold me back, but I wedged my way through the crowd on the dance floor, and the Village tilted, and I regained my balance by grabbing the shoulder of some girl, whose date pushed me away roughly, until the next thing I know I am at the edge of the stage looking up at Aron Hunter.

He looked down at me and grinned, and the next thing I know he leans down and draws me onto the stage. And he leans toward me *as all of Zuice goes into the chorus of "Yellow Submarine," and he shouts* Why don't you sing one, brother?

Now why that boy asked me onto the stage is beyond me to this day. What impulse of connection went through him and through me and what drawed us together on the stage. I knew I was supposed to deny it and to wave him off, but I had come to this point against all odds, and I think it surprised Aron Hunter more than it done me, because when he stepped back and started that rhythmic guitar strum like at the beginning of "Mystery Train," he switched keys at once when I told him no, higher, and all of Zuice bent their awaiting locks in my direction.

I swiveled my hips like the King, and some in the crowd laughed, and I don't remember whether they thought I was good or not when I begun to sing.

> Train arriiiive…16 coaches long
> Train arriiiive…16 coaches long
> Well that long black train
> Got my baby and gone…

And Aron shouts out yeah! and sets a hot crackling lick against the bass line and the drum, and some people started to dance and I tilted toward the edge of the stage and wailed it out like an old black blues man. And just as I start to thinking I'm going on from here, to hell with studies and the whole of Western Lit, the cops step into the back of Gypsy Village and all the lights go on.

∗∗∗

Of course it did not dawn on me that the police were there for anything more than checking for underage drinkers. But the riots were a done deal just east of the club, over on 28th Street in the heart of a black neighborhood, and even after four years, the white part of the city was jittery about the park being integrated, mommas and daddies afraid their children would rub elbows with Negroes.

So the first thing the police department had done around the park was send officers to Gypsy Village to make sure there was no trouble, even though it was the one lily white island remaining in the whole funfair.

But I was thinking of my own skin, and when the lights went on and I saw the blue uniforms at the back of the dance floor, I looked for the nearest exit. Aron was on his way through the instruments to the backstage, and I followed as he busted out onto a loading dock and down the stairs, stumbling, telling me now you're on your own, Elvis. The people inside were shouting and booing, upset that the music stopped, and Aron sat on the topmost step, drew out a pack of cigarettes, and motioned me away. I guess I realized he was stuck there, moored down by his amps and his expensive guitar, but I was a free agent and headed toward the park, where I climbed a chain link fence, straddled the chicken wire at its very top, and came tumbling down inside the kids' part of the establishment, right beside a carousel where a few little black kids were riding the horses, because after sundown the park pretty much changed its colors, and the white kids filtered east and south and north across the river.

I stood there for a moment, as the horses flashed by, from dark to light back into dark, and I watched people trailing out of the big white double-arched entrance. The lights were still on in the funhouse, and I left the club's commotion behind me and made my way toward the entrance of Hilarity Hall, which is what they called it, where two laughing manikins guarded the door, still shaking with electric animation.

I had heard so much about this place. The ceiling was ribbed, and it vaulted over you like the dome of some old gothic church. You could pass by the mirror maze, in which a body can grow and mash down and break into fragments, and find yourself at the center floor, where two slides descended from behind you—the Angel Slide, which stretched to the end of the funhouse at an incline just steep enough to excite you, and the Devil Slide, which made a sheer plunge and ended alongside the far wall, halfway the length of the hall. I had heard kids at school maintain that two children had been set afire by the friction down the Devil Slide, but by now I was too old to believe it, set instead on seeking refuge for a while until the club cleared and the police went away.

Of course I was not the only one there. The Sugar Bowl, this big circular ride that spun you around, was coming to a stop, and four dizzy black kids hopped off, recovered their footing, and headed for me.

Now as I was saying, the races weren't relating at that particular time of history, so as a boy who grew up in what was nearly an all-white small town in the south of the state, and whose black classmates in the city had sat quiet and buffaloed in the back of the classroom, I was now in their home territory, and I was frightened.

The old men by the courthouse in Yorktown had told me the stories: that they were better fighters than white boys, that they all carried knives, that they had extra bones in their feet that made them run faster. I was so scared I couldn't move, frozen by mythology as three of the boys approached me, followed at a distance by the fourth, a tall, lanky older kid about my age, who called back the other three, though they kept coming.

They asked me what I was doing here. Said that white people's time was over for the day in Hilarity Hall. I wanted to say I had as much right to be there as they did, but it seemed like the very worst thing to say at the time. I held my ground because I could not run, and the tall boy called out to them one last time, telling them to lay off, that three against one was unfair and below them.

One of my confronters, a short kid wearing a cap and the most menacing of the group, said, what you plan to do about it, DeMoyne? Are you fixing to take his side?

And the tall boy stood next to me and said, so everyone could hear, Market Street bus is leaving in a few minutes. This isn't the night for you to be out here late.

I may of been foolish in my college days, but in times dire and mortal I could hoist a little sense up from inside me. I made it out through the main gate, mingling with a crowd of white kids and some of their parents, following their current until we reached the bus stop. And that DeMoyne was right: the bus arrived shortly, and coasted north of 28th and Greenwood, where the faint sound of the commotion and the glow of the fires guided us away from all disturbance and safely on our way home. By the time I made it home it was nearly midnight, my route delayed and deflected by the rising riot, the whole city empty under the yellow light of the street lamps, and I fell asleep in my place and above my books, not knowing for years that I had met my future Representative, whom I would support and betray.

Buddy would show up at my place the next day, none the worse for wear but irritated at me for ditching him at the village. He had caught the bus after mine, and he said the streets had been a little more raucous, and he swore a rock had been thrown at the bus window.

But I barely listened to him, my thoughts on the confusion of the night before, on the mystery train and the low tide of whiskey buzz in my faculties, and of the morning's discovery: there, propped on the window sill, sat a cornshuck doll, its blank face dried and pressed against the pane.

✳✳✳

1968 was a big year of riots and disruptions. It don't take historical insight to let you know that much. But the summer passed for me in relative peace, as the world exploded in that terrible season. Out in California Robert Kennedy was assassinated, Nixon was nominated in Miami, and Humphrey in Chicago at that shit show of a convention, and most of this I missed by sitting through an Introduction to Religion class in a hot and crowded classroom where people raced for the window seats to get at the air, and the wasps buzzed in and out through the room.

And so it dragged on until Halloween, the holiday of my people on the street and the best night of all for the Witches' Tree. That night, barely twenty and midway through my second semester, I had gone to see the Doors at Freedom Hall.

The great god was subdued that night. Straight back from Europe and headed toward the American leg of the tour. Baggy white jeans and a t-shirt, no bombast of tight leather. 'Hello, I Love

You,' as his greeting, smoking and drunk evidently, theophany five days before the election that brought Nixon in, and something in history gone bad.

I listened through the set in solitude from the back of the house. Was in the leather jacket of my own, hair slicked back in a D.A. and packing my Elvis defiance in a crowd that had chosen new idols. "Soul Kitchen", then a couple of old blues covers. Then "Wake Up", then "Light my Fire" to the most applause of the night. And there was this young thing in a peasant blouse, her jeans so tight they conjure memories nearly fifty years later, and she was saying something to me in the first bars of "Not to Touch the Earth." I bent my head down so her lips brushed my ear as she spoke, and Morrison singing "Run with me / Run with me…"

Her breath give me shivers and got me hard, and she slips a little pink pill into my hand, and she bites my earlobe, and Morrison shouts from the stage that he is the Lizard King, he can do anything. And I looked back and the crowd had swallowed her, an apparition on All Hallows Eve.

I dropped the acid on the way home, thunderstorm rumbling out of the west. The last of the trick-or-treaters still on the street, the big kids, cheap masks and gerrymandered costumes—they were too old, had outstayed the holiday's welcome. And Nixon masks among them, as I tried to stay outside the trip while driving. I passed my apartment by mistake, headed toward school and a flash of lightning over the white gable of the old theater as I dismounted from Buddy's borrowed car. By the time I reached campus I was sure the Republican Party was out to get me, and of course the acid was prophetic.

All the buildings were closed down and locked for the night, and I rode the fear like someone in a bad Hunter Thompson story until I found a door ajar in Gottschalk Hall, where someone had propped it open and forgot, so I slipped in out of the rising storm.

There is a small seminar room on the third floor, above and across from the larger classrooms. I knew it because it was where I'd had the Moderns class—Pound and Eliot, Joyce and Faulkner, perched high up like Yeats in his tower, you can believe me or don't. There was a stairway off the room, and you could get to the roof, though it was unwise, they cautioned. And though it was unwise, I got there, and I looked out over the campus by night, through the trees toward the parkway and the old Confederate Monument.

And I felt it before I heard it, son, wild light and the top of my head sheared away and it was like my soles were soldered to the ground in sheer electric energy. For a moment I gained balance, and the branches opened and I saw city lights steady in a current of blackness, a current that broke across them and almost carried me with it, in rain and shadow, but I held my ground.

And that was when I saw it. A ring of lights fanning out from the white peaks of the university theater, extending west like ripples when you drop a stone into a still pond, but there was another stone to the north it seemed, a cascading circle of lights come down from the park north of campus until the two broke against each other in a vibrating surf of light and energy, and the lightning struck again, this time near the overpass way down by the parkway, and it was bright enough you could see the edges of colors rather than the grays of the night.

And there was a pattern forming, I was sure of it, though my hair was burning and my jaws tight and trembling. I saw something that connected the lights and the movement, and it didn't last, but it took me a trip down the stairs, stumbling on each landing, to forget that I was not and would never be alone.

✳✳✳

I stumbled out into the lyrical night, wounded and marveling at the sheets of rain on my face. It was a bath and a baptism, and I stayed on my feet until I had reached the underpass where the trains crossed over the parkway that ran by the school. And it was like I had circled around, almost eleven years to the day since I passed beneath that little railway bridge and the air bent and snapped around me on my way to see the King.

I was rain-battered, dizzy, still smoking from the lightning strike, and though I'd always heard it never struck in the same place, I didn't want to test the proverb. I made for the shelter of the bridge, *and was almost there when I saw the men on patrol in the shadows beneath it.*

Three men in slouch hats. One bearing a rifle, one a sword, the third a cannon ramrod. I stopped in the rain, showers soaking my hair and leather jacket, and I watched them patrol the dark passage out of which the parkway emerged like a road out of hell. What they were up to I could not tell you, and I could not place where I had seen them before—something to do with the death of a girl back in the day, but my memory was staggered and it would take days for me to recover it. In fact, I was still muddled enough to approach them, thinking nothing could be worse than the pounding rain and the prospect of lightning.

Then the rifleman lifted his gun, and lightning rocketed over the huge domed building behind me, and I felt something whine like a wasp past my ear, and I turned back, rushing toward where the bolt had just struck, thinking If there is any sense in the rules at all, if old wisdom holds on any count, then Grawmeyer Hall *had just been near-struck and therefore the safest place in this rising storm.*

Coming across the huge quad that led up to the building, I slipped in the mud and fell to my knees, looking up into the face of the Thinker. A copy of the original, the rain glistening off it in the lamplight. It looked thoughtful, all right, and it was like a voice echoing through layers of bronze when it told me to enjoy the downpour.

You think it's a big deal, it said. This contentious storm that passes through leather and skin and metal. But you don't feel the lesser things. You were headed toward shelter, but when someone raises a gun at you, the rain looks good, then, don't it?

When the mind's free, Tommy, the body's delicate.

It was a saying I did not know until I saw it played in full at the theater. Back then, I thought it was a jumble of the wet and the electric—words jostled out of place and into poetry, and so when the Thinker told me that from now on I would prefer no shelter, would favor the open skies and bathe in the sun and the rain and the night wind, I took it as false prophecy, until I woke up on the lawn in front of the statue, uncertain when the waking had passed into dream and the dream passed into waking.

It took me a year to grow hair back. I was magnetized, I still could not wear a watch if I was so inclined. I never returned to my apartment, returned to Mamma's only twice, but I have wandered elsewhere: I have blacked out many times and awakened on the balconies of buildings, sometimes naked, sometimes wrapped only in a blanket against imagined winds, sometimes in leather and denim, and sometimes in full lamé. And from then on I was asking alice. I was abstracted from things. I receded like something primeval and tidal, and I have washed ashore in this place, this is how I got here.

It was a good thing Tamar had not changed the locks.

Mickey was no cat burglar, and entering by the front door still aroused no suspicion among his neighbors. He knew the alarm code, and after a brief hung-over flurry of trying and failing to key it in, he shut off the device before its first whoop and stood in the middle of the living room among Tamar's too-expensive furnishings and a half dozen cardboard boxes, each partially packed with his belongings.

Jordan, the mynah creaked from the bedroom, but it was bearing no tales. Mickey thrashed through the closest box, dragging out two shirts and a pair of khakis.

It had been two weeks since Athena Bumpas's dinner party, and Mickey had established a life of sorts away from his old apartment, shuttling among the carrel and classroom, the bar and the bookstore. By now, instead of laundry, he was showering at the faculty gym, soaping his clothes while he wore them, then stepping into a dry alternative—another pair of pants, another shirt. Nobody noticed trousers on a man, so he could go for nearly a week, commando and alternating his three (and now five) shirts. The math and planning was more than he wanted to do, and his carrel smelled faintly of sweat and whiskey; however, before he left the apartment, he stripped naked, dropped the soiled clothes on the floor, and dressed in yet another shirt and pair of trousers, adding a brown linen jacket to replace his grass-stained blue seersucker, attempting a kind of dignity as he closed the door behind him and stepped out into the walking court.

He would have liked to miss Tamar more, to feel wronged in their falling off. There was a time when he had been fond of her—a woman twelve years his junior, bright and supportive of where he was headed until she recognized he was headed nowhere.

There had been a time when the birds had been a barometer of her discontent. Tamar brought in a cockatoo and a brace of finches to begin with: when Mickey received his only raise in his six years on the faculty, she had begun to collect silk rugs instead, so that the living room and the guest bedroom were layered like the floor of a harem. But two tenure track positions opened, only to be filled by younger faculty, and the birds stockpiled and the song grew louder.

He remembered once, when they were newly married, her working as a site artist on a dig to uncover Viking camps in Nova Scotia. Tamar had expected Sutton Hoo—gravesites filled with gold armor and jewelry, against all the recorded history of Viking burial—or at least a stark military camp, but the expedition found nothing, and by the end of the first week she called home early one morning, stirring him from sleep with her *Mickey, I miss you, come and get me.*

His heart had gone halfway out to her, and he told himself that talking Tamar off the ledge, rather than driving north to her rescue, was the greater act of love. Instead, he came to realize he was coveting solitude: even among his strongest affections for Tamar Walsh he would rather she were not around.

✳✳✳

When will it be my time, Mickey? she had asked him over and over, claiming that his ego, his preoccupations, his uncertainties were the order of the day when it came to their marriage.

They had spent time in the large front room of the apartment, one that had stretched the budget because Tamar needed space for a loom, and when the loom failed, for indoor arbors, and after that for easels, which receded to give space to bird cages. Mickey began to wonder early on if "her time" didn't change minute by minute: she wanted to have woven, have gardened, and have painted (what the birds were supposed to mean he had yet to figure out) but she didn't seem joyful in the process of any of her projects.

He could understand joylessness. So he left Tamar to hers. And the drift apart was gradual, almost undetectable, until one day Mickey was surprised to find himself sleeping on the sofa—not like the husband in trouble on a situation comedy, but inadvertently there and settled in, and thereby possibly more troubled still.

Mickey's carrel sat at the heart of a design he was just beginning to intuit.

It was an easy path from the library doors. The campus lay mapped before him in word and adventure. From there, the city spread south past the Thinker and the parkway overpass, north to his house, beyond to the theatre, to the Witches' Tree and to Broadway and Market Street beyond that, from where the landscape of dreams sloped slowly toward the river.

As he sat on the library steps, Mickey was thinking how Tommy's homelessness, glitter, and dereliction had somehow blocked knowing him.

Their looped and windowed raggedness was the line from the play.

Oh I have ta'en too little care of this.

Mickey walked north along Third Street, the traffic sluggish around construction cones, and he marveled that Tommy had read *Ulysses*, then wondered why he marveled. Notion by notion, Mickey was stripping away the things he assumed. And instead of turning toward home, he continued through the park, headed toward Fourth and Fellini, toward the book store and the bar.

His path took him by the Witches' Tree, and he stopped at the corner, looking up at the beads and feathers and talismans dangling from its branches. Mickey drew closer: huge bulbous knots peered from its trunk and its base was tunneled with a hollow that put Mickey in mind of a talking forest or the elves who inhabited it. A little cherub—or some other winged creature, Mickey was unsure—dressed harmlessly in a pink robe, strummed a lyre or harp in the a notch of a big lower branch beneath a sign that read whimsically "The Witch is in."

Barely thinking, operating at a level he would later describe as "below and above thought," Mickey hoisted himself through the lower branches of the Witches' Tree, setting his foot on one of the smaller galls and beginning his ascent. He straddled the first limb big enough to hold his weight, gasping and puffing, wondering what had possessed a fifty-year-old man to tree-climb.

These are the very notches, Mickey told himself, *the very galls and branches that Tommy Briscoe climbed as a child, and probably again as a man young and old.* And whether it was the summer sun or the exertion of the climb, he felt a tremor in the old tree, he clung to it in a panic. But the shock soon dispersed, settling into a vigilant calm in which the park's edge seemed to waver and vibrate, hovering between density and the wavering outline of mirage.

This is how he felt, Mickey told himself. *The little boy climbing the tree almost sixty years ago. The young man in the university tower a few years later. Wondering and curious and completely alone.*

From his vantage point he could see across the park and onto the court where he lived. Seen or imagined, figures dotted through the landscape like chess pieces. Large as the Thinker or Prentice by the library, small as the little winged figure hanging from a branch below him. Serene as the goddess atop the fountain or as raucous as the long-vanished mannequins that guarded the entrance to Hilarity Hall. In Tommy's version some of them had moved, others had spoken. Others, it seemed, guarded underpasses or stood like lions at the entrance to the park's long promenade. Slowly, the landscape was peopled with his own meditative walking and with Tommy's stories and memories. Like the weaving patterns of a novel, or like Ace Briscoe's long-ago aggressive games of chess, the city was coming alive for Mickey in ways that it had never lived before.

It brought tears to his eyes, and he hugged the bole of the Witches' Tree until an inner voice, reductive and dismissive, passed him off as *crybaby*, as *tree-hugger*. And though he drew back from the strange serenity, he knew he was brushing against something that linked him to Tommy's stories, and he dropped from the tree with new resolve, his rusty knees and ankles shivering from the quick descent, and the world around him riddled with a light he did not recognize.

It was time to get another tape from John Bulwer. And a drink at the Oscar Wilde. But it was more than Mickey bargained for, as he descended the tree into a world of stories.

"Up a tree? At our age?"

Alan Stack was incredulous, and Mickey was a little rankled, being cast into the age group of a man two decades his senior. But it was hard to be irritated at Alan, especially when the first pour of the Jameson was on the house.

There had been talk of his retirement, of his leaving the management of the bar to his partner Thanh. Mickey would miss him if he left. Would no doubt take his business to the collegy and grungy Mag Bar or to the Tavern right by the school, because life and alcohol would have to go on. But every time Stack approached that rite of passage, he backed away. The neighborhood was changing, for the better or sometimes for the worse, or Thanh's English was still not good enough after forty years stateside (an absurd opinion in Mickey's eyes). Or the economy was booming or adrift, depending on Stack's mood, on whatever financial shift that would necessitate his staying in charge of the establishment.

That time was not on the horizon as the two of them sat in the banked light beside the Wilde's long oak bar, drinking whiskey and musing on trees and outrageous birds in their branches.

"Up there among the winged fantastic," Stack observed ironically. "Right above the cherub with the harp, you say?"

Mickey finished his glass, beckoned for the bottle. "And what's that got to do with anything, Alan?"

"That's a fairy, not a cherub, Walsh. You were watched over."

Mickey shook his head, bracing for the story he was sure would come. And Alan began a tale, this time one not from their mutual New England (they were the two Yankees on the block— Mickey from Vermont, and Alan from upstate New York—so geography had sealed their accord early on) but from Vietnam, where he had served, been wounded, left for dead and presumed just as dead for two years afterwards. But this story wasn't about his harrowing time in country—at least not evidently—but a charming tale of love and loss.

"Once upon a time, Mickey," Stack began, leaning against the bar and circling his finger over the mouth of the Jameson bottle, "there was a young scholar named Từ Thức. In some versions of the story, he is an aristocrat, but that doesn't matter, not really. What matters is that his only goal in life was to find the Land of Bliss."

"Which is like...heaven?" Mickey asked, and Stack shrugged, pouring himself another shot.

"Like and not like. It's close to earthly paradise—birds and trees and gentle weather. Music on the wind. Probably not heaven, because it's not permanent. But it's the place to be until you get to Nirvana, if I understand it. You can ask Thanh if you're really interested. But as to Từ Thức.

"Some people might claim he was simply a wanderer, a vagrant, but I like the version of the story that has him headed toward the Land of Bliss alone. Not just imagining it, but on a quest, a journey. In search of a place on earth where, for a while, your dreams are steady and peaceful.

"One day, Từ Thức came to Bich Dao Grotto, a beautiful cave only miles south of Hanoi, which he had no idea was a passage into the very land he'd been searching for. He passed through the orchestra of musical stalactite leaves at the top of the cavern, then climbed down through the middle portion, shaped like a chessboard, stalagmites like chessmen rising from the grid of stone, then down to a crossroads in the tunnel, where one path ascended and the other declined into darkness. All the way he was guided by the sound of rustling water—water from somewhere deep in the cave.

"Từ Thức didn't notice that the cave had closed behind him: he had turned away from the sunlight some time back, and now he had only his torchlight to guide him.

"Just when it seemed the torch was about to go out, just when he'd be left in darkness and lost forever in the caverns, the pathway widened, and Từ Thức found himself in a circle of stone flowers, pink and smooth like the robes of a cherub. Flowering peach, mai, and lotus after lotus, as though the rock had shaped itself by remembering the gardens above ground.

"In the last flicker of Từ Thức's torch, one of the lotuses opened, and out came a beautiful winged creature, stretching wings in the cool cavern air.

"It was love at first sight, the story goes. Maybe it was the wings that did it, or maybe that the fairy had risen from the flower. Or very possibly, Từ Thức knew at once that it was the pathway that he'd been looking for, that even if the guide was unexpected, how beautiful a creature the fairy was.

"So he asked if he could join the fairy in the Land of Bliss, and though the answer was long in coming, as though the little winged creature was debating the answer, eventually it was yes, and Từ Thức followed the fairy, not on the upward path he had expected, but down a gentle incline until the whole corridor glowed in a rainbow of light ahead.

"And Từ Thức stayed happily in the Land of Bliss for a while. He basked in the perfect weather, the musical wind, the fairies who floated about, their wings glittering and their robes a thousand colors. He slept at night in a grotto of his own, his lover curled against him. It was everything he wanted, and should have been so forever.

"But soon, he began to miss his home country and all he had left behind. Though he was and had always been a wandering scholar, Từ Thức yearned at last for home. So he asked the queen of the fairies, who happened to be the mother of his fairy lover, for permission to return to the human world. The queen was not encouraging: she warned   Từ Thức that once he left the Land of Bliss, he would never be able to return. Having been taken out of this earthly paradise by his own desire, he would lose it all—the musical wind, the lovely caverns, and most of all, his fairy love."

"Seems like a bad bargain," Mickey observed. "I mean, why *not* stay?" He thought of his own mother, of Tamar and his bird-loud apartment not a mile away. Surely Từ Thức had better to return to.

And Tommy. Would Tommy have traded comfort and magic for a trip back home?"

"Oh, I can understand," Stack said. After all, Từ Thức was so lonely, that nostalgia where he imagined his homeland as more beautiful than any place, than even the Land of Bliss. Nor did the queen's warning that time moves differently in the earthly world—that for the fairies and for the Land of Bliss, time is fluid, moving much more slowly as part of the bargain of paradise— have any effect on his yearning. So when Từ Thức returned to the human world, he found that time had passed much more quickly than he could ever have dreamed. The buildings were strange in his home town, as were his family—those who were still alive, that is, and even the living were no longer familiar. And the customs had changed: even the greetings were alien, like they were offered in a different language. Từ Thức felt like a foreigner in his homeland. It was an unbearable sorrow and he took to the road again, alone and estranged, never to be seen inside or outside the Land of Bliss."

✳✳✳

They sat silently at the bar and finished their drinks. Stack was obviously moved by the story he had told, and despite his uncertainty, Mickey felt a sadness, a dislocation in the tale, as though it had touched on something intimate to them both. It was that discomfort that drinkers feel when a conversation pushes against borders, when you aren't drunk enough for trespass but drunk enough that you press against the fences.

"Think I'll go over to Salvages," Mickey said. "See what's up with Bulwer. Those Briscoe tapes are pretty interesting, you know: I think I'll take up the gauntlet."

Stack smiled. "We were hoping as much," he said. "And, Mickey? Don't let the stories affect you so."

Mickey turned at the door of the Wilde, raising an eyebrow.

"They just remind you of things," Stack explained. "They tell you where the story has been, not where it's headed. If you don't move past them, they haunt you, you know."

Mickey marked that down to Jameson's. To some vague disappointment of Stack's—perhaps domestic trouble or the old shadows of war. The sunlight outside the bar was relentless, and the temperature, as it often did midsummer in the city, had soared to unpleasant.

In contrast, Salvages was cool. Bulwer had never succumbed, it seemed, to the old man's malady of being cold in all places. Mickey entered to the smell of coffee and Marlboros, to the impeccable phrasing of Rene Marie's "Stronger Than You Think."

"I'll take the next tape," he said, getting right down to business, and Bulwer's laugh wheezed smoke across the counter

"So," the older man drawled. "Getting hooked at last, are we?" he ducked into the back office without waiting for Mickey's answer, and emerged immediately, a cassette in hand.

"Better not get a jones for these, Walsh. I'm running out."

Mickey took the cassette. "No matter where I go, Bulwer, I'm running into stories. I would say that there's no chance of running out now. This one's making me squirrely, though—I climbed the Witches' Tree a few hours back. Saw all the places Briscoe spoke about, from a vantage point where it was impossible to see them for real. Then I came down, had a whiskey with Stack, and heard some kind of Vietnamese myth that I can't figure why he was telling me, except that it moved him greatly. Then he tells me not to let the stories get to me, but I confess they've already gotten there. It looks like the world is becoming stories."

Bulwer shrugged. "Like it wasn't before? And every story opens into another one, and people from one story brush against another. The Japanese call it *engi*—arising in relation."

Mickey wasn't up for the dharma at the moment. He reached across the counter for Bulwer's pack of Marlboros, lighting one and noting that he was smoking more, drinking more, since this mystery and commotion over T. Tommy Briscoe. He started toward the stacks, lit cigarette in hand, but a soft throat-clearing from Bulwer reminded him that the stacks were forbidden country for anything burning.

"Say, Walsh?" Bulwer called as Mickey returned. "Was Stack's story the one about Từ Thức and the Land of Bliss?"

"You've heard it, too?"

"That I have. He always gets emotional when he tells it. Flashback from his tour of duty, I guess."

It was obvious that Bulwer was in a story-telling mood, too, and Mickey, in his heart of hearts an adventure novelist, preferred a war story to Zen parables or kōans. So he didn't have to pretend attentiveness as Bulwer went on about what he knew of Alan Stack's stint in the Củ Chi tunnels.

✳✳✳

A tunnel system, built over a period of twenty-five years, formed a warren underlying Củ Chi Province just north of what was then Saigon, now Ho Chi Minh City. During the war, outnumbered and outgunned by their American opponents, the North Vietnamese Army and the Viet Cong had taken refuge in this labyrinth their people had begun to dig, largely by hand, in the old war against the French. Now the tunnels housed outposts, refuges, even little villages, as larger communities burrowed into the landscape to avoid the American bombs and invasions.

Stack was what they called a "tunnel rat"—a skilled soldier small enough to descend into the cramped maze of burrows and clear out the guerrillas who garrisoned the dark. From '65 to '67, if Bulwer remembered correctly, the gentle little barkeep two doors down had undertaken one of the riskiest jobs in the war. Not only would Charlie wait for him in the shadows, but the corridors were teeming with traps: pits of punji sticks, bamboo vipers tied in your path, hornets, scorpions. There were even rumors that plague-carrying rats were unleashed at the margins of the tunnels, and even if this made no sense, the possibility that they were there increased the terror, made each step into what they called "the black echo" like a dance on the edge of a cliff.

Sergeant Alan Stack thrived in the darkness. With a flashlight and a pistol, he'd lead the way for his troops, going first in patrols where he would not send a man ahead of him, taking the brunt of the gunfire, killing more Charlie than he could put words or memory around, each time stepping deeper into nightmare.

It was apparently during the Tet Offensive in early '68 when, just south of Ben Duoc, not far from the surface, Stack caught a bullet in the shoulder and, more dangerously, another that passed through the side of his helmet, grazing his head and leaving him unconscious in the dark. He would awake being tended to. A cluster of children over him, so that at first he thought they were going through his pockets, but he was somewhere in twilight, had been lifted out of the tunnel and carried, apparently, to safety.

Stack never quite pinned down the location of the camp.

The families of the boys, though, would nurse him back to health, and several of the boys became his friends in the process, one of whom was (and Mickey had guessed it by this time in the story) Pham Thanh. Thirteen or fourteen at the time (Stack was very dodgy about the boy's age, for obvious reasons), his was the closest friendship the wounded sergeant would form.

In mid-69, an advance unit of American army regulars were surprised to encounter a white man, dressed in traditional Vietnamese black áo bà ba, the garment indistinguishable from what the soldiers recognized as pajamas. Stack was close-mouthed about where he had been for eighteen months, and he had always confided to Bulwer that, despite the hardship he had undergone with the villagers who rescued him, their land was "pure land" to him, a paradise or at least a memory of a cherished past.

Bulwer swore that it wasn't just the boy. Stack had found something in Cứ Chi Province, and Bulwer was certain that whatever he found, harmony or connection or simple accord, he had brought with him to the Oscar Wilde, and as long as Alan Stack ran the place, it would stay there and create abiding peace.

Whatever, Mickey thought. I bet he wakes up with the Cứ Chi nightmares. He decided to walk several blocks to the Third Avenue Cafe, another nest for afternoon drinkers, where he might spend some time free of Tommy's stories and the Asianized shape they were given by Bulwer and Stack. As he left Salvages, though, just to satisfy himself by telling himself "I told you so," he asked Bulwer what he made of Stack's war story.

"So, how do you think Stack fits with the Từ Thức legend? Did he find the Land of Bliss? Is he the best Từ Thức we have, the wandering scholar come back? And is the pure land somewhere in Cu Chi Province? After all, you believe in reincarnation, right?"

Bulwer shrugged. "Not always."

"Then what? Did Stack know the story when the bullets hit him? Did he see himself living the same pattern, walking the same road? Or did he learn the story later, told to him by Thanh in the safety of the village, or even read before he came back here? Thanh came over when?"

Bulwer reached for another cigarette. "'73 or '74, if I remember correctly. I'm thinking it was only weeks before Saigon fell, and Stack must have some serious political *metta* to have dragged the kid out of hell."

Mickey stood at the door now. "So, what then? Did his memory of what happened to him fall into a tunnel with Từ Thức?"

Bulwer blew smoke lazily into the bookstore air. "You know there's an old story about two monks quarreling over a flag. It's up on a pole in high wind, fluttering violently, and the monks, like monks do, are splitting hairs in a debate.

"The first one says that it's the wind that's moving. The second one says that it's the flag. So of course the master comes along to settle the issue. Neither one of you is right, he says. 'It's the *mind* that is moving.'"

Mickey folded his hands and bowed ironically. "I'm doing this instead of trying to find my Buddha nature with both hands. Because I don't think it's there."

Bulwer's laughter followed him out the door into the rising dusk.

$$***$$

Third Avenue Cafe had been pretty much the same since Mickey had moved to the neighborhood a decade ago. Widely windowed and open to an intersection, clean and crisp-smelling, it nonetheless drew its share of students, young people in search of a reasonably priced lunch and a well-lit corner to read in. But this time of evening, it was mainly the haunt of folks grabbing hamburgers or a quick beer before heading to more raucous or sleazy elsewheres.

Mickey sat at the bar and ordered whiskey, his current habits subject to no environs. He stared into the mirror behind the bar and wondered why the hell a raggedy man like that had been scaling trees like an Irish monkey only two hours before. As the bartender handed him his drink, he noticed Diana Chen seated at a table by the far window.

"Send her another of what she's drinking," he whispered to the bartender. "No...I know her."

Mickey leaned forward, rested his elbows on the bar. He tried not to look up into the mirror, suddenly a little embarrassed by his heedless gesture. Surely Diana wouldn't think he was hitting on her: if he'd been ten years younger, that would have been comical, perhaps creepy, but the thirty, thirty-five-year age difference had pushed it, he was sure, into the realm of completely unthinkable. Surely she'd get he was being nice, he thought, looking at himself in the mirror and brushing some wayward strands of hair to a neater position behind his ear, before his eyes lifted to Diana, to the approaching barman, to her glance at him and quick aversion of her eyes.

Damn, he thought. *I didn't even mean it that way, I don't think.*

He mantled above his whiskey. The clock read half past six, that crucial hour when a drinker decides whether even to bother with dinner. A hamburger might be wise, but another whiskey would be more venturesome and vague: he touched the lip of his glass and winked at the bartender.

Diana was nose-down in her book, her silky black hair aglow in the tilted sunlight from the window. Mickey felt sorry he had been so forward, and carefully checking his motives direct and ulterior, made his way to her table, where she looked up at him, frowned and sighed.

"I don't think it's what you're thinking," he said, and she sat down the book, giving him a perplexed but not unfriendly stare.

"And how could it be otherwise, Professor?" she asked. Before he could object, could offer a word in his defense, she continued, and the conversation veered.

"After all, he confessed to it. Asked my forgiveness, but I'm nowhere close to granting it. And I'm sorry, Professor. Though you know this is not my doing."

Puzzled, Mickey pulled back a chair, started to sit, but Diana rose and headed for the door. He started to call for her, thought otherwise, and stood there inanely as she stepped outside and around the corner, her slim frame swallowed by evening sunlight.

✳✳✳

Afloat on a final bourbon, he headed home about eight.

The nightly unruliness was already afoot around the neighborhood's most notorious intersection. Fourth and Oak, called "Fourth and Fellini" by the experts, was a convergence of hipsters, commuters, and crackheads. Just up the block lay Bulwer's store and Stack's bar, but it seemed later than it was, so Mickey turned left and headed home past the park.

King Lear was underway at the amphitheater, the old king raving about the ills of women and letting copulation thrive. Mickey thought about stopping, but his set path carried him past the park and onto the court, the fountain ahead of him and the gaslights on now, the summer evening sinking into dark.

He knew now he was trespassing. Something in him wanted to see what was now transpiring in the place he'd figured as home for so long, so he was both disappointed and relieved to find the lights off, the birds quiet, and nobody at home. He didn't bother calling for Tamar, but sat down at the table and poured a mug of lukewarm coffee, his ears hot and the barroom buzz receding. A smell of reefer laced the air, alien to his home and anathema to his wife, who had made him give it up weeks after the wedding.

The bed was rumpled, the spread half-covering a disarray of sheets, the weed smell stronger in this room than elsewhere. Still a little fuddled from the alcohol, he was nevertheless clear-headed enough to do the math.

Diana's emotion and reluctance to talk. Her cryptic account of some saga of penance and unforgiveness.

Jordan's chivalrous escort service the night of Athena Bumpas' uncomfortable dinner.

But he found he didn't care. And fell asleep fingering the next cassette in the sweat-damp pocket of his shirt.

XXI

The next morning, the signs began to appear once more.

The first was geometrical, chalked on the sidewalk outside the apartment door, so that Mickey stepped over it on his path to the bus stop.

✻✻✻

Nothing momentous, Mickey figured. A simple rhombus, a tilted square, a solitary line leading from its nearest corner, pointing a simple way back into the apartment.

Might have nothing to do with Tommy and his story. Might have nothing to do with Mickey himself, for that matter, though it unsettled him nonetheless: his thoughts filled with suspicion as to who might have put it there, who was signaling in a terse, almost mathematical graffiti that he (or she, for that matter—Mickey had no idea) was onto the fact that Tommy's paths through the neighborhood were being marked and perhaps followed.

Mickey rounded the usual suspects in memory. Daddy Chrome seemed out of the question: Mickey figured Chrome would say what he had to say face to face, without resorting to hoboglyphics. Furthermore, Chrome no doubt knew that hobo signs were opaque to Mickey, so if veiled communication were the way he rolled, he'd at least find a new alphabet to get across the message.

DJ Mel and Falcon Holly had dipped from sight since Tommy ended up dead. The police had searched for them, but kept coming up empty, and since Titus and Humphrey had confessed, finding two more of the victim's derelict friends seemed somehow less necessary. Gone for months and probably out of the neighborhood's circuit of rumor and gossip, the pair probably knew nothing of Mickey's connection to the Briscoe story, unless they had gotten wind of it through some kind of grapevine go-between.

Which seemed to be most likely Magnolia Street.

Mickey had mulled it as far as he could go for the moment. Instead of hoboglyphics it could just as well be the botched beginnings of a hopscotch field, a game negotiated better by foot than by low-grade paranoia.

Catching the southbound bus to campus, Mickey set all suspicions aside, now anxious only at the prospect of seeing Diana Chen. Last night had embarrassed them both: Diana because she had spilled the secret to an old man down on his luck, and he because…

Well, because of something less definite.

✳✳✳

Diana Chen, to his surprising great relief, was absent from class. They'd moved on to D.H. Lawrence, all that myth masquerading as steaminess, or steaminess masqueraded as myth, flag or wind paradox. Mickey thought that it was just better that Diana read this on her own.

A little sad, convinced that he had taught poorly again in the hot classroom, Mickey retired to the library, savoring the cool air in the stairwell, the musty smell of the stacks as he made his way to the sanctuary of his carrel. He was brought up short by the marking on the door:

***

This time there was no room to speculate: it was menacing, after all, that someone would climb four flights of steps to find his little office and leave this sign, regardless of what it might mean.

The carrel no longer felt like a refuge. As Mickey slipped into the office and gathered his belongings for the trip home, something rustled in the nearby stacks. He closed and locked the door behind him, sitting in the darkness for a long, unsteady time until he was certain there was nobody outside the door and nearby.

Outside the library, the air was still and dusk had arrived early. Mickey checked his watch, wondered if it had stopped, then set out on foot toward home. Past the 19th century brick townhouses that lined Fourth Street he walked, the calm weather foreboding, like a storm was waiting in the wings, but no evidence in the sky except for a stagnant layering of gray clouds.

As he approached the court, for a moment the statue of Venus (or Galatea, if he was to believe Diana Chen) seemed to vanish in a ripple of damp summer air. When Mickey looked again, though, she stood unperturbed atop the bowl of the fountain, her robes loosened and held apart to the adoration of the little water cherubs who crouched beneath her.

Mickey started to turn toward his apartment. Saw the light in the front room.

Decided once again it was too much trouble. That he'd take a stroll up through the park and banish anxiety.

***

A light shone from the amphitheater stage, where three figures sat in a rough triangle, facing each other. Mickey recognized Magnolia Street by the height and the blonde weave, but the other two were unfamiliar: a white woman in biker leathers and a black man, lean and conked and dressed for a 1970s film. It took little deduction to guess that it was Falcon Holly and D.J. Mel.

The three of them faced an oil lantern, burning disconsolately at center stage. Around the light they had placed trinkets and baubles: a lipstick case, political buttons from both the Roy Rausch and DeMoyne Troubles campaigns, a sprig of evergreen and what looked like a sheaf of bus transfers held together by a clip.

Mickey approached slowly, standing at the wings of the stage, until Magnolia saw him and beckoned him closer.

"This here's the professor," she announced to her friends, as the two made room for Mickey between them, and the triangle became a square. "These are my friends Falcon and Mel."

Mickey sat among them in silence for a minute or two, careful not to be the intruder, the colonizer of whatever was going on in this central and quiet place.

"We come now and then to honor Tommy," Magnolia explained, lifting her dark and quite beautiful eyes to Mickey's. "We brung offerings of love and long acquaintance."

It was like the graveside of a small child, Mickey noticed. The little artifacts were a kind of muted poetry, circling the lantern as though where they were placed was as important as what they were. A Viva Las Vegas marquis belt buckle and a Rick James keychain, a pair of large feathers knotted together with a ribbon.

Finally, Falcon Holly spoke up. "It's closing night of *King Lear*. We always celebrated a closing night."

Mel nodded gravely. "*The Tempest* starts up next week. I love me some *Tempest*."

They were silent again for a while, then Magnolia Street pointed to the lantern. "This the spot."

"The spot?" Mickey asked, and she nodded soberly.

"The spot where lightning struck the second time."

Mickey had heard the story. Tommy claimed he had been struck twice, once in the heights of the university building, then again on the stage where he had jammed old Stones songs with the doomed Vinnie DeChevre. But there were rumors that the lightning had missed him that second time, that instead it illumined the park and streets surrounding so that Tommy was party to visions once more.

And yet, Mickey could see, the story had its own legs. Already the Brischords were opting for the magical version, the hero-struck tale of lightning and wind. Mickey thought of a story he had heard, in a classroom or a bar or a place more reliable, about the minting of Roman coins: those minted in Italy, the story went, bore remarkable likenesses of the Emperor, but as you moved further from Rome, the imperial profile became more abstract, more geometrical, until at great distances the face was no longer recognizable as human. The story was told to illustrate the empire's vast geography, or the loose hold of Rome on its farthest regions, but Mickey had come to understand it otherwise. He saw it as a refinement, a distillation: that by the time the idea of the emperor had reached more far-flung places—Alexandria, perhaps, or Antioch—that he had become a force, a structure, an archetype rather than a man, a figure of legend rather than history, or at least someone who straddled carefully that constantly moving border.

Tommy was becoming the myth he had imagined.

Quietly, Mickey nudged the subject that had bothered him for days. "Too bad Norm Titus and Wayne Humphrey couldn't be here."

The stares he received in response were sullen and cold.

"Them boys was framed," Falcon Holly muttered, then fell silent when Mickey's eyes were on her.

Then the conversation wafted through the circle of celebrants. Already D.J. Mel was going on about the tornado, the one that had struck the city six years after Tommy's official exit—the one in which our hero claimed to have been lifted high into the unyielding air and transported over the city in an arc. He listened for a while to Mel's account, anticipating the version he figured would be on Tommy's recording, but drifting in and out of Mel's lively and smooth retelling, his thoughts still returning to Titus and Humphrey, wondering how they fit into the growing crowd of stories.

After a while, it became apparent that Mickey was not that welcome at the ritual. He rose, nodded, and backed away from the stage, turning reluctantly toward his apartment. A glance at the fountain showed that Galatea was stable atop the glittering water, and as he turned onto his court, he saw that the place was dark. Quietly, dreading that he might discover Tamar in a situation compromised and embarrassing for at least one of them, he opened the door and slipped into the front room.

She was still not at home. The alarm clock in the bedroom read 9:00 pm, and the LED numbers gave him purchase and steadiness. No doubt she wouldn't be back for a while—plenty of time to pack a light bag with several changes of clothes, his razor and toothbrush, then make a sandwich and head back out into the deceptive darkness, bound on a night bus to the university, where he hid in his carrel as the library lights winked out, committed to restless sleep, to not going home, to Tommy's story, and to a lean week of wandering and detection.

XXII

It gets stranger from here on out. My enkindlement atop Gottschalk did not get much better, and weeks into '69 I remembered only as shored-up fragments.

Patches of light on the brown leaves until the last fell and even the Witching Tree become bare limbs twisting into dark skies.

Broken glass reflecting the corner of Fourth and Oak, which was already being called "Fourth and Fellini". If you lay on the pavement at the right angle and looked at the shards of bottles and mirrors, the occasional window, you could see the buildings that were here before, the ones that would come later.

A snow fell in January right when Nixon took office. Bu then I had found shelter in the backstage of the amphitheater, blankets and Sunday Courier-Journals sealing me against winter and rough weather. Often I slept there, but sometimes I would wake up blocks away from the park, bearing no idea how I had steered myself from one spot to another.

Daddy Chrome stuck by me during those times. He was still Buddy Drake back then, could catch a bus east before nightfall and stay with his parents against inclemency. At first he would ask me along, saying his folks would not mind. But soon the large sky and the wind and the changing branches had wrapped me up and taken me in, and by January I was committed to the streets, and Daddy Chrome stopped asking me back with him.

Still, he rarely left my side. Chrome could tell me logical histories that got me from one place to another, connect the dots from my resting place in the park one night and finding myself on a doorstep four blocks over and four days later. Or how I could find myself on the campus, my socks damp and stinking with river water.

The histories were made up, and we both knew it, but they gave me a connection to a splintered world. He begun to fill up the country with lore, and I took it from there.

Took it from there, and slowly mapped my journeys, up to the head shops and book stores on Fourth Street, then south to the steps of the library, where the statues of Lincoln and Prentice sat in bronze or marble like they were fixing to jump at me, over to the hippie parks where the young folks gathered and ran me off when I drew too near. All the while, Daddy Chrome patched the gaps in my memory, and well into the spring of '69 I began to fill those gaps with stories and images of my own: the brick townhouses taking on new geometry, their roofs sharp and narrow like frozen blades of flame, the sidewalks tilted at angles like the tracks of the roller coasters over at Fontaine Ferry, the whole city gone strange and the park at its heart and epicenter, the statues all turning to follow me like the eyes of a painting in a haunted house.

Galatea.

Not Venus rising from the foam, like the tour guides will tell you, but Galatea, the statue of a girl brought to life by the sculptor Pygmalion.

The story goes that the young man could find no proper girl on earth. It probably says more about Pygmalion than the girls he went after, but regardless, it was that lack that set him to carving a substitute, a surrogate. And he done so until the girl come to life through the love in his hands and art, and the two of them lived happily ever after.

It was a fairy tale, for sure, but I understood it well enough, because I remembered how my clay sculpture of Elvis had hovered between the King and the Ace, like the topmost draw in a deck of cards. How I had sculpted the head towards something I lacked, and when it was finished I found that I still lacked something though my hands were dirty.

On one end of my park was Galatea, but the northern boundary—where Park Avenue straddled the block between Fourth and Sixth—was marked by the Witches' Tree. I had climbed it first in childhood, and now in my early times of exposure it was a gaudy companion, gnarled and done up with signs and talismans, with amulets and dream catchers, and with a little pink cherub someone had placed in the fork of two large branches—placed long ago so that the tree had started to grow over it, to clutch it and sink it in a sea of bark.

I stopped there often, and one evening when I had started drinking early, while the ground was still warm enough to be soft, I took up earth and started to mold it into the likeness of that cherub. It was small, strong, and delicate, and my hands could not imitate what I thought and imagined, and soon my eyes teared up for some reason, and I thought that like Pygmalion I would find me no girl. Not through the faults of the girls, but because of some wound of my own. And perhaps my children would be fashioned of mud and earth, like my bust of Ace and Elvis or like poor childless Dilly's ranks of clay men.

It was too much to bear. I would of been a horrible father, even worse than the chess-playing con artist who was my lot to begin with. It would of been another chance to disappoint, to let someone down. I think that when the clay cherub crumbled in my hand and I looked up through the branches of the Witches' Tree into the streetlit night sky, that it first dawned on me that I was home here, that I would spend the most of my life among these blocks and monuments.

***

The zoo opened in '69, and since I was free-floating and experimental following my enkindlement, I would visit on occasion and found places to linger after hours. There was good company in the animals, but the cages saddened me, the hopeless look of the orangutan and the big cats pacing. I understood by now that pull against confinement. I had heard in school of the German philosopher who went mad when he saw someone beating a horse, and I wondered if madness was my direction and part, when I would look at the leopard restless in his too-small environs and I begun to weep, and wept every time I saw him in the place.

Up until the afternoon he spoke to me, and I realized I was not mad but instead clarified.

'I know you,' he said to me first, and I questioned my sanity at the greeting, because such things seemed implausible, until he described the woods outside Aunt Coral's and the town square in Yorktown. After that our meeting seemed more rational, and we talked for a number of evenings near the border of his environment.

His name was Chandali. How I come to know that was through insinuation, through his whisper like the rustle of wind on dry grass, through the low rumble in his throat as he hovered between stalking me and counting me friend. It was the kind of back and forth I understood already from the world around me, the changing seasons and weather, the climate of police from kindly to harsh, and my fellow travelers drifting in and out of clarity. Chandali, in short, was my kind of creature, and we spent difficult hours in conversation—difficult because much was lost in the translation between our realms, and because I had to look out for security, having entered the zoo by guile.

Our conversations lasted from late winter into high summer. We talked while Vietnam tore itself apart, before Manson killed all them people in California, and before the Woodstock Festival. And it was during that festival, when the people gathered up north at Yasgur's Farm and I longed to be among them, that Chandali asked me to spring him loose.

It was really more intricate than it seemed. You would think that the turn of a lock, a crowbar applied to a vulnerable part of the caging would be enough. Something related to cat burglary. But the zoo was secure and tight and every possibility closed out until the night we landed on the moon.

Everyone's attention was in the heavens as I took the sidewalk path toward Chandali's environment. A huge peacock was perched on a branch above the trail, and he let out a scream as I passed beneath, and throughout the zoo his call was answered—big cat and coyote, a nation of birds, as if all the zoo was connected by sound. It was a network of noise that rousted trust, else I would not of climbed over the railing of Chandali's environment and lowered myself onto the flat, sandy ground.

He had encouraged me in this, saying that from the inside I could find the means to let him free, but once inside I could not find the exit. What was more, Chandali was not the only resident: from the other end of the environs I heard a low growl as something stalked the midsummer night, rumbling in an old predatory dream.

If Chandali could of packed, he would of been ready and waiting with his bags, but instead I guided him to the wall of the environs and lifted him with difficulty until, resting on my shoulders, he could spring over the railings into the wider freedom of the city. He must of weighed a hundred pounds, and I lofted him I caught the smell of blood and savannah, the twitch and tangle of his muscles that I now suspect meant he was contemplating giving up the venture and simply eating me. With an effortless leap from my shoulders, his back paws digging enough to break my skin and cause me pain, he leapt up into the night. My last sight of him was when, perched just the other side of the railing, his big head peered down at me through the shadows, and the stink of turned meat on his breath spackled the air.

'Keep to the wall,' he told me, in that wordless whisper of a voice. 'If you can make it till morning, the keepers will come and fish you out before the others can get you.'

And then gone, leaving me at the low point of the veldt, certain that my obituary would read like a gazelle's or a hartebeest's. But

Chandali was right, and no other cat stirred that evening, and the keepers had me back to safety just after sunrise, sending me into an old neighborhood north of the zoo. In the years that followed I would hear about strange sightings of a big cat in the city: once there was the sad situation of a young girl mauled over on Seventh Street down near the strip club where I saw the double of my erstwhile son, and then years later, a big creature rousted from undergrowth near the end of a suburban bus route, the one that teacher talked about when they produced the Greek play and I led the chorus.

Oh, yes, I am connected deeply to this town, as you could discover if you knew where to look. But so, as well, is Chandali or the memory of him, the hot breath of carrion borne on the summer wind, the rustle of old gods in the undergrowth. He left me that night at the zoo, and there was never again a definite sighting, but often I heard him as a recessed and smoky voice. And there were maulings and rendings at the margins of town, and many times I believe I caught wind of him in an alley, or when his voice rustled through the promenade in the park, and the stone lions that framed the walkway seemed to stir and ripple on their pedestals.

***

All the while, Chandali was my invisible companion, whispering guidance and blame and cajolery depending on where I was and what he wanted. It should of been a sign of my unraveling, my friends have told me: a young man all Elvised up in lamé, listening to the voices of a leopard in his head while performing impromptu concerts on street corners.

Because the lamé came in the spring of '73, after I had first seen the documentary of the King on tour. Glittering and revived and godlike in beauty, on tour in California and rehearsing his show in Vegas. I began then to think of Vegas as the place to get to, that if I could navigate the fog and maze of this city, could get to the center of its secrets, that it would become but a waystation on the road to Vegas, and I would look back on it as my trial and ordeal, my necessary passage to the center of things.

But then it was unhappy times. I was lost in the labyrinth, down among the statues and the wannabe gods. But the country had not yet turned cold, and there were people around me who had decided to pluck me out of madness. I received donations after singing, more money than Ace Briscoe could of dreamed of, and I did my own tour of the city, from the Armory to the amphitheater all the way down to the university, and I drew a crowd and coin and even a small following—hippies who thought they gained counterculture by circling me with approving smiles, showing the other hippies that they got me, that they understood, though back then I was a lousy Elvis and an even lousier singer.

It was on the steps of the Free Public Library, a place that I had discovered marked the outer boundaries of my powers, where intuition slowed and the sky to the north occasionally caught fire. I would set up there at sunset and sing a capella to the passersby, and in the warm autumn lamé was enough against the weather, and I could thrive on my own and in the elements.

One night I had no audience. The songs had lifted to the air unheeded, and I was fixing to pack it in for the evening, to head back to the park and the safety of the theater, when I noticed them standing by the statue of Mr. Prentice, listening to my slow version of "Dixie" as the sun settled on the buildings west of Third Street.

Three of them, teenagers by the look of them. At first they stood motionless, in file like a trio of soldiers, but a warm gust of evening breeze passed among them, and the jacket of the tallest one stirred in the wake. And when I looked again down the steps there was another, always another one beside them. A brown, hooded shadow I could not figure for a man or a woman, hanging back. Then the boys moved, tossed change into my hat, while their shadows grew longer, like they were not quite solid, like they were dissolving into the shadows around or inside them, and a faint smell of incense rode on the air.

The man placed his hand on the shoulder of the nearest boy, and the two forms wed together like they were mirages distant on a blacktop, and then the four of them come together in a single wheeling light, and I figured it was a flashback to my old bedroom, where Cousin Dilly's clay men stood sentinel and the world was safe.

I whispered my thanks to them, and I headed out toward the park and the theater and sanctuary. Grateful and at peace, I passed at the foot of the high-rise apartments, then thought I could hear them coming after me, though when turned around, there wasn't a pursuer to be seen, but the smell of flowers had faded, replaced by the faint whiff of turned meat and dried grass on the air. It was then I started to run, and I made my way to the amphitheater.

I would see them again, them boys. Or a version of them.

A month or a year later, because as I said the time was fragmented and my imagining unsteady, because they had not grown when I seen them the second time, this time around the margins of the stage where I had made my home. I know it was later because I had stopped my singing on the library steps for the season, and the tiered seats of the amphitheater were covered with leaves. I woke up and stretched myself and stepped onto the stage, and there were the boys on the tiered benches this time more solid, defined by morning's pink light.

And it was a man for sure behind them, and I recognized Nick Mays's beautiful hair beneath the brown hood, and this time he was whispering. 'If a man have a stubborn and rebellious son, which will not obey the voice of his father, or the voice of his mother, and [that], when they have chastened him, will not hearken unto them, then shall his father and his mother lay hold on him, and bring him out unto the elders of his city, and unto the gate of his place, and they shall say unto the elders of his city, This our son is stubborn and rebellious, he will not obey our voice; he is a glutton, and a drunkard. And all the men of his city shall stone him with stones, that he die: so shalt thou put evil away from among you; and all Israel shall hear, and fear.'

The first stone hit me then, and then another in the ribs, and I was headed backstage when another smacked the back of my head, and I could of sworn I heard hooded Nick say It's enough, Aldo, we have punished enough for a warning. When I looked back, the boys and their guide were dissolving into thin air, like the cloudy fabric of a vision, and I knew that these boys were not the same as the ones

I had met before and that nowhere, not even the sanctuary of my theater, was a safe place against the gathering night and the wars that rage around us among things unseen. I would look in the faces of young men for years, catching the memory of those boys in the narrowing of eyes, in the curl of their lips, but back then I hid in the wings for two days, and the night wind brushed by my hiding place carrying on it growls and laments and gibbering, and it was those nights of all the nights that I felt most lonely in the world.

Anyway, that night I had no visitors. The songs lifted into the air unheeded, and I was about to pack up and call it a night when Prentice moved on the little traffic island before me. He rose from his stone seat, stood and regarded me across the westward lane of Albany Street, and I knew at a moment's glance he was no longer Prentice but somehow streamlined and spruced up, the marble hair pomaded and red in the sunset until he was no longer the know-nothing of the older days but my old suitor Nicholas Mays, come out of nowhere to revisit me.

'Tommy,' he said, and his voice was dry as a late autumn wind, dry as Chandali's whisper. 'Tommy, it's time you come with me at last, for you have been ten years in the finding, and the Holy Spirit waits only a space before It moves on. For it goeth where it listeth, and thou hearest the sound thereof, but canst not tell whence it cometh, and whither it goeth.' I knew the voice then, knew it from childhood and way back home. I tried to back up the stairs, to get away from him, but the library doors were locked by now, and Prentice stood in the middle of Albany Street, regarding me with those white and sightless eyes and calling me down to testify.

I turned and ran then, headed south to the park and the theater and sanctuary. I thought I could hear the heavy marble footsteps chasing me, though when I ran at full tilt for a block and then turned around, there wasn't a pursuer to be seen. At last I made my way to the amphitheater and hid backstage, and the night wind brushed by my hiding place carrying on it growls and laments and gibberings, and it was that night of all the nights that I felt most lonely amid all my desolations.

✳✳✳

So it would continue, on through the long summer and the fall, as the Watergate hearings picked up and my sojourn deepened in the park and surrounding environs. I lived out of panhandling and shelters, my lamé jumpsuit becoming thin and crusty. I spent the night in some shelters, backstage at the open theater and under railway bridges. Near the end of the summer I tried traveling east on the new bus line—something, anything to get me out of the park and its whirlpool force. But not far up the expressway the light hit the windshield of the bus, and the road in front of us became blinding, and I saw in the glare there were figures dancing just beyond the glass, like they were shadows projected on a screen. It was enough to frighten me, so that when I reached the end of the line I stayed on board, took the bus back to Broadway and walked down to the park, which opened its leafy arms to my return. It was safe there, and I ventured east again only once, on the day of the tornado.

I thought I saw the statue of Prentice standing at Fourth and Fellini, a winter morning just after the turn of the year. He was standing in a crowd and because he was born of stone instead of flesh, he loomed large on the block by the book store and the bar. I tried to hide myself against the wall of the Baptist Church—the one that would go Church of Christ later, where the mob tore up the boy on the steps—and I could feel the marble eyes searching me out, like he could sense me by smell, sense my heart fluttering. And my breathing come short, and my chest tightened, and I am thinking here it comes, hysterica passio, like the play says. My back against the stone, I held still until his gaze passed over and by me, and then I could breathe even though his eyes were blue and familiar and his body transformed into something panther-like and lean under the folded marble of his nineteenth century suit.

I knew he was hunting, and I hoped he was not hunting me. I headed through traffic over Fourth Street and made my way toward Mamma's, to find her not around and the door locked against me. I sat on the stoop to wait her out, but I could tell after a while from faces in the windows and the passers-by that I was embarrassing.

Once or twice I tried visiting my mother. Ace was nowhere to be found in all the city, and so Mamma became my one connection with an idea of home. But I was no longer moored to the world around me, spending my nights in the safety of the park, my days on familiar and nearby streets where night would not catch me too far from the theater and the Witches' Tree and home.

All the while, around me the city darkened. Cars would swerve away from me, and the first group of my transients dwindled as autumn settled in and the air turned cold. I was the one who lingered in the park. The police would roust you, and they let harsh things go on, like the time that a man who might have been Prentice and might have been Nick Mays or someone else come by with a gaggle of schoolboys, stood on the topmost tier of the amphitheater, and egged on his company as they threw stones at me until I crept behind the stage and shook, hearing the rocks rattle against the sets and fearing each moment they would come down to get me. I would look in the faces of young men for years, catching the memory of those boys in the scorn that their gazes returned.

And the nights were darker still: the hustlers were starting to trade up by the promenade—some of the girls I knew, but the teenaged boys were a new ripple in the business. Standing at the corners, they huddled against the cold and smoked until the cars passed by, the windows rolled down, and they would lean against the hood and talk and then, opening the car door, vanish into the night.

✳✳✳

I was awakened one morning by a soft call from the stage and a pretty girl who had brought me sandwiches and coffee.

Jasodhara was a godsend that winter when the air turned cold. She was twenty-one and red-haired and ruddy, probably an Irish girl from her up-East accent. Had on a blue anorak, the hood lifted at first against the cold, so that she looked much younger, like a child bundled up. It made me nervous until she pushed the hood back.

She smelled of patchouli and running brook water. In later times, after she was no longer around me, I would catch the smell

185

in a sharp switching of summer air, and she would almost appear before me, like the light grown bold and reflectant on a summer road. And I would think of her, and be almost but not quite in love again.

Dhara, as she later asked me to call her, was there with a pair of friends about her age—a tall, goofy-looking black kid named Roderick and a girl named Armeet. I learned later that the girls had taken Indian names, but we had not reached that revelation on the day when they stood at the theater apron, and the morning sun was just peeking over the backstage so that the three of them cast linked shadows across the first few rows of seats, like snow angels formed of sun and fog, or like the angels on the library steps before the weather changed and the world went cold.

Months in the open had taught me caution. I'd been through all I told you before, and that winter I'd been beat up twice, once pretty bad. One time an older guy had dangled himself in front of me, but I was able to elude him. All of this had lent some caution to my encounters, so I peeked out from backstage and small talked until Roderick come closer and gave me the sandwich. It was peanut butter and thankfully no jelly, and it sat well on a liquored stomach like they might know what they were doing.

My angels stayed a while to talk to me, even though you could tell the girls were nervous: after all, my lamé jumpsuit was gamey by now, wine-stained and grubby though the weather had been too cold to sweat through it. By that time a residual buzz guided me into most afternoons, and it was enough to make me believe that Dhara might fancy me, after all. Armeet had a bindi on her forehead and long blonde dreadlocks. She seemed to be more than friendly with Roderick, for as much as you can tell after a few minutes acquaintance; however, I was more certain that she was less than friendly to me, considering how she was urging Dhara to go, claiming they had places to be.

The three were college students from up north, taking their junior years to be involved with some program that provided the sandwiches. I was never sure about the names of the places and the programs, so struck I was with Dhara and her green eyes and the faint whiff of patchouli she left in the air. She came with her companions a couple of times more before she got up the courage to come by herself. We sat downstage after that, as her sunniness brought me out of hiding in the wings, and then as the first hints of spring come into the park, we moved into the first row of seats, where we sat and talked about the town and the larger world, and she asked me about Yorktown but never said where she was from, and it pains me sometimes that I did not ask, being wrapped up in the immediacy.

After a while, whereabouts didn't seem important. And Dhara started on her path to curing me. Sometime in early March, she asked if I would be willing to do some tests at a wellness center a few blocks east of the park. I asked her what was in it for me, and she replied that I already got sandwiches and coffee, so I liked her even better. She went on to tell me it would be like giving blood without the needles, a small sum of money I could spend how I liked, but please not on more wine because she could smell it on me. She was this strange combination of social worker and flirt and strict librarian, and I got to know and admire her at the center where she worked.

The center was a little bit pop psychology, a little bit rock star Buddhism. They would teach you to meditate, and counsel you with yoga. Mostly the people there were the rich suburbans, but on Sundays and Tuesdays they would close up shop and let us in to dispense the dharma to the derelicts. About the second week I was there, they passed out paper and crayons, Armeet drawing circles on the paper for us because they were skittish about putting compasses in our hands.

Then the circles were drawn and we sat before them, Armeet telling us to fill them in and don't judge what we were putting there. Some of us colored them solid, but it seemed better to me to draw and imagine. Blue for Thusa Creek, winding through the center of my circle like a benign python, on one side of it the red clay, on the other the green of my native woods. The yellow of the summer sun and the white of the winter sky promising snow, a circle of nature lost under the asphalt and brick. And suddenly it made me sad, and I stared *it down until the city went away, and Dhara put her hand on my shoulder and told me it was time to close the center for the evening.*

I took the circle with me, and looked at it under the streetlights behind the amphitheater, but it seemed as though the night had bleached its colors, and it seemed like residue rather than treatment, like one of those memorial cards you get from a funeral home. In the full sunlight of day, though, when you stood on the stage, the colors returned and even deepened, so bright with poetry that it made me sad again. I folded my drawing and put it in my pocket, so that wherever I went it would put me at the center of things and radiate out from me, and thereby I could know my whereabouts.

I would discover that Dhara's first name had been Bridget. Her last name remains a mystery. And yes, she was from up around Boston, a refugee from the Irish Catholics, turning instead to extempore Buddhism she had picked up from the Beat Poets.

Where some people up her way were headed abroad for their junior years, Dhara had taken charity as her destination. She delighted in getting her hands dirty, she told me, and Europe was to her no place for that. So instead she had come to a Southern city to help with the needs, and for a long while I felt fortunate to have found her.

Our ages were not much different when I figured it. I turned twenty-four on Election Day '72, and she was four or five years younger, old enough to be legal and young enough not to have had aspiration beat out of her. I was perhaps her friend and perhaps a project, a kind of duty she paid to a world that was spiraling downward though neither of us knew it.

For the park and the surrounding streets were in decline, the beautiful old homes whose bricks were now sun-bleached or water-blasted, the mortar powdery and sparse, the wooden porches and window frames pocked and shredded now by generations of rain. There were disturbances as nearby as Ninth Street, where at night you could hear the brief, solitary whoop of police sirens and sometimes the long and drawn-out bray when the cops were chasing someone, but nights backstage were no longer quiet, filled with disruption and new vagrancy. I feared for Dhara then, because the new people were surly and undone, the drug trade high and no longer diversion. A man was stabbed in the promenade that January, and though I found the body it seemed better for others to seem to find it, and I tried to crash at Mamma's again, and this time she let me in because I was noisy on the stoop.

She fed me on Campbell's soup and apathy. Made up her sofa the first night, a pallet in the parlor the second, and by the third there was the fidgeting I had come to know while I stayed there, the bird-flutter of her hands that let me know I had outstayed my welcome. By then, news of the knifing had spread through the neighborhood, and you could tell that a part of her had passed from impatient to afraid. She stood by the window and faced the room, and the steak knives vanished from the cabinet, so that I was carving nothing more solid than butter.

Dhara got me lodging at the place over on East Jefferson, and there was a television there where you could keep track and wait until investigations dropped from the horizon and you could go back to the park. The others seemed to me feral and vague: I met Miss Eleanor Rigby for the first time there, the little drag queen who worked the Wilde under previous ownership, but otherwise I could not tell apart the clientele, a sea of tattered men woven together at the edges of energy. A block east of the premises you could see the wall of fire spread across the city—the smokeless flames cold and brilliant, which my people can tell you burn only those of us destined not to cross into the country of lawns and sprawling houses. Once I tried to pass through the firewall, and it seared my clothing and blinded me for a spell, and I smelled the watery ozonous wind as it pushed me back toward town.

It was then the first maulings occurred to the west, three of them along the double-digited streets of the black neighborhoods. Two old women and a four-year-old child, the child the third one when maybe the animal had found out the old folks tasted of gristle and urine. The police were mum about it, like they usually were on *anything west of Ninth Street, but the men in the shelter claimed at first that it was wild dogs, and then, when the child's remains showed up, claimed that it was more than a dog, something powerful and beyond this city.*

I was afraid for Dhara then. Not so much for myself, because I, too, was a mass of elusive tendons and lamé, but Dhara was smaller and plump and from the looks and smell of her, would taste good to a wild creature. I escorted her the times she would let me, out of the park and north toward Broadway, where she would insist I turned back, that she would be safe from there. I knew she didn't want me knowing where she lived, but I pretended to believe what she said. And it is strange how pretending to believe can lead you to faith itself, so that one night when I lingered, just south of the library, I saw her catch a bus east and realized she was headed out of the city, she had found comfortable lodgings in the suburbs. I explained it on the spot, as the statues of Prentice and Lincoln looked down on me in pity: she was sharing an apartment with other girls, it wasn't that the burbs were cleaner and more posh, but just that a student could be closer to better things if she moved her belongings east. By late March of '74 I thought nothing of it, no longer misgave.

We had smoked weed together twice, once with her friends and the second time just the two of us. I was constantly trying to sit closer to her, being ever so careful because I knew that a forward move from a guy like me just might be the thing to drive her from the city altogether. On that second time, we approached the matter of trust. Dhara claimed that she did not mistrust me, not at all, and finally, when the cannabis kicked in and we both became relaxed and more talkative, she gave me her address out east off Lexington Road, which was then very much a rich neighborhood until the suburbs moved further east and became richer still. I promised I would not visit, and she said she wouldn't really mind if I did, but I could tell my promise eased her worries. She set her hand on my shoulder, a touch that passed through me and rousted my tears, and she claimed on the first of April that she was getting a good ounce from Roderick and that if I'd come to the center with her on the 3rd, we could get together at the theater that afternoon to smoke some of it.

So I turned that moment again and again in my imagination and fancy, because I had yet to touch Dhara, or to initiate the touch is more like it. And of course I wanted to, but I feared to try unassisted by wine or weed, afraid that my hand might pass through assembled air, that she might be cloud or a wisp of fog.

And all through the winter the statue on the court took on her shape, or what I imagined that shape to be beneath the layers of anorak and down vest and flannel shirt: Galatea spiraled up from the fountain waters, turning and draping about her a bronze scarf that hung in the wind and suspended thought, and beneath her the adoring cherubs looking up to her, dizzy with water and desire, their arms outstretched through the spray.

At times I had imagined her little breasts half-covered by the scarf, like the cleft between her thighs, had stood beneath the bowl of the fountain and look up until I felt myself turning to bronze from the knees up. And at times snow had covered her shoulders, and once some hippie had placed a slouch hat upon her head against the weather, and I would stand there as the pooled water took on a film of ice and imagine what her legs would feel like beneath my hands, her lips against my lips. And into the spring, when the city began to warm we had talked longer hours, until she had touched me and promised me weed.

The afternoon of the 3rd when she was supposed to come, it was dark and still, like something foreboding was set loose, and I waited for a time at the center, then afterwards by the theater, and when she did not show I collared a trio of vagrants headed past the Witches' Tree and south toward the courts. One of them was Eleanor Rigby, and he claimed there had been another animal mauling, this time as close as 9th Street, the victim a young woman who wasn't from the city.

By the time I reached 9th and Kentucky, standing on the grounds of the old apartment complex that would wait forty years for the fire that would level it, I had found that the clawed and mangled woman was both black and younger than Dhara, and I felt joyful and relieved, and regretted the feeling for the dead woman's sake.

I waited at the bus stop for the line that took you east, and around me there was a premonition of smoke and a hint of patchouli oil on the air—the smell of Dhara and of the last summers of love before the storm and the next hard decade. At the time I did not recognize the prophecy of things to come—that I would never see Dhara again, though I would hear rumors of her from the north, and that I would not yet recognize this moment as the time when my last ties come unsettled and I would float adrift into the world of vagary and dark clouds.

Because now my eyes were on the immediate darkness, as the skies went foreboding, and even the locusts in the trees hushed their rattle as the air settled on the central blocks of the city. Now the storm was approaching for real, the dimensions of which I had no way of foreseeing, especially since my imagining stayed on Dhara, wondering what had kept her from our rendezvous. My thoughts spiraled and quickened, and the concern I once had felt over anonymous victims descended now upon my friend, and I resolved to ride the bus to her place anyway, and I swear that the skies first rumbled when I decided to break my promise.

It was what the locals called 'the mall bus', and it made a path through the side streets of the city, past the park where the fountain and the goat boy made their home, onto an eastern thoroughfare until we hit Lexington Road and the blinding fiery light shook the darkness, like it done before, and fearful and knowing my walk was but a few blocks from here, I pulled the cord and disembarked by the Catholic school.

The trees that surrounded the campus were bent by the winds over the statues of Mary and the saints, and if I had been paying attention, I would have noticed there was not much traffic on the road. But this was east, as far east in the town as I had ever ventured, and the wall of light pushed and crackled against my skin as the few passing cars rushed through it. It resisted me, pushed me back under the trees, and I hugged the edge of it but could find no way to get through. Dhara's place was still several blocks beyond it, I guessed, but it took all my strength to navigate the edges of the wall, and by then the rumbling had begun, a distant chugging like a train at full speed growing nearer and nearer, the air completely still and *anticipating, the sky black, and it was only then I suspected what was approaching and curled into a ball on the curb as the twister swept me up.*

✳✳✳

They tell stories of miraculous survival. How the baby was lifted from the crib and settled softly a hundred yards away, the grieving parents finding their infant laughing and kicking in the midst of the rubble, only a little wet for the journey. The same force that drove broom straws through telephone poles, that lifted a car across the river and crashed it mercilessly against a shanty or a dock, would suddenly turn benign and almost gentle as it settled the child on the ground in a cradling wind, evidence to some folks that the forces behind nature loved us and cared for us, despite flood and cyclone and the slaughter of earthquakes in Central America.

I remember my journey in fragments, that rush into the sky and then losing consciousness, waking up gasping in a whirlwind and then again knocked out, the path of the storm sweeping me north above the river, where the old snake coiled against the rising wind, its eyes aloft, no doubt taking in the young man in torn lamé as the tornado took me past the falls before it turned slowly over the old amusement park and sped east over the westernmost part of the town, past parks once segregated and over streets huddled against approaching damage.

And then I saw it again. The enormous wheels within wheels that made up the city and spiraled down into the park that was my home. I rode the top of the tornado, people, and from the height I could see the design of things, how wind and water come together in a large and mysterious pattern. It was all connected, it was all on the move, from the shadowlights out east to the serpent and the leopards prowling the north and the east, to the statues in the south, all circling the seed at the center of the pattern, the subtle swirl of water and wind on the stage of my home in the theater.

I suppose it was then that I opened my arms and rode the storm back over the city, followed the downward spiral as leaves and grass and branches whipped around me and I hovered over the theater and then, with a last surge, hurtled west across abandoned streets, the rubble and ruin of convenience stores and gutted churches until my jumpsuit snatched on a limb, people, and I dangled helplessly, left hanging by the wind a dozen feet above a green city lot, and I blacked out again for a moment, and when I awakened, black hands had lifted me from the branches, black hands were tending me in the storm's wake.

XXII

"He always claimed that it was love lifted him from the branches," Bulwer explained, raising the cassette to the light after Mickey handed it to him. "*When no one else would help*, like the hymn goes.

"But DeMoyne Troubles got him down from that tree. This much was verified, because the Councilman told me roughly the same story about the aftermath of the storm. How they'd huddled in the house—all eight of the Troubles brood—and when the sky cleared and the storm at last passed over, they emerged to find a white boy dangling from the water maple in the front yard."

"So the Councilman recurred in Tommy's life," Mickey said, explaining the story to himself, apparently, because the others in his company knew it already.

They were seated at the bar of the Oscar Wilde. The place had just opened for the day, and Faj had poured them each a shot of the house bourbon as Alan Stack turned on the lights and the stereo.

"The old eternal return," Bulwer pronounced, drawing a laugh from the barkeep. "Tommy went on much as he had before, though the death of Elvis sent him into hiding for a while, and he seemed to move to the margins, almost, and there were times when I wondered about him. Because the store was up and running by then, and when Tommy vanished from the neighborhood, people noticed. When one of us drops away, no matter how slightly he's brushed against the rest of us, we tend to see the absence, we tend to miss him.

"But he came back for DeMoyne Troubles. He came back out of gratitude."

Mickey took a sip of the bourbon, cleared his throat. "So. I've heard Troubles lived up to his name, even if he was a minor hero on this occasion."

"Ah, Troubles was pretty much a problem from the beginning," Stack called from the corner. "Corrupt as hell in his later years, a foe to my clientele simply because he kept his mouth shut when the plague ran through our numbers. Lip service to the whole community, but a cherry-picker when it came to who he *really* looked out for."

"Now, Alan," Bulwer soothed. "But who hasn't done that? And then last year the candidacy of Aldo Wooters. Surely he's worse."

Stack nodded, and turned on the television above the bar. "Can't argue with that. Wooters is a sugary monster."

Mickey shuddered to think. Grubby and brilliantined, smelling of Aqua Velva and moldy Bibles, Wooters had been a deacon at Heart Ministries Outreach, a charismatic church out beyond the statuary and the underpass. When the city had tilted politically rightward in the last election, he had ridden the surge to a council seat, but only after DeMoyne Troubles had been linked to involvement with a fifteen-year-old girl. The circumstances remained suspicious: throughout the city's black community there were claims that the accusations were part of a heavily funded set-up, money channeled to Wooters' attack squads by the bottomless real estate coffers of Rausch Enterprises, a faceless corporation headed by Roy Rausch, the former U.S. Representative from the district across the river. Reporters were sent out to play Watergate investigation, but as everyone had figured, the energy failed by January of the next year, and Wooters had spent a bumbling and ambitious term as a Councilman, his pockets full and his eyes on a national office.

But it was DeMoyne Troubles—now running the family liquor store and contemplating another political run, shamed in the larger venue but still loved in his community—whose path had crossed Tommy's a number of times while in and out of office. Though Alan Stack had little truck with the former councilman, he had to allow that Troubles looked good next to his successor, and John Bulwer, situated to the left of any politician in the city, still liked "Brother DeMoyne" and considered him a great source of lore.

"You see, Tommy joined Troubles' first campaign back in the '80s out of gratitude. He always wanted to pay his debts, and he sang for the would-be alderman at a number of the rallies in whiter parts of the district. It didn't take long for Troubles to see that Tommy was an embarrassment to voting people wherever he went, and for different reasons depending on where he went. The sideburns, the lamé jumpsuit, the accrued glitter—all of it was soon a liability. But Troubles had hangers-on throughout the campaign. Intoning ministers, community organizers, performance artists, crackheads, grifters and grafters, all flocked to the banner, and the candidate had learned early on how to use liabilities as assets.

His placing Tommy outside select precincts was sage calculation: whether intentionally or not, Tommy's act had the knack of scaring off white Republicans, who could never quite put their finger on why he turned them away from the polls: after all, they told themselves, it was Elvis whom he imitated, and the songs were all pre-Beatle and therefore clean and Christian. But something about him pushed them away, while the black voters walked past Tommy calmly on the way to the machines, convinced that it was just another white guy doing Elvis and that was all.

So once through the primary, Brother DeMoyne coasted to the first of six consecutive victories, as Reagan passed into Bush

I and Bush I passed into Clinton, while the position Troubles ran for changed its name from Alderman to Councilman, the makeup of the city from "city/county" to "metro". The creature evolved and transformed around Troubles and his entourage, and to hear Bulwer tell it, the head man was up to the challenge. And Tommy, though never taken on formally as a campaign operative or even a regular sideshow, was always allowed for as the rallies wound up their quadrennial patterns.

Which was why it seemed strange when Troubles dropped Tommy altogether at the turn of the new century.

Stack was the cynic about this sudden change. "No invitations after 9/11," he said. "'All ye who are strange and othered, who walk this city by different roads and sidewalks, get the hell out of town'. That kind of thing."

"Oh, it was later than that," Bulwer said. "It was after that performance down at the theater. When Aron Starr was killed."

"Wait, wait," Mickey protested. "*What* performance? *What* killing?"

"You were here by then, Mick," Bulwer insisted. "But I'm not surprised you haven't heard the story. Disastrous production of the Bacchae down at the theater. People in the cast ended up missing. Some of them feared dead. Tommy and the Brischords were part of the play's tragic chorus, but they all went underground after its opening night. Tommy surfaced a few days later with some batshit story about how Aron Starr had been castrated before the crowd killed him, how some huge yellow python crawled out from beneath the stage and swallowed the play's director."

"Talk of bad reviews," Faj said, and everyone but Mickey snickered. Mickey, who was still gaping at this strange, preposterous turn in the story, insisted that someone tell him what he's missed, and it fell upon Bulwer to fill in the details.

The story Tommy told, according to Bulwer, was Euripides mixed with a pint of Rosie. The production was a disaster from the start, and when the director brought in half of the neighborhood's vagrancy to play the chorus, Stephen Thorne's

Bacchae could go nowhere but spiraling into disaster.

"They never found the boy in the end," Bulwer said. "Aron Starr was his name. So there was some kind of foul play took place in the neighborhood, after all. And yet to hear Tommy tell it, the whole thing was *Bacchae* inside *Bacchae*, the world of the actors mirroring the world of the play."

"Breaking the fourth wall," Mickey said.

"And adding on a room," Faj said, pouring them all another round.

"But Tommy was always one for imagined drama," Stack observed, brushing by Faj to wipe down the bar. "So maybe his 'Dorothy in the twister' was just another embroidery."

"Like the girl?" Bulwer asked, and suddenly Mickey was attentive, pulling back from the bourbon blur at the new tidings.

"How do you mean. Surely Dhara—"

"Oh, you didn't think that Dhara was real, hon?" Stack asked ironically, draping the bar cloth over the faucet. "Johnny and I tried to find her while the taping was going on. Searched white pages in Boston, university records, accounts of any charitable programs running in the city during the early 'seventies. No Dharas, no Bridgets, no psychology-for-the-homeless crusades, at least nothing that looked like what Tommy described. Internet's a wonderful thing: if you aren't there, you don't exist."

Mickey wasn't buying it. "But that was forty years ago, Alan. The accounts would be sketchy. Perhaps Tommy was remembering some unrecorded kindness, an encounter that slipped out of history but remained in his memory. In his gratitude. The way we've all remembered things now and then..."

"Like Becky Thatcher?" Bulwer asked, and it seemed like everything Mickey had heard was unraveling at its edges. For some reason he had accepted Becky Thatcher and her mother, the witch-goddess of creeks. Accepted moving statues and talking leopards as all part of hallucination, whether drug or madness. He imagined Tommy at the foot of the fountain, looking up at the lithe bend of Galatea, imagining her metal transforming to flesh, the glow of the skin softening in the late winter sky, his chapped hands yearning to touch her, to touch a girl he had fashioned from dreams.

***

"I still don't understand why me," Mickey said, after his fifth drink and everyone else's third. He was flushed now, warm at the temples, sitting alone with Bulwer as Alan and Faj set up drinks for the Wilde's earliest customers.

"I have to get to the shop, Mickey," Bulwer insisted. "As much as I'd like, I can't linger in the bar all afternoon."

For a moment the comment stung. Mickey was sure that Bulwer was casting aspersions, something about laziness and alcoholism. But there was no verdict in his old friend's expression, nothing but needing to open Salvages for the day.

"One more, John?" he asked, almost plaintively. "Or at least don't leave before explaining why you chose me? I mean, I'm no historian, no detective. Not even a reporter, for God's sake. Why did you draft me to begin with?"

Bulwer brushed his hand through the air, dismissing a thought. "Oh, Mickey. It was simple intuition. Look at you, now. Have you thought of anything other than Tommy Briscoe for the last couple of weeks? It's taken you by storm, this story. It's rousting your instincts. And not just as a novelist, mind you."

Mickey stirred the ice in his glass. Motioned to Faj, who frowned and poured him another. "So, why, then?"

Bulwer met his gaze. "Because you're outside of things, Mickey. You're on the border between worlds. And I suppose by now you recognize that as Tommy's country, too. What better biographer? That is, if you have the *cojones* for it."

Mickey smiled blearily. "*Cojones. Cojones* and *samprasada.* Sure, I do."

Bulwer grinned back. "One more tape, then. Don't go home without it."

But Mickey had no intention of going home. Instead, groggy

with bourbon, he took the 4th Street bus south. At this hour on a Sunday afternoon, not many people were aboard: an old granny with a brace of toddlers, and behind her, in the back row of the bus, another drunk.

As the bus sped past his usual stop, Mickey caught a sharp, feral stench in the vehicle, and the windows darkened slightly, as though the route was headed under the bridge on the south end of the campus—a sign that he had ridden too far. Awkwardly, seized by a panic that was disproportionate for the situation, he tugged at the bell cord, and lurched from the bus at a stop two blocks north of the university. It was as though the compass points were shifting, and though he felt entirely lost, the stench rode with him as he embarked from the bus.

He blamed it on alcohol that the buildings had shifted once more, and he felt trapped in a mid-game of strategy, when in fact the only thing he needed to do was to make his way to the damned library. The old campus theater behind him now, Mickey thought he had recovered directions, but then there was a parking garage before him, a squat brick building he didn't recognize, and he weaved through the new-laid maze toward the high roof of the library.

Slowly the harsh, carnal smell grew fainter. At least it wasn't me, Mickey joked to himself, though he had known all along it was something else, something that barely reached him over memory and distance. He disciplined himself not to run, on the superstition that whatever it was, the thing would pursue a running quarry. As the sidewalk gave way to the plaza behind the art museum, Mickey heard a skittering sound, the shuffle of claw against concrete, he would tell himself later, and despite all thinking, an instinct beneath all thought kicked in, and he sprinted toward the library steps, now in sight.

He took the stairs three at a time, and burst into the front lobby, his lungs heaving, the fear and exertion having just about undone a drunk in his fifties. Eyes looked up from book, and the work-study student behind the circulation desk frowned self-righteously. Mickey shushed them all—a little loudly, considering it was a library lobby—and stepped into the elevator.

It seemed the student was not the only critic. A note taped to Mickey's carrel door, dated Thursday afternoon, informed him that Dr. Athena Bumpas had come by to see him, figuring he was in his office since the phone line had been busy all morning, both before and after the class that Mickey had apparently missed.

It couldn't bode well. Nor could the phone messages from said department head—two from Friday and one from Saturday afternoon—and then a fourth one, an older woman not recognizable at first, who turned out to be neighbor across the court. She was *just letting him know* that Tamara had tossed a number of items onto the sidewalk in front of the apartment. *Mostly men's clothing*, the neighbor explained. *Though I'm guessing there might be other things in the boxes.*

I've brought in the clothes and the boxes I could carry, the neighbor, an older woman, confided. *If you could pick them up within the next week or so, I'd be glad to hold them for you.*

Mickey was not sure he could keep such a rigorous schedule. On the other hand, he was fairly sure none of the silverware his mother had bequeathed them had made it to the curb, though Tamara might have decided that the paper plates were his by inheritance. He sat at his desk, the momentary irritation and despair giving way to a surprising sense of elation.

Because there was another tape. Bulwer had given him yet more treasure.

Mickey slipped the cassette into the player, retrieved a legal pad and a pen from the desk drawer, then thinking twice, set aside everything but the listening.

XXIII

Next came the season I vanished. I can tell you the surrounding story, its prologue and its aftermath, but if you're looking for details, you'll have to ask the Brischords.

It all started in the crawl space under John Bulwer's store.

Just that morning I had awakened in the cemetery rising under stone angels, one of which I had glyphed on the previous evening, the base of its statue now bearing a sign I had done while liquored up and well-oiled with irony which somehow seemed faithless and violent in the morning light.

But I could never imagine the real violence that would come by the turn of the day. By afternoon, wandering back home, taking a wide course around the library and around Prentice lying in wait. I must admit my purposes were not lawful, as I headed past Fourth and Fellini and right, past the bank and to the back of this very place. I was in search, I admit, of copper pipe.

Copper, as you must know, is the currency of my brothers in meth and crack, traded to pay for their substances. I was of the old school, traditional in cheap wine and Duggan's on a good day, but I had discovered that copper traded just as well for liquor. I wouldn't of tried to pirate Dry Salvages had I known Johnny then, and known that within a year I would start history with the place. There in the back alley, I made my strategies, which I confess were little more than crawling under the building and stripping it of what availed. I had forgotten however, the gaunt mobility of crack and meth addicts, the thinness that would let them negotiate the tightest of crawl spaces.

Indeed, for a moment, with the late afternoon light just right, I thought I saw another in the passage—someone moving toward me, angular, scuttling like a crab, mirroring his movement in the shadows underneath the house, bound toward the copper.

Not that I was stuck. Nor that I was scared. But I was compressed enough and startled enough by this intruder to make noise, to cry out. Which of course aroused Johnny over here, who of course came outside and exercised Second Amendment rights in rock salt upon a poor man's backside. God bless him for the lenience of no further pursuit, and God bless the crawl space with manifold entries, for I squeezed into light and hurried up Sixth Street and away from there.

I was limping, felt the rock salt burrow into my bottom so that it hurt to run. A distant siren startled me, and I hid by the Witches' Tree until it was clear that the authorities were headed elsewhere. The weather was stifling and the lamé, I confess, was tattered behind, so I looked for interior shelter until commotion died away. I had heard about a free movie preview at the Shangri-La. Remembered the theatre had a balcony, and figured it as a high, air-conditioned retreat where I could sit in darkness for a couple of hours and lick my wounds—a figure of speech, of course.

I had been to the Shangri-La before, in the company of Ace back in the fifties, when it was the Horizon. Together we had seen The Ten Commandments, Heston dangling the Tablets over a cast of thousands. Back then my clothing and spirit had been cleaner, and I had been provided for—at least as much as Ace was able to provide for anything.

That was what I thought of as I entered the theater from the alley between Third and Fourth, slipping by some kid with a joint and a man-bun who I guessed to be working the concessions in the place. The lobby was beautiful—a mural of what seemed to be the

Garden of Eden and above it the faces of a hundred death masks, some of which I recognized as the likenesses of the great artists. I did not stop to consider, but took a back stairway to the balcony, which seemed pretty much closed to the public that night. And it was a patron's eye view I caught from up there, far different from the old Horizon, with red velvet curtains and filigrees painted gold, statues of Greek gods in the alcoves, and above me, high in the theater vault, a canopy of imitation stars.

It was the old days layered on top of the new. It was happiness imagined in a rear-view mirror, an elegance recovered from nowhere. This time the film was about Dr. Caligari, an old German silent classic with its monstrous buildings and sleepwalkers. It was like the world when you'd been drinking, like you could step outside onto Fourth Street and watch as the carnival come to town.

Alone I watched from up in the balcony, taking it all in there amidst the cool and the dark, my bottom still smarting from the rock salt. I remembered enough about the film from college—enough to know it starts out about a fair in a small town, about this evil Dr. Caligari who comes onto the midway with a sleepwalker he has trained to murder. Our hero Franzis loses his best friend to these partners in crime, but when he sorts things and solves the murder, it turns out he has dreamed it all out of his own insanity, that he is a patient in a madhouse and old Caligari is not the serial-killing villain, but a respectable psychologist whose job was all along to cure our hero.

That's what I remembered about the film. But what I had forgotten was what Caligari himself had done, how he seized you from out of the film, broke the fourth wall and pulled you inside. The old villain had me from the beginning. He duckwalked through a tilted city street, the camera iris closing slowly around him until his face was the only thing on screen.

It took me a few seconds to recognize that my backside was no longer hurting.

I lost my breath. I felt occupied. Someone was sitting beside me in the darkness, hunkered over, glittering. I thought perhaps I was called to Jesus or even by Jesus, or maybe that I had lost all sense *in my extremities and that death was creeping up the somatic ladder, but the back of my pants had rewoven, and I could take up my bed and walk. The man beside me whirled with contained light, and the theater seat crackled and glowed at the edge of bursting into flame.*

I shouted out, and made for the light of the lobby. My legs were healthy, and I took the stairs in bounds, begging the pardon of two ushers who grabbed ahold of me, showed them my backside to their puzzlement, for they saw nothing wrong with my trousers beyond the scuff and soil of wear. I told them my story, and when I made motion to leave, one of them, a Eurasion boy older than the other but still young enough to be my son made the sign of the cross over me, and he said, 'Behold, thou art made whole: sin no more, lest a worse thing come unto thee.'

I could no longer tell whether the boy or Caligari had cured me, but I felt doubly occupied, like a second soul had set up lodging in my breast. The death masks on the ceiling of the lobby looked down at me as though the gods were breathing life into them, and I crossed through the murals of Eden toward the Fourth Street exit. I looked back once, and caught the eye of the boy who had blessed me, and all of a sudden I felt tears rise up and I walked out into evening light and the sound of an ambulance scarcely a block away.

✳✳✳

I do not remember as much from this stretch of my life. I saw the usher at the theater again, several times, in that way that someone has always been in the vicinity but it takes one important encounter to make you notice: he was a happy youth with friends and working toward a girlfriend, and I was uncommonly glad to recognize that, as though it lay in my power to grant him blessings in return.

And I took up with the Brischords again, this time singing less at the street corner but more receding, to serenades under the Witches' Tree and then by the promenade between the lions, nightly until the police began to question, then once or twice a week only, our concerts receding until we performed now only on the theater stage, site of the second time the lightning had come close. And I remember these things in only fragments, but constant was the shape who had sat by me that night in the theater, the other man in gaudy lamé.

At first he moved in accord with my movements, a shape dancing at my peripheral vision, vanishing when I turned toward him like a speck in the eye, like a floater. But it was not long before he—or she or it, because I never saw him full on, never directly— would start up actions of his own, and I begun to wonder if all that imitation, all that mirroring, was not me following his lead instead of what I had supposed at first. I could see the figure in the wings of the theater, moving and dancing to his imagined music, to his solo concert, and there was once or twice when I could of sworn he joined in harmony with me, and I could hear blended voices in the chorus of "Suspicious Minds" or "You Were Always on My Mind". The mind songs, the ones about imagining or remembering.

Together we roamed the customary blocks—my double and me—straying as far east and north as the hospital streets, where projects and ghettos were rising and crumbling in the streets just south of Broadway. Then we would wander as far south and west as the long stretch of road leading out of the city toward Yorktown and home, where at night you could sit at the crest of another park and look out to where the huge smokestacks of the cement company belched dusty smoke into the sunset and, even after midnight, winked their lights into the sky's deep blackness like they were twinned towers, doomed like the new ones up in New York.

All the while we never spoke. The shape from the Shangri-La was my companion, always walking beside me. Sometimes I would stop to count us, and then it was only me, standing there on the sidewalk or beneath the awning of the promenade, and then I would look up and see him glitter with borrowed sunlight. Gliding, wrapped sometimes in gold lamé, other times in a color I could only call pale, because it gathered light and gave nothing back. I could not tell whether it was me or someone else.

I had heard long ago that Nick Mays had fallen beneath the streets,

victim to tremor and collapse on that February night in '81 when the sewers exploded from a processing plant releasing hexane gas beneath our streets. And yet now I almost suspected otherwise, because a young man who was the spitting image of Mays was running for council against my old rescuer DeMoyne Troubles.

Aldo Wooters was a piece of work, earnest snake oil up against Troubles' apparent goodness. Wooters was from some charismatic church at the edge of the district, and where everyone knew that Troubles liked sweetheart business deals with friends and cousins, not to mention business with friendly young sweethearts, Wooters come across with the kind of cleanliness you knew couldn't exist. He was the one who claimed righteousness when a body was downright certain there was some tweaked-out boy hustler in his basement along with the gas generator and two sets of golf clubs.

I could tell from early on that Wooters was nothing but trouble, and I made plans to unmask him as soon as I could find out what needed unmasking. Problem was that my other devices—my devices of misguided revenge—were already underway.

When DeMoyne had disavowed me in his last campaign, I had shunned him back, and by the summer of election year I had dirt on my old benefactor, switchery born out of my own self-righteousness and desire for revenge. All of which I regret now, because I have entered a world beneath and beyond and above our customary stories, where the simple judgments no longer work or matter.

Back then it was like my devices were set forth only to become entangled: Daddy Chrome took me aside and scolded me for going to Wooters' campaign manager Bucky Trabue with an eyewitness account of DeMoyne in his old maroon Lincoln with yet another underage girl. Good thing it was me spreading the story, Chrome says, on account of Trabue was supposed to of said that any of my qualities—homeless or half-drunk or Elvis impersonator—was enough to disqualify anything I said. But it set Trabue to fishing in other spots of the stream, which Republicans do quite well when they have to, and he come up with a scandal that done in the councilman and lifted Wooters up instead.

Everyone I knew hated Wooters, and it pained me to think that

I had been somehow responsible for his time in office. Because one of the first things he done was twist some arms at City Hall and double the police presence in the district: it made the voters feel safer but the terrain more suspect for yours truly and my associates.

So I set about to follow Aldo Wooters. Word on the sidewalks was that Troubles was still the overwhelming favorite in the November election, but that this time there was a backlash, and that the party out of power might be the one in power if the incumbent didn't watch himself. It was my opportunity for independent research, since I had lost my standing with the Troubles campaign following my performance in the Stephen Thorne play that ended so horribly that people were arrested for simply having been in the audience.

Once again I had no attachments. I was flying solo in a desperate country, and so I sought belonging among the outfits that moved and shook the city. I figured that the Councilman would award me once more with affections if I was to come up with the truth about his opponent, so I set out to Watergate Aldo Wooters.

The whole adventure started privately in public, at the most confusing political rally in the city's history. It started out as an event for the first opposition candidate, a janitor name of Jerry Jeff Pfeiffer who doubled as a faith healer, but at the rally Pfeiffer got out of the race and the powers that be replaced him with Wooters. I was there when it happened: it was in the South End, down by the famous racetrack, and I lingered near the back of the crowd as church people mingled with hot walkers and strippers, and Pfeiffer resigned and Wooters come forth for the laurels.

That was when I first seen him, and something electric passed between Wooters and the man he followed, and I knew that both of them were and were not who they claimed to be. There was a light around their bodies which I wrote off at first as a mix of Richards and weed, but that turned out to be genuine, on account of I saw the boys from the Shangri-La there at the same event, and they were exclaiming over it, and I saw the part-Asian once more, the one who had blessed me that night after the theater healed my ass, and the day become a spectacle of doubles.

That Asian boy. There was something about him that beckoned

me, something like what I had felt that time under the Witches' Tree when I shaped the figure from mud and thought of the sons I did not have. I know a fatherless boy when I see one, and that night he had all the symptoms. I know the Brischords come to suspect I was sweet on him or something, but it wasn't that. It was that powerful loneliness that spoke to me, a loneliness even among his hipster friends.

But not so much loneliness on that cloudy afternoon when he come up to join the multitudes, a stripper hanging on each arm. He was wearing a gray suit and wire-rimmed glasses, looking so much older and more refined that I doubt I would of recognized him had I not dwelt on him so much already.

Pfeiffer had gathered a whole mess of creation into his following. There were the churchy folks, the high-haired Evangelicals. There was a couple of black people who had not given up on Pfeiffer's political party, though it had long given up on them. There was some suited kids from the college, who were as out of place everywhere as I was, as folks like me. Mostly it was what they used to call the great unwashed, and I knew I was the most unwashed among them.

Pfeiffer spoke at first, thanking the powers that be and God and his party, but I had stopped listening because my thoughts were on the young man.

This was and was not the same boy I had seen at the Shangri-La. There was something harsh in him now, something cruel as he muttered things and showed off for the girls.

And of course they approved, leaning against him and laughing at the jokes, as Mr. Pfeiffer's voice trailed off into nothing, and it was like the whole scene was a silent movie, all tilted and blurred like Caligari. And when I say 'not the same boy,' I mean it exactly. It was like something had stepped up to inhabit him or took him as a shell or resembled him. But whoever he was, the gray-suited man was occupied with the speech and the girls, heckling Pfeiffer more loudly as the girls laughed.

Bucky Trabue, who by now I knew in passing, approached the kid and begun to talk. The girls glared at the intruder, and I knew the story at once from my long experience: they were unwelcome, they *were being ushered away.*

But the boy wasn't budging. So introductions began, and false handshakes: the campaign worker was Bucky, and both of the girls was Chantelle. The trespasser introduced himself as Dominic.

'Well, Bucky,' says Dominic. 'I guess they don't do fascism like they used to.'

You could see the fight brewing from my distance, could feel the boding of violence in the air. The dancers were giggling, and this Bucky says something, still polite and even genial, says something about how it is too bad that Dominic thinks so, and I knew this was headed for trouble and that the kid was on foreign turf and that somebody ought to stop it.

There was light in the young man's wire-rims. You could not augur his intentions. Bucky asks him if the three of them could keep it down a little, seeing as this was church property and that Pfeiffer was still speaking and that he was a man of the cloth.

But Dominic was going on about church and state, and the thing escalates, and I feared for the boy on account of he would be the one the crowd would turn on, not Bucky, and I wondered if the whole stand-off wasn't too far gone to defuse.

All of this while, on the podium, Pfeiffer is talking about how all things, when you seen and understood them truly, how they touch upon and relate to each other, don't stand apart but they stand together. He said it was like we lived in a big net woven out of each other, each of us a net and each of us connected, he said, and each of us watching the others from a distance and from up close. And he said the Lord had come to him, and likened us all as a net of brilliant jewels, each with a countless number of facets. Each jewel reflects in itself every other jewel in the net and is, in fact, one with every other jewel...

Like the jewels in my sequined raiment.

It was time for me to step between two adversaries. To protect the boy or to call him out, as any good father would do in the times of tension and strife. I had taken so much from the huge, impossible world, that I figured it was time to give back.

Dominic stiffened at my approach, and the two of us stood face to face as Bucky stepped away.

Dominic commented upon my fashion, and then I saw behind the swimming light of his glasses and the old smell of rotting meat and the savannah settled in the air, and I knew this was not the boy from the movie theater, but something I had released long ago.

'Yes, we are both kind of a pair,' I said. 'Aren't we, old buddy? I think we have met before, in the dark backward and abysm of time. I thought at first we met on the night of the preview. You and a younger man come to the balcony, brought me out to the lobby, and effected rescue from my seizures. Or at least you resemble my hero, sir, and if you are, upon your deeds the gods themselves throw incense.

'It's like a film, ain't it, son?,' I asked him. 'Like the whole body of cinematic endeavor was one film and one only, all plots and sets and actors and characters connected in a huge tapestry of stories, kind of like the preacher was saying when he talked about the glittering net. So that the Duke is a cowboy and a Marine and a fighter pilot, simultaneously and in sequence, because space and time get jumbled all together in this film, you see...'

He called me crazy and stepped back, fixing to fight me, but I stood my ground. Spoke to him about the dancer and the dance, how we couldn't tell where one leaves off and the other begins. That it was like Pfeiffer was saying up there at the podium, that we were all connected like stars in a raiment of sky, and that he was my son same time he was my enemy, that he was my own—all of him.

No accident he stomped off toward the dancers' club with the girls in tow. Said something in German and vanished into Seventh Heaven, that bright pink club topped by the purple thoroughbred, and around me the crowd gathered closer to the podium to bear shocked witness to Pfeiffer's suspending his campaign and Wooters taking over, all oil and Bible, popping his cuffs because his suit jacket was too short, and hooking his arm around his big-haired wife, who smiled all martyrly and begun to consider the curtains for the Councilman's office.

And I begun the slow mourning, the prospect that something was fixing to defeat DeMoyne Troubles, had overtaken Dominic, something had spread into them and out from them into the city I loved, and that they were thereby ruined by the world inside and around.

And to make it worse, I suspected I had some hand in the arrangements.

✳✳✳

In a matter of weeks, the big fire hit the Shangri-La, the fire that all of you remember, the one that burned down the premises and scattered the young people who had worked on its staff and preserved its beauties and guided winos down from its balconies.

By then I was into harder times. Roses, or the Carnaby's that come in the plastic bottles. I seldom strayed from the park theater, finding comfort in the epicenter of things, right by the omphalos since the summer plays had closed and the structure gave me a place to hide from vicissitude.

I saw Dominic several times during that dark stretch. He was drawn to the theater as well, and you could look up and peer through the sets and see him, dark and slight, seated in the amphitheater, watching nothing unfold on the stage. On occasion his friends were there—the red-haired boy and the pretty little blond who had been burned in the cinema fire and whose face recalled the flames, the wound like wax cupping her chin and the right side of her face.

When Dominic was among friends I would recede backstage, watching through a balcony door or from a shadowy wing. When he was alone I was tempted to step out into light, but the encounter at the rally, when I had dowsed a monster in him behind his glittering glasses, was something that lingered with me, like the scarring did the girl, so I did not speak to him, not until chance brought us together at the Greyhound station in the city.

I had thought for a long time that I would travel up north before the weather turned. Boston seemed like a town to visit, to perhaps find Dhara. I was near sure she had reverted to Bridget after forty years, even more sure that she would no longer remember me. She might very well have moved elsewhere, I figured, and that would leave me in a cold Yankee city just as the weather turned, a bad place for an alfresco man like myself. But it still seemed like an unraveled thread in the bright glittering web that Pfeiffer had talked about that day at the rally, and I thought of a last journey far away, a last quest in which I could weave a strand into the fabric of things and maybe understand how all my wanderings fit together.

The pull of desire instead of right intent. But there at the station, Dominic gifted me, as I was the last to see him off to a deep New England of his own.

I had followed him in a manner close to stalking. His grandmother lived not far from where Mamma had lived for her short stay in the city; likely they would have been friends, would of connected, if they had been there at the same time. But what it meant was that I knew the porches and corridors of the court, knew where to scout him among the statuary and the Venetian Gothic arches. At first it was curiosity, my wonderment that he could of changed so much from the night at the Shangri-La to the cloudy afternoon in the crowd at the rally, draped with exotic dancers, his eyes aglitter with borrowed light. Then it dawned on me—what had brushed against my thoughts along with the liquor that day when Pfeiffer gave up his campaign—that we had passed through a time of transmigration, which I had read of when I went to the library and researched the Reverend Mays.

It was no surprise, then, to see a Dominic like the one in the cinema—sweet and solitary and sad, probably since he lost his job when the Shangri-La burned. I seldom come close enough that he could see me, on account of I did not want to seem a stalker. But that day we met at the Greyhound station, he seemed the boy of old, and he greeted me there with a nod and a smile.

I asked him where he was headed, and he told me 'home'. Somewhere in Vermont, he said. Up there, he told me, home was the place where, when you have to go there, they have to take you in.

And in reply, I told him I would of called it something you somehow haven't to deserve, and our eyes met, and he says, I remember you from the Shangri-La. How's your wound? he asked, and I told him it was almost healed. Then he placed a wad of money in my hand, like he was divesting himself of all belongings or giving me a talisman, and he says, find your home, my friend, and he dips his head and gets on the bus and I lose him in the long array of tinted windows.

After he pulled away, I looked at what he gave me. $27.00 was not enough to make it to Chicago, much less to New England and the Dhara I imagined. So I looked up to the schedule for the next departure, and it was to Nashville, headed south, brushing past Yorktown on its way past Bowling Green.

I was packed lightly with belongings and connections. But the city had been my home, supplanting Yorktown in another transmigration, and I hovered on the dock before I turned around and headed back inside.

XXIV

"And damn it if the tapes don't stop with this one," Bulwer said.

He lit a cigarette and pushed the packet to Mickey, as though it was a poor substitute for the returned cassette.

Again, Mickey lit a Marlboro, embarrassed to confess that the day before, he had purchased two packs of his own and had already just about run through them. By now his friends had no doubt noticed he was inhabiting hard times: the seersucker jacket so clean in June was frayed and soiled at the cuffs, a grass stain on the left elbow, and the practice of alternating the khakis worked well until right before Mickey's laundry day.

Slowly he was coming to resemble the man whose life he had been enlisted to chronicle.

"So what do we do from here?" he asked.

Bulwer and Stack looked at each other, and Stack pushed away from the Salvages counter.

"Looks like your job, Johnny," he muttered. "I have to open the bar."

Bulwer grabbed his old friend by the arm. "No, Alan," he said. "Stay a while. Faj can open, and I need you here for the rest of the story."

He turned to Mickey, then leaned forward against the counter. "We were hoping you'd have some ideas," he confessed. "We're tapped out, Alan and me. The rest is hearsay."

As if Tommy's tapes were a reliable source, Mickey thought bleakly. *As if they aren't asking for a handoff from one suspected liar to a proven one.*

He sighed. "So what do you know, John? What're we working with?"

"As I understand it," he began, "Tommy went straight from the station onto the Nashville bus. If he got off at the nearest stop, it would have put him in Yorktown by late that afternoon. We have no idea how he got from point to point out in the country, but when he came back and started recording these tapes, he claimed to have spent a week there. Claimed he came back changed."

"I don't know how he meant 'changed'," Stack said, folding his arms and looking over and across the shelves of books in the front room of Salvages. "I do know that when he returned he had more money than he knew what to do with."

Mickey's cigarette poised before his lips, his eyes shooting directly to Stack. "More money? He got money in Yorktown?"

"Don't know for sure," Stack said. "He got it somewhere, at any rate. A few days after he returned—or said he returned, we weren't sure when he came back, or whether he left at all, to be honest—he was out there on the promenade, scattering money to his fellows like some homeless Diamond Jim. Small bills, for the most part, but each day it was a few hundred dollars, and as you might imagine, it didn't take long for the news to get around the neighborhood.

"People started to gather each afternoon. First it was the Brischords, of course, but as each of them knew others and those others knew others...well it became a map or a flow chart of the whole indigent population of the city. Each day there was another band of brothers and sisters, and you would think it might be dangerous, but the homeless people are no fools, and by the second day they had clued in to Tommy's having a huge stash of money somewhere in the vicinity, and that doing him harm for a day's chump change might interrupt the steady flow that came to those who waited."

"All the time," Bulwer added, "Tommy was making the tapes here in the store. As it went on, people started to gather, and what at first I thought would be good for business became just its opposite—panhandlings and fistfights, a brother with gold-dyed dreadlocks playing a panpipe right in the middle of Oak Street, then threats to Tommy so that, of all people, it's Norman Titus and Wayne Humphrey showing up as body guards, stationing themselves right over there at the front door, blocking traffic like they were crowd control at an exclusive club, keeping out their fellows and letting my customers in. Of course, eventually someone pushed around one of my regulars—a young student from the university, who happened to have connections, a daddy on the board of ChemCon and a mother who lawyered for Rausch, Standish, and Rausch.

"It had all the prospects of getting worse, but then the last tape, and Tommy vanishing. Only to turn up drowned, with the bodyguards responsible."

Mickey blew smoke out across the shadowy stacks. "I've heard they weren't responsible."

Stack raised an eyebrow. "Who told you that?"

"Magnolia Street. Met her in the park not long ago."

Stack laughed and turned toward the door. "Magnolia Street has never met a guilty party," he pronounced, and opened the door into the humid sunlight, as he squinted, waved, and headed two doors down.

✳✳✳

Mickey walked toward the bus stop in the dark, his thoughts still orbiting the end of the evidence, the last of Tommy's tapes.

Somehow during the listening, he had been lulled into laziness. Half-promising Bulwer and Stack that he would write this man's story, he knew that every day the stakes were arising because of his own inaction. Now that the history had spun its course, they were all left with guesswork and conjecture.

Which was probably why Bulwer wanted a novelist to write the story.

On his way across Ormsby, Mickey marveled at the gaps in his own life. How something in him continued to imagine himself as exceptional, extraordinary, while the world around him told a different story.

The promise of youth in the snowy north had melted in his southward movement, as the family had relocated—from Vermont to western Massachusetts, then to upstate New York, where Mickey had attended college with no distinction. He ended up in a graduate program so second-shelf that his mother had revealed loudly to her friends that he'd probably get a doctorate by correspondence. A few short stories published, followed by an often-rejected novel, a four-month marriage and a year's work in a Fotomat kiosk brought him face to face with diminished promise. The South, with its slowness and (he had been told) laxity of intellect began to call to him, and late in his twenties, he had re-enrolled in a doctoral program and scraped through its hazings, then, hooded with a marginal Ph.D., his novel self-published but at least in hand, he had latched like a barnacle to the hull of the city's university, teaching part-time and eventually full-time under annual contract, until the millennium turned and he looked up, newly married, mired in the academic rutted road, and pretty much stuck where he was.

Now, judging from the belongings he culled daily from his apartment doorstep, he and Tamara had struck an unspoken understanding that things between them were over. As he picked up his clothes and notebooks, through the windows Mickey could see his things replaced by those of a younger life. He assumed that Diana's Jordan had made the leap and was moving in with Tamara. Or perhaps it was more mythical and strange: perhaps, freed of her old rhapsode of a husband, Tamara was rejuvenating—turning back the clock and growing young once more. She imagined them, he figured, like the old Tithonus myth, where she was the goddess of dawn and he was her human husband, immortalized but not free from aging, dwindling into a desperate cricket on the doorstep, with his creaking song summoning a death that refused to come.

Either way, Mickey told himself, he wished her well. Though, in fact, he did not.

From what he could tell, aloft in his fourth-floor library carrel, his job was past jeopardy and fallen into a waiting out of the year's contract. Athena Bumpas, it was rumored, was interviewing candidates for a job in Literary Modernism, and Mickey considered himself forewarned. The books, both scholarly and fictional, lay in undisturbed stacks of paper on his carrel table, and he even had forgotten his place in his own writing, his thoughts on these tapes, these tall tales, this glittering derelict.

And it was to the carrel he was headed now. The library closed at eleven o'clock, and he needed to be on the fourth floor by ten, safe behind his door with the lights out, elusive to any patrolling security guard. It was a good bargain for the early curfew: a roof above his head and air conditioning, as comfortable as any book on the shelf while others in the same social boat, cut loose by landlords or parents or spouses, would nest beneath inclement stars tonight.

When the bus sighed closed and pulled away from the stop at the corner of Fourth and Park, Mickey was still half a block away. He waved, shouted, but the driver moved on, and he was left to wait for the next bus, thirty minutes or so north of here, prowling the downtown streets before swinging into the old city and past the park.

It was middle August, and the park was in its seasonal lull between the summer of plays and the autumn of foliage tours. The stage was dark now, though you could still see the outline of the sets from the streetlights above the visitors' center and the promenade, and shadows cast by another light Mickey could not locate, at least not yet. The park was waiting for the next turn, its silence interrupted only by the electric sputter of the lamps and the rush of traffic down Fourth Street.

Someone had carved a sign into the bus stop bench. A hoboglyph, he guessed at first, but carved more skillfully than the ones he had seen elsewhere in the park, the others Daddy Chrome had deciphered for him at Salvages:

Broken by the slats of the bus stop bench, it pointed in all directions, like a compass of reeds. Mickey used it as a sextant or a gunsight, standing in front of it and framing the park by its spreading lines.

There in the loneliness the grounds before him seemed to reconfigure, to promise a kind of symmetry. Squares of brightness led into squares of shadow, and a kind of grid spread out before him, sometimes almost an order, at other times a random scattering of light. Beyond the line of shrubbery and down a dark slope, the theater stage rose, its backstage highlighted by the burnt gold flicker of firelight. For a moment, Mickey was alarmed, remembering the burning of the Shangri-La, the way fire plagued the old houses in this neighborhood, but the light settled, and he could see someone had set it, that the flame was banked against disaster and the eyes of the police. He squinted and looked across the park, then, forgetting his bus entirely, burst through the shrubbery and headed toward the amphitheater.

✱✱✱

How Mickey crossed the dark terrain to lie on a front-row bench at the amphitheater he would later have no way of explaining. He slipped in and out of thought, dimly aware of being guided by the flicker of flame, only to awake and find himself conveniently on his back in what the Greeks called the *orkhēstra*, the home of the chorus and dancers in front of and below the stage, in sight of the central bum fire up on the boards, the steel barrel trash can circled by shadowy figures, rising taller in their own cast shadows, whom he recognized, as his eyes adjusted, to be the Brischords he had expected.

Who, this time, motioned him into their presence.

Among them this night was Daddy Chrome, a surprising turn since the man had a steady job as resident cataloger and savant at Dry Salvages. It was Chrome who made a place in the circle where Mickey could stand and warm his hands (as if that was needed in humid August).

"Welcome Professor," he said. "Headed home?"

The others looked up cautiously. D.J. Mel nodded in greeting, but Magnolia and Falcon kept their gazes on the fire.

"Where's home?" Mickey asked. Then regretted the question in this company. "I mean…things have changed."

None of the Brischords acted as though they had heard him. Instead, they passed around the ragged white linen duster that Mickey had seen draped across the set weeks and generations past. There seemed to be some ritual involved with circulating the old coat: each of them held it as Mickey stood at the circle's edge, watching the duster move slowly around the fire, borne in weathered hands.

As the duster passed from Brischord to Brischord, a change came over the face of each celebrant. It was as though each of them was rising to a role, hands tracing across the folds and borders of the old coat, feeling memories and stories in its weaving. A joint moved from hand to hand in the opposite direction, and the nutty smell of reefer hung in the humid air.

Finally, after the coat had passed twice through the hands of each Brischord, Daddy Chrome beckoned Mickey into the center of the circle, and quietly, as though he was in the presence of something entirely outside his experience and powerful beyond his knowing, he stepped among his new fellows.

"I remember," Mel said, his eyes on the fire, "the time when the city blew up."

Falcon and Daddy Chrome nodded. Magnolia, on the other hand, took a hit from the joint, then looked to her elders attentively and whispered, "Then speak to it, D.J. Mel."

"It was February of '81," Mel began. "Reagan was in office, but he had yet to be shot. Right before Valentine's Day, when that processing plant over to Floyd Street had been dumping chemicals into the sewers for years. But they'd had a containment system, they claimed, so down here we were not in danger. Until the system failed, and hexane gas come up through the sewer grates in the earliest part of the morning, before people went out to work.

"They say it was a car somewhere over on 9th. A spark from the engine, or friction from the wheels. I don't know what to believe, because I don't know the mechanics of things. But at the time we thought it was the world's end. That son of a bitch in the White House..."

"Yes, Lord," Magnolia exclaimed, exhaling a billow of smoke. "Six letters in each name, and six six six the Mark of the Beast..."

Daddy Chrome stared into the fire. "More than that, darlin'. There had been signs and portents among the community. Falcon and Mel would remember. We all knew the Preacher, and how he came back into Tommy's life, and thereby into ours."

"This was the Reverend Mays?" Mickey asked, as the joint came to him and he partook past reluctance.

Daddy Chrome nodded. "By one name, yes. But he came to the city with other names as well—credit cards, checking accounts, drivers' licences under a dozen names. Falcon over there saw him once, and D.J. Mel saw him twice, so though I never saw the man he was verified by hearsay.

"According to Tommy, Mays had quit preaching years ago. Had stayed as a presence in the city's South End, where he sold smokeless tobacco and hustled stolen cars. Had been arrested once for stealing teddy bears off children's graves over at Cave

Hill, then reselling them at flea markets."

"My, my," D.J. Mel said. "Never heard that escapade till now. Wish I hadn't ever."

Daddy Chrome continued. "Anyway, late in 1980, for one reason or another, Mays took his ministry out of mothballs. Went southeast of the city, to where folks were setting up Heart Ministries in a Quonset. There he offered his services, claiming a divinity degree from Southern Seminary, going by the name of Foursquare Banks."

"I thought that was always Billy Hightower's church," Magnolia said. "From the ground up."

She was interested mainly because everyone in the city's gay community knew Billy Hightower, famous for Bible and bigotry, with some race-baiting thrown in for good measure.

"Naw, honey," Falcon said. "First was Mays or Banks or whoever, though he didn't last long. Then Raymond Hightower, then his son Billy. The church has been a nest of Hightowers since the sewers exploded. Dependent arising, John Bulwer calls it. How all things depend on all things—is that right, Daddy?"

Deliberately, as if to a shared prompt or signal, the Brischords seated themselves around the trash barrel, illumined by the firelight winking through its rust holes and cracks. Mickey followed suit, hunkering between Magnolia and Falcon as the dope kicked in and the world bobbed and settled. He marvelled at the level of talk he was hearing on stage, like these people were the hobos of fiction and romance rather than the actual item.

He was not sure how to think about this revelation. He was not sure whether it was Daddy Chrome's bookishness that had spread contagion, or whether it was an accident that these particular people had gathered together to know and understand. Or perhaps it was something else owing to the strangeness of the place and the cannabis and the night: or perhaps when he had burst through the hedges, his head filled with shadows and firelight and the stories of T. Tommy Briscoe, he had brushed against one of those pockets of the city where time stilled and the rules dropped away—one of those places in Tommy's childhood stories where the surroundings "swallowed sound".

All the while Daddy Chrome was continuing his story about the eruption of the city streets. How it had burst and buckled streets throughout the neighborhood, so that residents had gone without power and water for days to the great amusement of Daddy Chrome's people. Now what Nick Mays had been doing in the area was anyone's guess, but apparently the whole thing had been engineered by Tommy, who claimed to have foreknowledge of the "crapocalypse", as they came to call the sewer explosion.

"Months before it happened," Daddy Chrome said, "Just about the time Reagan got elected, Tommy started prowling around Heart Ministries. By that time, he figured he would not be recognizable to anyone but those who had kept track of him over the last few years, and I expect he was right. By then he had a beard, his hair was shaggy and streaking with premature gray. Nature had masked him as a woodland creature—as a faun, perhaps, or a satyr—and he swore that he was satisfied in giving Mays a start.

Tommy said there was an immediate bond between them. He suspected that Mays knew who he was, as he knew Mays, but that neither of them was ready to unmask the other, because the unmasking would lead to unmasking himself. It was like some kind of duet, Daddy Chrome said, and as the weeks went by, the two of them became complicit. Like Mays had wanted them to be years ago, when the two had met down in the southern part of the state.

They worked a simple faith healing, Daddy Chrome said. Mickey saw its roots in the scams and misdirection Tommy had learned under the teaching of Ace Briscoe, but the whole caper seemed to be based on Tommy's disguises. Entering the church the first time as himself, he returned as an older man, then shaved and veiled, once preposterously as an old woman. Each time he bore a malady that Mays would heal by a laying on of hands, and each time they would divide the offering—50/50, Mays told him at first, but on inspection of the plates one night after the revival, Tommy discovered that his own portion was closer to a third of the take.

"I think it was then that Tommy began to plot the dismantling of Nicholas Mays," Daddy Chrome said softly, and the other Brischords responded with a *yes* in unison. Mickey realized they had heard the tale before, that there was something in it they awaited.

His audience rapt, Daddy Chrome continued. "So Tommy played the rube. Set up a Friday morning sunrise revival over around Eighth and Jefferson—an area he was hoping Nick Mays did not know so well, did not know was simply two intersecting blocks of warehouses. After a long negotiation, Mays dispensed enough cash for a rental tent and two dozen chairs: it wasn't much, but Tommy was never one to covet money, being more about the honor and respect. And what was more, he would tell me later that he knew by that February how the arc of event had reached its conclusion, how at long last there was no more of this story to be told."

To this, the Brischords nodded. And Mickey, though troubled by where he saw the story heading, was nonetheless inclined to agree.

"So Mays was there at the street corner, there a little after five in the morning, when it was not yet dawn but it was dawning on him that he'd been hoodwinked, though to what end he had yet to discern. I like to think that he was looking up into the dark sky, seeing the Twins at their angular distance, when the auto spark—if it was an auto spark, all said and done—ignited the hexane in the sewers at his feet.

"The news would report the great good fortune of the disaster's timing. How, had the explosion happened but a short while later, the streets would have been busy with rush hour traffic, and lives would have been lost. Many lives. Instead, the news would tell us that none were killed nor injured by the blast. Though we, the ones inside the circle, know otherwise. Know that one died in a sacrifice by impact and fire."

The Brischords laughed meaningfully, and the dry leaves rustled in the trees in a kind of call and response. Mickey knew that they all believed Tommy had caused the explosion, though he did not know what to believe himself. Even doubted, the story was alarming: Tommy's closest companions thought him capable of murder, and all of a sudden, Mickey's entire image of the man as part Huck Finn, part bodhisattva, was unsettled for the first time in a while.

All of the stories he had known regarding Tommy Briscoe were filtered, he realized at last, through those who had wanted to see him as kindly, as well-meaning—from Bulwer's stories of Tommy as an urban wise man, through Tommy's own, in which he was a folk hero, a saint in the making. And now he was hearing from the Brischords, this dark and discordant version of the man.

Again a Fourth Street bus passed at a distance on its way toward the fringes of the town. This time Mickey didn't try to catch it, didn't bother to stand. It appeared as though he would be up late, and he leaned back, propping himself on his arms.

Daddy Chrome ended his cautionary tale, and the park fell silent, only to be disrupted by a rising whirr of cicadas. Now Daddy passed the coat to D.J. Mel in exchange for a second joint, and a new story was underway—one that took place in the very spot they were seated, as though Tommy's legend had narrowed its wide orbit and come to rest here among them on a still summer night.

"There was the play a couple years back," Mel began. He looked straight at Mickey, and continued.

"This was an amateur gig. Stephen Thorne was directing it. Yeah, he done some TV commercials, and he was a guest guide on that cable ghost show. But he had dreams of larger things, and had fallen from grace. So he done this Greek tragedy right here a year ago last spring. Brought in actors from the schools, and hired us as an afterthought chorus. Tommy was excited about it, went down to that novelty store on Main, brung us back a half dozen masks. Leopards, big hunting cats. He said they had to do with the Greek god who was big in tragedy…"

"Dionysus," Mickey interrupted, but D.J. Mel didn't care

about the name.

"Whatever. We got leopard masks. Upset the talent, so the director axed us to revise the props, and Tommy come up with these plain masks made out of corn shucks, smooth with little eye holes in them so we looked safer to the uprights, like something out of the plant kingdom but like a serial killer's hockey mask if you ax me.

"And Tommy taught us our lines and he took us into strange country. I come to believe that when we said those words, standing in front of the stage, that we made the story by what we were saying. Not made up the story, but put it together out of words, like if you was to say 'here, fire', and look at that barrel among us, that the fire would start within it and the flames walk up its sides.

"It would of give you power," Mel continued. "It would of made you think there was magic in your speaking, except Tommy had give us the words, which he had from the script, of course. And some of us began thinking that there was old magic or mojo in the script, or that Tommy goophered the words some when he taught them to us. All of that is urban legend to me, but it did feel like it wasn't commentary so much as conjuring something to life.

"By opening night the air was thick with it, and the weather was the city in early summer, humid and hot and wailing with mosquitoes. There was white people all up and down them seats behind you, Professor, all of them sweating and waiting for culture. So of course, after Dionysus had his speech, we come on stage..."

"*Hard are the labors of god*," Falcon interrupted. Then joined by the other Brischords,

> *Hard, but his service is sweet.*
> *Sweet to serve, sweet to cry:*
> *Bacchus! Evohé!*"

All of them laughed, then, and Mickey felt like he was outside of something, awaiting initiation or a least a clue to the present mystery.

"But it all went to shit from there. Because no matter what you allow that the words bring to life, they only touch a thread of a web, and the whole thing shivers all over, every part of it tense and vibrating and drawing the spider. Because there was that riot over by the Church of Christ, and then they brought the boy in, carrying him in parts like they was the madwomen in the play."

Mickey's jaw dropped. "Wait a minute," he said. "What's this about..."

The Brischords looked at him knowingly, a kind of condescending pity on their faces.

"That's right, Professor," Mel said. "Was the purpose of the commotion over at Fourth. Them women tore that boy the fuck up."

Magnolia brushed her hair back delicately. "You had heard the mother dropped the head right about where you was standing, right?"

Mickey resisted the impulse to look down, to jump. "I thought that was..."

"An urban legend?" Mel's question hung harsh in the damp air. "That's what y'all always say over to the university." He paused, lifted his hands above the fire. "Even the legend sugars the truth, Doctor. On account of the legend you heard was that the boy's own mama dropped his head down there in the orchestra, know what I'm sayin'?"

Mickey nodded, uncertain where the story was bound.

"Well, that wasn't the only organ she dropped there, if you understand. The press threw a blanket on it like we threw a blanket over the boy's head and jimmy. Some deaths don't bear witness, but we all seen them drop from the sack she carried."

"And you see Tommy behind this?" Mickey asked after a long, shocked silence.

Mel shook his head. "No, but maybe yes. He was surprised

as the rest of us, but I can't help thinking that something in his speaking was what cast out a line that reeled in a monstrous thing."

Mickey was unconvinced. "But why wouldn't someone have reported…"

"The Deep State," Daddy Chrome replied. All of the Brischords nodded in agreement, and Mickey could see Mel's words touch every filament of the vast and imagined web. The story was spreading out now, touching other stories in the city, bringing home mysteries that had long slept here, on the stage, in the park, in the city.

"That might of been why Tommy become so generous there in his last days," Falcon said. "He knew ever thing he done was linked to ever other thing, and so he spent accordingly."

"I've heard something of that," Mickey said. "The generosity, that is. Alan Stack says Tommy left town and came back with money."

Falcon scowled. "Never heard the part about leaving town. But what I do know is that the time come when he was dispensing to all of us. Not that I cared what he done with what was his. But flashing cash is drawing danger. And what was more, something had addled him."

It was Mickey's turn to frown. From the tapes, Tommy had seemed far-flung and fanciful, but the sentences had come together, time and space cohered. He knew he was thinking like a novelist rather than a shrink, and that in itself was consolation.

Falcon said that it all came down to a kind of honesty. That instead of the guards and subterfuges of the homeless life, Tommy had opened to the elements. There was that young man, she said, that Tommy followed around, almost stalked for a spell, and she had come to believe that Tommy might even be sweet on the boy, though there had never been any sign that he bent that way. Later she had come to believe it was misplaced fatherhood—that Tommy had come to that time when what might of been rushed from behind to catch up with him. It was sad, she said, but at least it made some sense.

The unsettling thing, she repeated, was the money. You would see Tommy standing in the rain, dispensing dollar bills—sometimes fives or tens—to passersby. And the funny thing was, to hear her tell it, that the rich white folks took the money more often than the people she knew.

But it was drawing danger, no matter how you looked at it.

"I guess I can see," Mickey said at last, "the motives of Norman Titus and Wayne Humphrey." It was a line cast into the water: he waited for Magnolia Street to rise to the bait, remembering how she had told him, in the park not that long ago, how she didn't *think them boys should be lethal injected for something neither of them had a hand in.*

She rose as expected. "Them boys didn't do it. Why, Wayne was simple, pretty much a halfwit, and Norman minded him. I know it: I seen it myself."

Falcon leaned close to Mickey and whispered, "Magnolia and Norm had a thing betwixt them."

Magnolia glared at Falcon. "That don't change what I know," she snapped. "Them boys didn't kill Tommy Briscoe."

The stage fell silent. And finally Magnolia spoke, this time more softly, and the cicadas seemed to hush in the park to allow for her confession.

"I was there," she said, her eyes on the dying flame in the barrel. "Seen him walk into the river. I run away at the blue lights flashing. But Wayne was out in the water, waist deep, and Norman went to fetch him. The cops must of caught up with them right after."

There might have been witnesses, Magnolia claimed. The path down to the river, she said, took them past bars and up through the renovated, yuppiefied sections of town northernmost in the city.

Tommy was agitated that night, she said. Told them he was headed uptown, past Broadway. They knew his route would take him out of his comfort, but he wouldn't let on why he was doing this. He said it was something about what his daddy had told him, how he was headed for *the world that was all a body was promised*.

And no, she didn't know what it meant, but it didn't sound right. Norman agreed they should follow him, and of course they had to take Wayne with them because.

Mickey knew what Tommy had meant. Ace and his thirteen-year-old son waist-deep in the river. An icy baptism meant to school the boy away from fancy. Baptism paired with a strong current and with fatherly betrayal, like Ace had set the boy on a journey that lasted almost sixty years, only to end at the same spot and altar where it began.

A weariness passed over him as he left the comfort and light of the Brischords' fire and stumbled off alone into the dark. Intending to head for the university, Mickey became disoriented by the night and the dope and even the earlier liquor. He found himself at the fringe of the park, befuddled in shade, night-blind and barely navigating, low branches rustling and rubbing against his arms and face, the smell of black mulberries, some of which he picked and tasted, then the needling brush of evergreen and the astringency of juniper, then light, then light and dark, light and dark as he moved toward the edge of the park, drowsing in a net of branches.

Mickey's steps brought him once again below the Witches' Tree. The burled trunk was adorned with new gifts and tokens. Mardi Gras beads, an opalescent costume ring, plastic and plaster statues of babies and children and autumnal clowns—all of them shimmering in refracted moonlight and from the glow of the streetlamps above the tennis courts, where a solitary couple batted the ball back and forth over the sad, ill-attended net.

Mickey hoisted himself into the branches, past the dolls and costume jewelry. Yes, he had done this once before, but not at night, and not with this drunken knowledge and resolve. Tommy's story had its own legs: Mickey would follow it through, though it was leeching his energies and time, and for the first time Mickey thought of his own age, thought of it long and dolefully, propped in a crotch of the tree and looking behind him, out over the patterns the park displayed this time of evening.

Then the Witches' Tree slid up Sixth Street with a scrape of root against concrete, its movement slow, almost tidal, in the opposite direction from where it had taken Tommy those long years ago. Mickey clung to the branch, afraid he would fall, afraid to drop onto uncertain pavement. There in the branches Mickey nodded to sleep, his dreams of Tommy on the river, body afloat with the current, the lamé glittering in a dark, amniotic flow.

***

He awoke to familiar sunlight, in a wooden booth opposite a span of vaguely familiar windows. Faj was stacking new bottles on the shelves, inattentive to Mickey's stirrings and dramatic groans.

"All right. How'd I get here?" Mickey asked at last.

Faj smiled. "On the doorstep. You a foundling. You smell of ganja and bourbon, I think."

Mickey looked blearily out into the sunlight.

"You want dog hair, then?" Faj reached for the top shelf bourbon, and Mickey decided not to correct the idiom, that dog hair was certainly better than hair of the dog.

Across the street, just beyond the intersection, the old Victorian houses glowed in the summer sun, a long line of ruddy brick past the heat-shimmer, like treasure glimpsed underwater. They led the eye toward the heart of town and the on-ramps to the interstates, the path Mickey had chosen, the long drive to the state penitentiary where he would talk to Titus and Humphrey, who would no doubt face execution after a number of ill-starred appeals by harried public defenders—appeals to which, it seemed, the boys were either indifferent or downright opposed.

This morning, though, buoyed with new optimism that came from deciding to do this, to do this at last, Mickey saw himself as a rescuer, almost like one of those Greek heroes who made the descent into the underworld to retrieve loved ones from the shadow of death. If Titus and Humphrey were innocent after all, then surely it was at last like the Dr. King quote, that the arc of the moral universe *did* tend toward justice.

Somehow, though, Mickey could barely buy the idealism. He looked down into the freshly poured bourbon on the rocks, watched the ice glitter in the amber, and tried to imagine just what Magnolia Street and Norm Titus had done with one another. The arc of his own moral path, it seemed, tended more toward the immodest, and he tried to banish the thought. What the truth was about Titus had no doubt been filtered through

Magnolia's desires, and whatever she made of Tommy's death—even if she was a witness, as she claimed—was clouded by her defense of her boy lover, a young man barely nineteen on his way to lethal injection, who seemed to have given up for some reason.

Borrowing Alan Stack's old Volvo, assuring Faj he was sober enough to drive and that yes, Stack had given him loan of the vehicle, Mickey lurched onto the interstate and headed south, bound for an intersection where a broad parkway took a westward turn and followed the river, six lanes knifing through rolling farmland and limestone cuts.

At first the drive was picturesque, as he took in scenery quite different from the Vermont countryside he had visited occasionally as a boy. The South was beautiful, Mickey conceded, but after a while, the landscape settled into a pleasant monotony that lulled him into a kind of driver's drowsiness.

He turned off the radio as rock music submerged into static, replaced by country gospel and hacking Holiness preachers. Twice he startled himself into vigilance, and finally, after a truck stop lunch of coffee and doughnuts, took the off road toward the state penitentiary, his thoughts rambling and melancholy.

The people here were like the countryside they inhabited, Mickey reckoned—pleasant and welcoming surfaces that covered a confining sameness. *After all, what remarkable good had ever come out of country like this?* he asked himself more than a little smugly. *Or for that matter, what remarkable evil?* He suspected that all the tides that carried a person to something large and notable flowed away from this neck of the woods rather than into it.

As he pulled into the penitentiary lot, then passed through the metal detector under watchful eyes, Mickey thought about the enormity of Titus and Humphrey. He had seen the pictures in the paper: Titus looking slightly away from the camera, eyes sharp and vulpine, a contrast to his so-called partner in crime, who gaped straight ahead, bottom lip distended and moist, eyes half-hooded.

It was like something from *Of Mice and Men*, which made

it hard to think of either boy as a martyr, but even harder to think of them as monsters. Their pictures, blurred and abstracted into black and white, positioned deep in the second section of the paper, had made them seem imagined rather than creatures of fact. Mickey wondered about his own involvement, whether he was as bad as Magnolia in his hope to see things otherwise.

The moment, however, he reached the door of the building, the world burst out upon him. With a huge, electric sigh, the bulletproof glass in front of him parted carefully, and a pregnant woman on a gurney rolled into the summer heat barely guided by two EMT techs. Mickey stepped back as the cart wheeled sharply in front of him, shuddering down a ramp toward the waiting ambulance.

"Went into labor talking to her man," a heavy woman in a tank top and capris observed from the bottom of the steps. "I know them both."

Mickey feigned interest as he went on through the door. Behind him, as though she had an audience at last, the heavy woman called out.

"Dude's in there for killing his wife. Some world, huh?"

✳✳✳

"Dead man walking," Norm Titus said with a grim little laugh as he seated himself at the table opposite Mickey Walsh.

For some reason, Mickey had expected Wayne Humphrey to be there as well, but it wasn't going to turn out that way. As Titus explained early on, Humphrey had stayed in his cell to work on a project, *because some motherfucker told him how this story ends, and he was all freaked, but I told him he could have anything he wanted for that last meal, so he's back there planning it. Two Big Macs and a Big Red, so far. Maybe a Payday if it don't hurt his teeth.*

They weren't there to talk about last meals, though. The place did look like a cafeteria of sorts, sparsely furnished with long, wide tables, around which the guards stood, carefully

237

watching the handful of prisoners and their visitors. Titus and Mickey were an unusual pair that day: almost all the convicts had female visitors—mothers, perhaps, or girlfriends, most of them tearful.

With some reluctance, and probably from boredom ultimately, Norman Titus had added Mickey to his list of visitors. He had heard from Magnolia via Daddy Chrome that there was some writer named Walsh who wanted to talk, wanted *the real story*, which he was prepared to tell under one condition: that Mickey would not write or repeat it until after the last meals and the three-drug arm cocktail.

Mickey agreed, but it was a promise he was not sure he would keep. Perhaps they both knew he might be lying, or perhaps neither. At any rate, Titus was willing to tell how the four of them walked to the river that warm night in June. He shifted the number to three at Mickey's questioning, then returned to four when he realized the slip was no slip—that Mickey knew about Magnolia—correcting himself with well-acted earnestness, assuring Mickey that he *just wanted to stick with all the facts.*

That night, Titus claimed, Tommy was showing them a spot in his history. "But we was all there for different reasons, even if we didn't know that when we set out. Got a cigarette?"

When Mickey waved away the question, Titus continued, his eyes darting toward the doors, toward the guard, as though he was plotting an escape. "Tommy rode on the handlebars of Wayne's bicycle, and Magnolia on mine. It's a long way from the park to the river, and Tommy was almost 70, you know, and more than a little looped up since he come back with the money."

"Was this about the money?" Mickey asked.

Titus shook his head. "You don't know nothing. So we go downtown then west to the old 14th Street Bridge, which is not much more than rusty scaffolding and track these days, though Tommy said it was better when his daddy first took him there.

"This side of the river, at the spot where the tracks begin to span the water, it's pretty near desolate, the interstate way above you and the cars passing at all hours. Somebody seen us, though, which is why they called the police.

"But that wasn't yet. Not before everything happened.

And down by the abutment, there's graffiti from a hundred years, and that's where we hid the bikes in the high weeds and Tommy took off that damn lamé cape."

"I thought they found him in the jumpsuit."

"Oh, they did, Professor. Thought I said 'cape'. And he left it on the handlebars of Wayne's bike up there, and the three—the four—of us walk down to the banks. Tommy wades out about waist-deep in the water, and said this was about the spot, that his father held him under water just about here. It seemed strange and inhuman to me, but what was to happen next made me stretch what I call inhuman.

"Because there was murder in the air, Professor. See, what Wayne had in his simple mind was to kill Tommy off for all that money he had found somewhere—the money the old man was scattering like seeds over his part of the city. Wayne didn't think ahead, though—I don't believe he *can* think ahead so good—and if he was just killing the old man for the money he had on him, well, where do you hide anything in a lamé jumpsuit?

"He only told me about the plan in the back of the squad car, after they'd read us our rights and cuffed us. By then Tommy was floating down river, and things had changed entire. Still, Wayne was guilty of thinking through to murder. Wrong intention, wrong mind, all of that's a factor. This I know, Professor, because I was planning a murder that night myself.

"But not of Tommy, out there in the water, that lamé all ashine from the lights atop the struts of the bridge, and the river glowing right in front of him like it was some kind of underwater treasure. The next thing we know Tommy is pointing to the light on the current like it was something beyond price, like it was the pot of gold at the end. And he says *there it is*, and something about the *wholeness beyond confusion*, whatever the hell that means. Then he's face-down in the water, floating downstream, and Wayne forgets himself for all his plots of murder and is about to wade out after Tommy, but Wayne can't swim and I remember and I hold him back.

"Last I seen of Tommy before he went under was this flicker of moonlight off his jumpsuit over to the far west. And I hear the police sirens as they come to get us, because they were already on it."

"How did they know so soon?" Mickey asked.

Norm Titus glared through the glass. "Fuck Magnolia Street. Hated him, even when he became she and was all right."

Mickey let it go, though he couldn't believe Magnolia had snitched on her lover. There were stories behind stories here, and more to determine. The account of Tommy's death was coded, obscure, like a landscape where all the stories connected, a place deep in some peaceful country, marked with glyphs he could not read, not yet.

Mickey cleared his throat. "So you said you were plotting murder yourself? But not of Tommy, you said?"

"You *sure* you don't have a cigarette, Professor? Yeah, but not of Tommy."

A long pause, as Titus gathered himself, looked at the guard again, then confessed to what he believed needed confessing, his voice low and urgent.

"He was not gonna get better, Professor. Big hulking body and mind like a child, like an idiot in the movies. I couldn't take care of him no more. And part of why I'd come to the river with Tommy was that I figured on doing what needed to be done, what was the only kind thing in this horror of a world. And figured of all people Tommy would understand, would help me with Wayne. And that Magnolia, who should go get fucked, would stay silent because of me.

"I was wrong about all of them. It all went in different directions. And when the time had come, I had held Wayne back from drowning alongside T. Tommy, so there was something that held me back as well. But bad intention, bad mind: contemplating murder is murder, ain't it? And who knows how long the two of us will go with a shelter over our head, square meals and warmth against the weather—which is something we never had while we wandered.

"So I'm asking you. I'm trusting your word that you won't say nothing until it's over. Justice should be entire, or you can do pretty near anything. I was after justice entire, a story where ever thing falls in place. But the truth worked itself out in the world, and I'm stuck with the outcome.

"So do I have your word, Professor? Are you good for this?"

✳✳✳

That afternoon, before he started on the second leg of his journey, a pilgrimage to Yorktown, Mickey called the police department back home. There was no longer a McCarthy or McCartney in Homicide. The officer who took the call assured him that, in this case, the conviction and sentence would fit the confessions of the defendants, though the public defender was all over the issue of mental competence when it came to Wayne Humphrey.

Mickey thought about what such justice meant as he headed to Yorktown, this part of the journey more winding, down narrow county roads past cave country souvenir shops, past churches and diners. He questioned whether his silence, his obedience to a promise he had given Norman Titus, was the next worst thing to murder.

He had no reason to doubt that some of Titus's account was true, or at least not a lie: both prisoners had intended to kill someone that night by the river. But intention was not commission, and knowing all, the court would no doubt find them innocent of the charges. But that was knowing all: we stumble through cause and effect, Mickey told himself, trammeling up consequences that lead to other consequences until the world is a whole impossible net of connection. Mickey could spend the rest of his days—or, rather, the remaining days of Titus and Humphrey—in a crusade that would fail anyway.

Still, it had not been an easy decision, Mickey told himself, to leave the two boys in the grinder of the justice system. Prosecutors and politicians loved to execute some hapless soul now and then, nearly as much as they loved to pull the switch on or inject some unrepentant monster. It was all one to them, and they came out looking tough and judicious to the body politic. Titus was slated be executed, because the state loved its executions, and Humphrey…well, Humphrey was the principal subject of the appeals. He would be at best institutionalized, but more likely follow the path of his more able protector, his last sight the eyes of onlookers as the lethal chemicals rode his veins toward his perplexed and slowing heart.

Tough and judicious, indeed. Basically human sacrifice, Mickey decided. He pulled behind a plodding tractor, tried to pass, slipped back into his lane to avoid an oncoming pickup.

Didn't his own quietude mean that he held the rope, threw the switch, pushed the plunger on the syringe? Mickey could keep calling, give aid to an idealistic lawyer, stand as witness to evidence that only he and a transgendered vagrant might corroborate. Even at best, if his testimony had bent the will of judge and jury, Mickey figured his life would have ended up devoured in the pursuit of freedom for those who, given that freedom, would again throw away their lives.

But perhaps his surrender was something other than simply giving up: Titus and Humphrey (or Titus, and Titus *for* Humphrey) knew, somewhere in the depths of their knowing, that a legend demands a sacrifice. Whatever the tale, someone suffers for it. Suffers, because that's the kind of place that the world is, a world without closure and resolution, where the story exalts some creatures and throws the rest under. Tommy had passed into the country of myth, and myth was seldom the clean and triumphant saga of the hero, but more often the mire of the others who didn't quite make it, who looked for stories to tell them what might have been or what might be, a fable to seal them away from what is unmistakably and unchangeably the way things already are.

Or stories into which they could step. That gave them meaning. The helper, the adversary, the one who gives directions or poses the hero's first test. The one who prophesies or warns.

The sacrifice or martyr, whose loss becomes the hero's triumph.

A story wide enough to contain the rest of us.

The county roads led Mickey into country more confined than the landscape along the interstate, a stunted little region seldom changed in the last seventy years. Tommy would have seen the farms this way: unkempt fences, hills of dry grass, Black Angus huddled against the sun under solitary trees. Up close it was not as desolate as it seemed from a distance, but still it was depressed, blank sky descending on nearly blank terrain, a route of sameness and red dirt that wound toward the southernmost parts of the state, the hill country that had housed Confederate guerrillas and moonshiners, meth labs and militias over the two hundred years the place had been settled. It took the shine off of dreams, this country, and Mickey wondered whether Tommy had gladly traded it in for the homelessness of the city.

The mile numbers on the signs brought Yorktown closer, though Mickey could see no changes in the landscape. The occasional "Welcome" sign was followed in a breath by "You Are Now Leaving," as he drove past small towns bunched on the highway, gas station and diners and always the churches, their graveyards teeming, white tombstones in tiers rising from the edge of the road. He became conscious of the rainbow sticker on the rear window of Stack's old Volvo, wondered if he was passing through country where the symbol would be troublesome, or whether he had already passed through that country into territory where it was no longer recognizable.

The listless gaze of the gas station attendant told him nothing about symbols or directions, or even the time of day, as he filled up the car and drove on, past hours of farmland until a water tower seemed to rise from the road ahead of him, *Yorktown* painted in black on its massive, globular top.

Mickey was where the story began. Searching for the last clues, the last keys to understanding Tommy Briscoe.

He had started this road trip with the old investigative idea: *follow the money.* The unaccounted week or so in Tommy Briscoe's life, the time from when he stood at the bus station until he re-appeared days later, trashy rich and dispensing dollars, seemed like time enough for him to have revisited Yorktown. Why he would have done so was a mystery: perhaps it had only been sentimental, but from all accounts Tommy was handing out money once he returned, and Mickey was set on solving the puzzle.

He imagined the old man returning to the banks of Thusa Creek, digging at a spot marked with the first hoboglyphics he had learned, uncovering pirate treasure caked with red clay, left from an unremembered time and exploit. But the story didn't fit exactly: instead, Mickey would follow the lie of the country, would see what he would see.

A trip to the courthouse gave him directions to the old farm of Medgar and Coral Downes, but the clerical assistant, made up like a drag queen, a pencil skewering her high hair, warned him that it *wadn't no sentimental journey, Mister. The farmhouse is long gone and most of the land give over to subdivision. But they's woods remaining, and I think one of the Stockton girls is still alive, on up the road at the nursing home.*

It was not an encouraging prospect, and at first the old farm delivered exactly what the girl had promised. From what Mickey could tell, the farmhouse had been replaced by a subdivision center—a clubhouse, pool, and a pair of tennis courts. Cautious of snakes, leery of even the ratcheting sound of insects rising from the shade of the little woods, Mickey paused for a moment at the edge of the road.

But the woods could wait. The next stop would be the nursing home, where from simple deduction and Tommy's accounts, Mickey stood to meet with Pearl Stockton Briscoe, and perhaps with the solution to the mystery of Tommy's sudden wealth.

XXVI

York Haven was what they called it. A sprawling, single-story residence made of Roman brick, lawn chairs lining its long, covered porch.

When Mickey's car pulled into the lot, it drew the attention of every eye in the shadows. One of the old men waved vaguely, but Mickey was in search of Pearl Briscoe, passing by his frail welcoming party and through the automatic front door, into a lobby that smelled of urine and overcooked vegetables. Others watched him from a makeshift television room, as he spoke to the nurse at the front desk, who pointed him down the stifling corridor to Pearl's little quarters.

Mickey's throat constricted as he passed beneath sputtering fluorescent lights, past an old man leaning against a walker jury-rigged with tennis balls on its feet. The old man beckoned, but Mickey didn't stop: the hall felt like a gauntlet, like he was fast approaching the key to Tommy's mystery.

As far as he had figured, Pearl was a few years into her second century. But for a moment as he entered her room, the light swelled, and an old woman nodding in a wheelchair, a movie magazine open in her lap, seemed younger by generations.

Dust motes dodged and wavered in the close air, and the cloying pine smell of room freshener snatched Mickey's breath. His eyes adjusting to the light, he immediately saw the old woman as she was, but for that moment she had passed beyond herself into surprising country.

"Miss Pearl?" he called out twice. On the third time she stirred awake, and Mickey introduced himself, took her frail hand in greeting, then made to sit in the chair facing her.

"Did I say you could make yourself at home?" she asked.

Mickey bent halfway into the chair, and Pearl let him linger a minute in half-crouch before she motioned him down.

"You from the government?" she asked, dim brown eyes darting over her visitor.

"Miss Pearl?" Mickey began, respectfully and tentatively. "I'm an old friend of your son."

She looked out the window as though in search of something.

Mickey moved his chair closer. "When was the last time you spoke with him?

"Dilly was killed in Korea, young man. So it's been twenty years. Maybe thirty."

Mickey sighed. Everything about this meeting was wildly wrong already. Now he regretted the four-hour drive, the passage through dismal country that seemed to have ended here, in the still air of forgetfulness, with an old woman looking out a window onto nothing.

What had he been thinking?

"Well, you see, Miss Pearl," he offered weakly. "Tommy claimed to have visited you a few months back."

The old woman remained silent. Dust motes caught in the sunlight as it passed through the window.

"I gave that one enough already," Pearl said at last. She leaned back, stared at Mickey with more focus, more clarity. "When Coral and Med died, it was only the two of us left, so what could I do but help him after I sold the farm to the developers? But it did no good for that Tommy. The dollars just passed through my hands into his."

Mickey nodded, feigning sympathy.

"You here on his behalf?" she asked. "Because there isn't more money. I gave him what the nursing home didn't take."

Mickey started to explain, to justify himself, to claim pure motive in the stillness of Pearl's room. But the words settled and faded, as "pure motive" became yet another set of self-serving words.

"I'm here for the rest of my days," Pearl said. "Nothing more than food and shelter. I even have to accept charity for the clothing. Meanwhile he's up in the city, doing God knows what with God knows whom. He and his father and that wayward minister who tried to kidnap him, all of them tied up in high society, or so I hear."

Pearl continued in the same vein, and the story slowly shifted into a world unknown to Mickey Walsh.

✱✱✱

Pearl had tried to maintain her teaching post after the scandal with Ace. In the one gentlemanly moment the boy had ever mustered, he had dropped out of her English class, out of high school, and taken a job at the quarry.

Meanwhile, Pearl tried to create a respectable middle-class home for the son or daughter on the way. But Ace couldn't hold down decent work, and he resented her rich preparations for the child's arrival. Five months pregnant, she had come home from school near the end of the term to find him packing, driving off to God knew where, though she would find out later that his destination was the city they all hated, that Babylon to the north that was the center of all corruption and crime and race-mixing.

When the baby came, she continued to stay with Coral and Med, because after all, Pearl claimed, the property was half hers. Mickey found that easy to believe: even in a world of men where the property would by nature be called *Med's farm*, there was a whole streak of Southern matriarchy in the region that would have allowed the property to be that of the Stockton girls, provided the deed and the tradition said that it was. Whatever the case, Pearl soon discovered that she would no longer be able to afford the luxuries she had planned for.

She hated Coral's hand-me-downs. Saw it as a return to childhood.

When the teaching post was not renewed in the fall, Pearl took a job as a waitress in a local restaurant. The tips were good, she said, because of her charisma and charm, but she was ashamed to be working at Marlene's Corner Café and Bakeshop, because she saw it as common, saw herself as a transplant, like a cowbird's egg laid in the nest of another, less powerful bird. She hid her job, as much as possible, from the knowledge of the more privileged girls in town, because she knew she was by nature one of them, that after a rough patch she would recover and rejoin polite society.

When the baby was born, things became just overwhelming. Pearl took to the house, she claimed, after a nightmarish afternoon in Hutchins Market when she thought about leaving the child in a shopping basket, thought about setting out on her own and starting all over, though her true sense of duty kept her from that kind of abandonment.

Later on, though, she had left little Tommy for a while in the care of his Aunt Coral and Uncle Med, gone south and picked up a Library Science degree in a part of the country that didn't judge her or know her. It was a woman's adventure story back in the '50s, she said. She was paving a life for the two of them, and after all, she wrote the boy daily, sweet letters that showed how devoted she was, how miles away she was a better mother than those who lived in the same house as their children nowadays.

It was down south that she met the man who could have changed things for her, for Tommy, for all of them involved. Soon after she filed for divorce from Ace, she met the dashing Monte Thrasher, decorated bomber pilot in the recent war, vice president in a prominent insurance company, himself freshly divorced. Pearl reacted quickly, pushing through the papers on her absent husband, and taking her own apartment near the university where she studied.

Soon Monte Thrasher was paying her rent, though not sharing her bed, she claimed. And she began to plan her second wedding until Ace Briscoe, returning like a nightmare or a bout with a chronic illness, disrupted her plans by abducting her son, taking him away to the city.

She was grief-stricken, she claimed. Threw herself into her studies, her intensity so fierce that, for a while, Monte Thrasher stepped back from her, and her world became darker, unhappier because of the burden of Tommy Briscoe and his reiver of a father.

Mickey wondered, but did not say, what had kept a devoted mother miles away from her growing son for eleven years. In the hands of Pearl Stockton Briscoe, facts were apparently embroidered and knotted, and though he had doubted many things in Tommy's story, it had become a lens through which he saw the entwined history of this weird and hapless family, and now each fact was faceted, beveled, each side with an opposite— mirrored and obverse in the telling.

Hearing of Ace's taking Tommy to the city, where he used him for confidence scams and sympathy swindles, Pearl said she made her way north, settling in the walking court just south of the park that would later become Tommy's home. For a while Tommy lived with her (this part, Mickey noted, the stories held in common), but the boy was too wild, she said. Things ended up missing from her apartment, and Tommy was flashing all kinds of money, which he always claimed was Ace's gift or payment from a part-time job.

Nevertheless, Pearl said, she continued to labor in hope. She took part of her inheritance to enroll the boy at the university, but he threw it away—both education and the money to pay for it— on race music, beat poetry, and drugs. In October of 1968—she remembered it well, because it was almost Halloween—Tommy came to her for yet another handout, and when she told him her money was exhausted, that an assistant librarian didn't make enough to send a boy to college and finance his sporting life, he slapped her and she kicked him out for good.

Not long after that, Pearl said, she made her retreat to Yorktown. Stayed in the family house with her sister and brother-in-law. Survived them both. Med had died first, she said, but near her end, Coral claimed to have received a letter from Tommy, begging forgiveness. Tommy returned for his Aunt Coral's funeral, and the two of them, mother and son, had shared a tearful reunion in which a repentant Tommy promised to change his ways, if she would only lend him some money to tide him over. "Over" what, Pearl didn't say. But Tommy's return was not the only reunion: only a day after her son returned, Pearl opened the door to Monte Thrasher, also repentant, also seeking to make things right.

Mickey watched the stories branch and contradict, wondering where any truth lay in these dark, submerged labyrinths of words. The return of the betrothed, the prodigal son, the struggle of child and potential stepfather—whatever the folktales might offer was brewing in a farmhouse on the outskirts of a little Southern town.

It was as though, Pearl said, that every happy ending you could imagine was offered to her by God, only to be yanked away by men. For almost a week—the happiest week ever, she called it—the son and the mother and the adoptive father shared quarters in harmony. Tommy and Monte treated each other with respect, and it was even better than that, almost affectionate, mind you, as the older man responded to the younger man's tales, to the glamor of thunderstorms and tornadoes, of talking leopards and stalking statuary. Not that she believed any of it, Pearl said, but she was torn between wanting the history and her odd fascination with the tall tale her son was spinning.

Mickey understood that feeling all too well. Pearl's story contradicted the stretched account he had gathered from Bulwer's tapes; he could feel both versions veer from the plausible, Pearl's soap opera weaving its way in and out of Tommy's hero-legend. He listened, absorbed, not believing but not wanting the telling to end.

"Now comes the real tragedy," Pearl told him. "Because Tommy Briscoe ruined it all by seducing the man who could have become his father. No, not in some forbidden and ugly way, but with those tales he was telling. And Monte saying at last to me, 'Pearl, I know it's dressed up like a tall tale, but dadgum if I'm not starting to believe him.'

"He made my son his heir. Tommy Briscoe became the scion of the Thrasher family fortune, and I expect there are relatives of Monte's down south who continue to curse his contrivance and his name. The will was handled by Gavin Stevens, rest his soul, whose family firm has handled our affairs since the Reconstruction, and with everything in place, Tommy could have abided easily, his inheritance only a matter of time.

"But he was not a boy to wait, as you must know by knowing him, sir. The night after they all signed off on the will and Monte had withdrawn ten thousand dollars for the boy's immediate succor and use, Tommy came to me triumphant and said, 'Mother, now I have from Mr. Thrasher all that I need from him. As you took from me my first father through lies and your own defeats and resentments, I have taken back a father in this Monte Thrasher, but with esteem and financial support and without the female smothering that is your motherhood'.

"And so it was for several nights, until, returning home from the library, I was met at the door by my distraught son. Monte Thrasher's body lay in the guest bedroom, shot dead with Ace's old revolver, which we had kept in the top drawer of the highboy as defense against intruders. Tommy begged for my help, begged me to hide his ill deed, then gathered what money I had remaining for a bus ticket back to the city. I did not know at the time that he carried so much of dear Monte's money with him.

"The next day I went downtown to Mr. Stevens' office and confessed. I told him that Monte had been more forceful and brutal than I had at first imagined, and the arguments had become violent over the last several days, resulting in the tragedy of the night before. I begged Mr. Stevens not to call in the police, that the affair would damage the good Stockton name, that we could perhaps dispose of the matter quietly and secretly.

"Because what was a mother to do but protect her only child? I suspect that Mr. Stevens saw through my flimsy alibis, but I suspect as well that he knew what a can of worms a sheriff and a handful of forensic evidence might open on a poor widow and her indigent son. So Mr. Stevens helped me bury the body, out in the woods on the eastern border of our property, and I have not seen my son again, but on occasion have sent him money to tide him over until the next time he goes wanting.

"And if he has ever known, sir, what sacrifices I have made for him and for his well-being, he has given no indication."

✳✳✳

He could have driven Alan Stack's Volvo, rainbow sticker and all, through the holes in the old woman's story.

It was all disjointed, Mickey thought. Dislocated, its timeline uncertain, contradicting almost all of what Tommy had recounted in the tapes, and not just the mythical parts. As he sped down the narrow road from the nursing home to the center of Yorktown, he realized with frustration that this trip to Tommy's home town was providing no simple closure, that the story he had been recruited to write was branching into shadow. For a moment he dwelt in its mysteries, in the whole growing awareness that, just as Tommy's story brushed against myth, his own tale of rescue and discovery was now following a parallel path.

The August sun was relentless as he backed the Volvo onto a recently paved frontage road and walked down the hill, away from the subdivision toward a copse of trees, all that was left of the boundary woods that divided Downes and Guthrie back in another century.

He stepped off pavement and approached the shade through the high weeds, bramble clinging to his pant legs. The trees were less than twenty feet from the roadside, and through the shadows Mickey could catch a glimpse of Thusa Creek glittering and flowing at the edge of the sunlight. Here was where the story began, and if you believed Pearl Briscoe, her part in it ended here as well. Mickey doubted he could unearth bones, much less a body, from the woods ahead of him, but there was a part of him—a part schooled on endings not necessarily happy but settled—that held out the hope that he would find the remains of Monte Thrasher and that somehow this would make the story clear.

But instead, the insects in the shade fell quiet once Mickey was fully among the trees. For a moment it seemed like he had dropped into complete silence, then a solitary gnat whined against his ear, and listening to and through it, he caught the trickling sound of a brook deeper in the woods. He moved toward the water, sidling through patches of brightness and dusk.

He almost expected to hear a voice as he reached a ruinous stone fence that at one time must have marked the border of Downes's land. What the voice would have been, Mickey could not begin to guess: perhaps a plaintive call from the Guthrie graveyard not fifty yards to the east, or something darker, perhaps, and more vengeful, like the bones of this Monte Thrasher crying for revenge out of a nearby shallow grave. But instead there was only the stream and the occasional, dodging call of birds, and it seemed as though anything passing for civilization in this backwater country had dropped away as well, and that Mickey's path through the woods was a path back in time.

A blue brightness surged over the path in front of him. The humid air boded a shape, then dissolved back into shadow. Mickey came to a stop, looked around him, listened.

There was a hint of blue again, something in the corner of his sight, but when he turned, the woods lay before him, unremarkable and unruffled. The air was palpably cooler here by the fragmentary stone wall, and as he laid a hand on one of the topmost boulders, he felt a tremor of energy pass from wrist to forearm. He looked up and saw a horse on the path ahead of him, formed of fog and slanted sun. Atop it a blue light straddled, then a cloud passed above the trees and horse and insubstantial rider vanished, leaving him alone at the fence.

Cautiously, Mickey lifted his leg across the stones and stepped down into Guthrie property. Moving along the wall, left hand extended to stay in constant touch with the makeshift masonry, he came at last to the Guthrie graveyard.

The graves were weathered and, in some cases, covered by weeds. The ground was flat now, and Mickey stood amid knee-high grass, peering over headstones and crosses metal and wooden. What words remained on limestone had been worn by almost two centuries: here and there a string of letters suggesting at a name, giving identity and form to bones buried underneath.

Only one inscription was clear: it seemed that Velma Guthrie, whose name Mickey remembered from the tapes, was the last one buried in the graveyard. The mound by the stone was still raised, still patchy in spots, but whoever had buried the old woman had not followed up, had not carved in her date of death.

The clouds that had been passing across the canopy of woods seemed to stall and settle over the clearing in which the graveyard lay. Suddenly the world slipped into evening, and standing in front of the grave, Mickey imagined the loneliness of Velma Guthrie, the fine and private place of her burial. Something in him yearned toward her quietude, and he felt his shoes sink past the soles into the spongy earth.

It was dark now, and the sounds of the woods stirred up again, the scuttling of something on the move through the undergrowth, and the chaos of wings as birds began settling for the night in the encircling trees. It drew out something basic, something primal: no longer was Mickey looking for evidence, for something to verify a story, whether Tommy's or Pearl's. Instead, he moved toward what he thought was the west, toward the Downes edge of the woods, toward the subdivision and Alan's car parked nearby.

Mickey followed a faint light, perhaps the moon, perhaps the lamps from the subdivision streets—he was too far among the trees to tell. He stumbled over exposed roots, his face brushing branches. He smelled juniper against his skin, the tart undersmell of mulberry, and something swept down from a branch, a wing brushing by him as though something had scouted him, found him too large for prey. The hunter flashed between trees, and the distant moonlight caught on her broad white wings.

An owl, the size of which he could barely imagine. Banking into the darkness, her wings steady.

He was in alien country. The stories from childhood of wanderers lost in the woods darted through Mickey's thoughts: he remembered hearing of two students—two young men, first year of college—lost in the Vermont woods back when he was a child and those woods were familiar by daylight. But their story took place in winter, and though one of them froze to death, irrecoverable in the snows just south of the city where he grew up, he could mark it off as the weather, as a tragic but explainable accident.

These woods held something outside of weather and chance and history. Once Mickey thought he caught a glimpse of someone dancing in a glade off to his right—bronze and gleaming, clad only in a thin scarf and a slouch cap, her small breasts catching moonlight. Then he stumbled through the water, knee-deep in the little Thusa, and he was the only thing moving for miles, headed toward open ground, toward breathing, crashing like a bear or bull through the edge of the woods...

And what lay before him was country so familiar it was strange: a long slope of mowed grass headed down to a stone promenade, to the tiered seats of an amphitheater, to the stage where a banked light glowed and where shadows crouched and danced.

In defiance of all possibility, Mickey found himself on his threshold, fifty yards from the place he knew as home. He stepped from the woods, still not believing...

And the landscape settled into a short field, rolling up to a file of houses, of streetlamps, of the drab suburban neighborhood next to which he had parked the car.

Epilogue

"So, no grave for Monte Thrasher? No stone, no mound, no solution to the mystery?"

Bulwer's tone was teasing, as he and Mickey leaned against the bar, sharing a noontime drink with Alan Stack.

The trip back home had been uneventful. One night in a Yorktown motel and four hours on the road Sunday morning, and Mickey was back to the city and to the Wilde, where he returned the car and recounted his adventures at York Haven.

For some reason he held back when it came to the time in the woods. It was all too hallucinatory, too intimate, as though he had adopted Tommy's way of seeing and lost the story in the process. And yet he told them Pearl's story, believing that it filled some of the gaps in what they knew of Tommy and his last days. Believing that, if they found the source of Tommy's unexpected wealth, it would solve the greatest of his mysteries.

But as he reached the end of the story, Mickey saw the way Bulwer and Stack were looking at each other. Mickey trailed off, stirred the bourbon through the ice, and waited for whatever was coming.

Bulwer began. "Mickey, a literary type like you, and you

don't recognize the name 'Gavin Stevens'?"

"It sounded familiar, I admit," Mickey lied.

"The lawyer in just about every Faulkner novel. The best educated man in Yoknapatawpha County. The old woman's demented, or she's just plain having you on."

"I will confess that after I talked to her, I realized there were holes in the story. Tommy's rich in one sentence, indigent in another. She's two places at the same time, like particles and waves. So's Monte Thrasher. If there was a grave site in the woods I missed it, or the developers had paved it under the subdivision or the side roads. So I can't figure what to take away from Pearl's story. But there's always a chance I missed a hoboglyph marking a hollow tree under which *someone* buried the family fortune—Stockton and Briscoe and Thrasher combined, a treasure beyond recounting."

Stack refilled Mickey's glass. "Honey, that's not all when it comes to Pearl, though. Her whole story of abandonment and betrayal by offspring…she's mixed together *Mildred Pierce* and *Stella Dallas*."

Mickey let settle on him the very thing he feared. Out of a patchwork of stories, of Southern Gothic and old Hollywood, Pearl Briscoe had quilted a cover for her past.

"We're not going to find the key to this, are we?" he asked, to neither of them in particular, his words still and a little despairing in the close air of the Oscar Wilde.

Bulwer finished his glass, set it on the bar firmly, and patted the top of it for closure. "That's all for me, Alan. I have a store to consider.

"And Mickey. I'm coming to think that finding the key isn't nearly as important, at least for this, as fumbling around for it in the dark as you stand at the door."

Mickey exhaled. He looked into the mirror behind the racked and rainbowed array of liquor bottles. Someone strange was seated at the bar between Bulwer and Alan Stack, looking up at him through a haze of bourbon and acquiescence.

At last he knew he wasn't going to write the biography.

Hell, they all knew—Bulwer and Stack and Faj, the crew by the barrel fire on the stage blocks away.

Mickey himself had probably been the last to realize. He wondered if the women in his life—Tamara and Diana, and strangely Pearl, and even more strangely his own mother, blocks away herself in a grave he had forgotten to visit—whether all of them knew he was failing at this as well.

"Put it on my tab, Alan?" he asked, and the old barkeep thought about saying something, but instead simply nodded.

✳✳✳

And he was out into the Sunday sun, catching a bus bound for the university. Sweating by the time he reached the library, he searched the stairs by habit, looking for signs that the imagined chess game had shifted, that the opponent he had fashioned out of myth and paranoia had made another move in a game neither of them understood yet. But everything seemed the same: the revolving doors mirrored him as he pushed through them into the lobby and climbed the stairs, which seemed a little steeper than they were before he left for Yorktown.

The notes hung on the door like icicles. The first Mickey opened was from Diana Chen, lamenting, to his surprise, his absence during the last two weeks of the course, though she was sure he had his reasons, and she hoped he was all right. She also wanted to tell him that she was not taking his Modernism seminar, mainly since the course had been assigned to someone else. She went on to ask what he was teaching instead, but he let the note drop.

And moved to the next one—from the Library Administration Office, telling him he had until the first of September to remove his belongings, that *a grace period of three weeks is given to carrel occupants who are no longer employed with or through the University.*

The third note was in a department stationary envelope, from Athena Bumpas. He didn't need to open it.

✳✳✳

Late Monday afternoon, Mickey caught a bus west along Main Street, disembarking near the trestle of the 14th Street Bridge.

Why was it that he needed to see the spot where Tommy had been drowned? The river would have washed away the evidence, all proof of Titus' and Humphrey's guilt or innocence, though by now he had come to believe Titus' testimony from the prison visit.

Nothing could be proved these days. Mickey stayed on the bus, though, impelled by a deeper sense of closure, of a sense that places should be visited and sights seen, that the story should have a sense of beginning, middle, and end.

The place at the foot of the bridge was desolate. Flattened, bare ground, and dry, because August was setting up to be a rainless month. The cicadas kept at it, whirring in the hot afternoon, falling silent as Mickey walked through the high reeds down to the river. There, standing at the edge of the mud, he looked out on the current, trying to catch a singular glint of light on the water, something noticeable in the continual flow.

He soon realized that such hopes were the wishful thinking of a novelist. Tommy was gone, and the loose ends of the story were trailing off into dozens of places and times, branching into creeks and streams and rivulets on their way west, and all an observer could do was note them and let them go as they passed. But this resignation tilted and refocused when, coming up the bank, Mickey caught sight of a bicycle leaning against the riverbank side of the abutment, above it yet another hobo sign, made hastily and scratched with a rock instead of drawn onto the abutment:

Infinity, he thought at first, but later on, when he spoke with Daddy Chrome, he found that in hoboglyphics, it was nothing so lofty.

Don't give up, its simple message. There at the city outskirts, at the edge of the powerful river.

The bike was beginning to rust, the spokes on the back wheel dented as though someone had thrown an object against them. Over the handlebars draped a lamé cape, stiffened by having endured the changeable weather but nonetheless sheltered under the bridge so that it had missed the worst inclemency. Its hem was soiled by wear and soot and mildew, yet another glyph glued in sequins on its back:

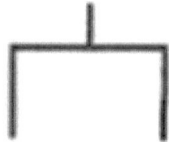

He had seen it before, on the back of the linen duster. Perhaps it had been how Tommy marked all things he wore, all things on his elusive person.

When Mickey picked it up, the cape seemed heavier than he imagined.

Swiftly, almost without thought, Mickey slung the cape over his shoulders and mounted the bike. The ride was rickety at first through the weeds and over the sloped ground, nor did the damaged back wheel help matters.

Not to mention Mickey hadn't been on a bicycle in more than forty years.

Puffing, wrestling the handlebars, Mickey fought his way to level pavement, picking up balance and speed as he rode off in the general direction of the university. Lifted by the wind, the cape tied around his neck managed a flutter at last. People on the sidewalk barely looked up as he passed, no doubt thinking no more of his odd presence than simply observing, writing it off as simply an old man on a bicycle.

But Mickey's inner landscape was alive and attentive. The half-familiar double-digit streets passed from their half-familiarity into accustomed ground. He steered the bike east, then south by the beautiful stone Catholic church where he had taken his mother to attend mass, then past the Witches' Tree and skirting the edge of the park. He could see the top of the theater barely, then it sank from sight as he passed the court and the apartment where he and Tamara had kept stormy residence, now bound south, past Confederate sentinels and the overpass.

All the while, the city was shifting into new terrain as his bicycle sped past: the houses seemed washed with light, the leaves on the maples and mulberries no longer dry but damp and vibrant. Mickey felt his movement through the vastness of things, so much of his world having taken place within the confines of two dozen city blocks, all of it tightly interconnected by architecture and roadway and a landscape almost inscrutable unless you were moving after all, seeing it as a continuous flow from one home to another, like a river itself with innumerable and veiled tributaries, connected to real rivers, to the outlying fields, by extension to everything he breathed in and understood. And he felt lifted out of himself, no longer guiding the bike but simply riding it along a route that hovered between chosen and predetermined, a lacing of honeysuckle in the air, the streets open and sunny and suddenly wider, as though they were leading to somewhere serene and perpetually promised.

About the Author

Over the past 25 years, Michael Williams has written a number of strange novels, from the early Weasel's Luck and Galen Beknighted in the best-selling DRAGONLANCE series to the more recent lyrical and experimental Arcady, singled out for praise by Locus and Asimov's magazines. In Trajan's Arch, his eleventh novel, stories fold into stories and a boy grows up with ghostly mentors, and the recently published Vine mingles Greek tragedy and urban legend, as a local dramatic production in a small city goes humorously, then horrifically, awry.

Trajan's Arch and Vine are two of the books in Williams's highly anticipated City Quartet, to be joined in 2018 by Dominic's Ghosts and Tattered Men.

Williams was born in Louisville, Kentucky, and spent much of his childhood in the south central part of the state, the red-dirt gothic home of Appalachian foothills and stories of Confederate guerrillas. Through good luck and a roundabout journey he made his way through through New England, New York, Wisconsin, Britain and Ireland, and has ended up less than thirty miles from where he began. He has a Ph.D. in Humanities, and teaches at the University of Louisville, where he focuses on the he Modern Fantastic in fiction and film. He is married, and has two grown sons.

www.ingramcontent.com/pod-product-compliance
Lightning Source LLC
Chambersburg PA
CBHW031941010726
47493CB00007B/2018